Rhapsody in Black

AN ELENA DEL CARRAL MYSTERY

RHAPSODY IN... MYSTERIES
BOOK ONE

MARIA ELENA ALONSO-SIERRA

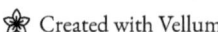

Rhapsody
in BLACK

An Elena del Carral Mystery

In honor of my mother, Elena del Cueto. Prima ballerina and choreographer extraordinaire in the golden age of dance in Cuba, who sacrificed home, country, career, social/professional standing, and fame for my sister and me.

The bravest woman I have ever known.

Chapter One

DEMI-PLIÉ.

With eyes closed, Elena del Carral sank and rose slowly into her warm-up routine. She was alone in Studio 4 of the National Terpsichore Ballet in New York City, taking advantage of the forty minutes of personal time before the rehearsal, which was to be followed by *the* audition.

The role of a lifetime, if chosen as principal.

Or so everyone said.

Elena wasn't that enthused. She suspected there was more to this invitation to audition than met the eye. Add to that her own personal reluctance and fears about finally disclosing the secret her mother had held close to her vest for more than ten years, and she'd have a problem of major proportions. Well, not a problem, per se. But Elena knew her revelations about *Black Rhapsody* would not be welcomed or applauded. Uh-uh. After the initial shock, the brokering would be fierce, not to mention the jealousy and bickering that would ensue. Elena simply wasn't ready for it. Ergo, her dithering during the past five years after her mother's death whether to disclose the secret or not.

And yet, this time, they'd forced her hand. Things could not remain as they'd been. And all because of the stubborn arrogance and conceit of

Broderick Newsom, Terpsichore's in-house choreographer cum artistic director.

Warm up. Warm up. Warm up. Ignore everything for the moment.

Elena forced herself to tune out conflicting thoughts and the normal murmurs, piano undertones, thuds from jumps, and the occasional *seven, eight, and a one* filtering through the walls and closed doors. She needed to warm up to her own music, her own tempo—detach from the world. She must focus on her body and muscles, her form, even when, today, her routine wasn't going smoothly. She was not at her best, by any measure. Her muscles groaned and protested. Her feet popped. She was stiff and tight. Then again, what the heck did she expect?

She was still jet-lagged, pissed, and disturbed. In that order.

Well...no, that wasn't the order, exactly. Elena sighed. Disturbed and pissed should be the sequence of priority. The lingering jet lag was not an issue. She could handle that at any given day.

FO-CUS, she chided.

Tendu front. Flex. Point. Close fifth. Demi-plié.

Leg movement sequenced into a *grand port de bras*, stretching her arm and lower back forward until her nose pressed against her knees. She crossed her arms behind her ankles and leaned further into the stretch, her upper body melding into her thighs in a seamless line. Her spine popped in two places. *Now that felt good.* She feline stretched out and up, bent waist sideways into the barre, and continued the three-hundred-and-sixty-degree *port de bras*, ensuring an overall lengthening of her deltoids and... Her sudden chuckle bounced around the empty room. Good grief. She was now spouting jargon like the company's physical therapist.

Elena studied her form on the wall-to-wall mirror opposite the barre. In the reflected image of the cavernous rehearsal room, she resembled a stick figure bisecting the wall. She squinted, corrected a few things and, a few neck pops later, *sous-sused* into fifth, lifted her left leg into a high *passé*, and held her balance for a few seconds. Ever so slowly, she closed on fifth.

Soutenu.

Repeat.

Demi-plié.

She started humming a familiar Chopin piano piece and added more *dégagés*, followed with *grands pliés*, and finished the sequence with *ronds de jambes par terre* and *en l'air*. By the time she reached her *développés* and *grands battements*, her entire body was soaked in sweat. When she walked over to her overstuffed bag by the door after she finished, her ballet slippers left small imprints on the floor.

Flopping on the floor, she drank long and hard from her favorite hydration drink mix and blotted her sweat with her hand towel. Scavenging through her ballet bag, she found pointe shoes and rehearsal skirt, and dropped both by her hips. She spread her legs in a final *à la seconde* split, shifted her split position right and left to maximize stretch, mopped up more sweat, and, finally, lay supine.

She hoped Fredrik Boelens, her colleague from Ballet Etudes and partner for the gala, would arrive soon. She wanted busy. She wanted light fun. Fred's cheerfulness was contagious, and his lack of guile was always refreshing. She really didn't want to think about the audition and what the reveal would entail.

Once that happened, the rest of her day would be, well, interesting, to say the least.

Elena draped her damp towel on the lower barre to air, grabbed her toe shoes, and wound the ribbons around her ankles as if trying to strangle them. Let's face it—she hated confrontation. That was why she wanted out of New York as soon as possible. Wanted the performance gala to be O-VER. Where the heck was Fred?

After wrapping her rehearsal skirt around her waist, she *bourréed* a few times to make sure she hadn't cut off circulation to her ankles. A few seconds later, she knew she'd tied her left pointe shoe too tight. She bent down and began adjusting the ribbons.

"Well, that is an interesting position. New ballet pose?"

Upside down, and without bothering to fix her stance, Elena looked in the direction of the stranger's voice from between her legs. Her eyes roamed up from jeans that molded muscled legs stretching into forever, followed by a well-defined chest expanding a muted green T-shirt to fullness, the image finally topped by the man's head to create an upended exclamation point. She didn't recognize him. Then again, even though she knew most in the company, she'd been away for more than five years and the man could have come onboard after her departure.

"May I help you?" she asked, returning to her task. She balanced on her left foot and grunted with satisfaction. *That was better.*

"Doubt it," the man said and walked closer. Curly hair, like eddies of sunshine, framed a golden ratio, symmetrical face. Light brown eyes studied Elena with curiosity and a tinge of humor.

"I must admit, though, you are a much-improved version from Derek." At her expression, he laughed—deep, paced, like molasses. "Reception said he'd be here for the rehearsal and the audition," he clarified.

"That's in fifteen minutes."

"I'm Jake Forrester, by the way." He extended his hand. "Haven't had the pleasure, but I'm assuming you are one of the guest artists for the gala?"

Elena shook smooth, strong hands, the grip solid.

Wow. Not only a killer smile, laugh, and body, but this man could be awesome at lifts.

"Elena del Carral," she answered, and wondered if he was administration or dancer at Terpsichore.

He snapped his fingers.

"*You're* the invited principal from Ballet Etudes." Admiration coated his voice. "I saw a short video of you dancing the adagio of *Concerto in D* with Fredrik Boelens. Impressive falls short as a descriptor."

Elena blushed. She wasn't yet quite used to people gushing over the piece. *Her* piece. *Her* choreography. She thanked the good Lord every single day that the director of Ballet Etudes had been receptive to her idea and, once he had seen a small sample of the choreography she'd staged, had placed her work as part of the repertoire of the company. The European premiere two months ago had been a success, ranking her as one of the new, up-and-coming ballet choreographers in Europe. She'd already had requests to stage *Concerto* in Stuttgart and London.

"Ah. Stop the press. The prodigal returns. Time to kill the fatted calf."

Oh hell.

Elena recognized the mockery and voice immediately. Justin. Justin Bakare. Ex-lover, conniver, exploiter, and all-around son of a bitch.

She gave him a quick once-over as he strode into the room. Sleek muscled and an inch shy of six feet, he walked with the same arrogance and verve as five years ago. But there were slight differences. His black hair, cut in his usual boyish bob, framed a square jaw that stretched skin, and his dark, penetrating eyes were puffy, his face not concealing the fact he looked older and...used? His cheekbones protruded further than before, and his thoracic cage stood out substantially, much more than she remembered. This image of Justin did not correlate with hers from five years ago, where he'd been fleshier, for lack of a better description. This Justin looked as if he'd melted all excess fat and sported only sinew.

A look that didn't quite suit him.

"I see the years haven't changed your sunny disposition," she said, her voice dripping with a slight touch of venom. "Praise just gushes out from your viper tongue, as always."

"And I see your bitchiness hasn't improved in five years," Justin responded, throwing his ballet duffle on the floor. He realized who was in the room with her, and looked slightly abashed.

"Hi, Jake."

Jake Forrester's lips twitched upward for the briefest of seconds. Her cheeks flared hot, like she'd poked her face too close to a fire. She never said anything disparaging of anyone, especially not in front of a stranger. But she couldn't help being snarky whenever Justin was around. Instinctual reaction.

"Sorry," she whispered to Jake and *bourréed* to the back of the room.

Forrester's smile grew wider.

The ringtone of one of her brother's film scores echoed inside the room. She automatically went for her cell, then realized it was not her phone, but Jake's, that was ringing.

She stared at him in surprise.

"Hang on a sec." Jake strode toward the doors and stopped short of where Elena stood by them. He leaned forward, catching her by surprise, lips grazing her ear.

"Never apologize about Justin," he whispered, and left the studio, phone pressed to his ear.

Elena released a breath she hadn't known she'd kept holding. The man filled his surroundings like dark matter in space, affecting and irradiating everything within reach. Unsettling energy. And not in a bad way, no. It was simply she hadn't felt this awareness in a long while. Not even with Justin, when she'd first met him and fallen in love with him in youthful naïveté, had she felt this disturbance in the force, to quote from her favorite science fiction movie. And after the disaster of her relationship with Justin (*no, you can't quite call it a relationship*) and her abrupt departure from Terpsichore and New York, Elena hadn't even looked at a man, nor had considered dating one. She'd been too busy in her new home, learning the ropes in Ballet Etudes, performing, and creating her choreography.

Maybe she was just out of practice where men were concerned.

A wave of energy and noise erupted around her. The rehearsal group had arrived.

Company class was over.

"Elena!" The squeal and voice warned Elena that Francesca Mori had arrived. She braced for the upcoming hug, which was usually nothing but intense.

"Hey, Frannie."

Francesca Mori was, and had been, Elena's best friend since they'd met in dance school. At her friend's first *développé*, all their teachers had recognized innate talent. As a matter of fact, Elena knew many dancers who would kill for Francesca's ease of extensions, perfect pointe, arch, and jumping strength. It had steadily propelled her friend forward within the company, until she'd made principal. Which placed a bullseye on any dancer, had they not been Francesca. Her friend was one of those rarities in the dance world—she was not ambitious. Her passion was to dance—and dance only. Dance anything. Francesca didn't care if she did it in the corps, as an extra, guest artist, or as a soloist. Her saving grace? Seeing the world with the guileless eyes of a child and imparting good intentions to all. If it weren't for that fact, the aggressive harpies within the company would have destroyed her years ago.

"OMG. I'm so glad you are here." She gave Elena a peck. "Why didn't you take class with us this morning?"

Elena's eyes glanced at Justin for a second.

"Oh."

"Besides, I wanted to say hi to Rick and Nat, take their class."

"Who's Rick and Nat?" came a voice from behind them.

"Fred!" Another squeal and a hug.

"Previous teachers of ours," Elena told her partner and messed up his hair. "Boelens, you are late," she chided.

"I was on the phone with Amèlie."

"Is the morning sickness under control?" Elena asked. Fred's wife was pregnant with their first child.

"The doctor gave her something for it today and guaranteed it will help. She should be taking classes by the end of the week."

"Ok, everyone. Gather round." Staccato claps centered everyone's attention on Analisse Menia, the company's *répétiteur*. She marched toward the center of the room. Patrick Tadana, the company's rehearsal pianist, continued on to his corner.

"Elena and Fred, you're rehearsing first. You can dance the balcony scene blindfolded, so I don't expect to give you too many corrections. Francesca, you and Justin are next. Mario and..." She looked around. "Where's Caro?"

"Our diva must be on the phone with her latest," Justin said.

"Oh, shoosh," Francesca said and bumped him with her shoulder.

Analisse ignored the exchange.

"Mario, you and she are next to last. Martina will cap rehearsals. Mr. Derek and Broderick should arrive shortly to welcome our guests," she nodded to Fred and Elena and scanned her schedule.

"A crew from *Dance America* will join us here tomorrow. They'll be taping rehearsals for the gala to use as a promo clip, which will air in the local news. We'll be uploading that to our YouTube channel and website, as well. Best behavior goes without saying. Best rehearsal outfit. No soiled shoes." She looked at Francesca. "None of your scraggly leg warmers, and..." Her eyes landed on each of the men. "No bare chests either. Light makeup, everyone, and ladies, jewelry at a minimum. Ok, people," she walked over to where the chairs were stacked behind the piano and dragged two of them center front, by the mirrors.

"Places, please." She sat and turned to Patrick Tadana, waiting at the piano. "From measure fifty-four, Patrick. Elena. Fred. From the top."

And so, rehearsal began.

After a half hour of grueling work as Juliet in MacMillan's brilliant, but mega-demanding balcony-scene variation, Elena reached the locker assigned to her in the changing rooms of the studio. Stripping off her soaked rehearsal clothes, she wriggled into fresh tights, leotard, leg warmers, and meshed top.

"You've got a lot of nerve coming back."

Elena didn't even have to turn around.

"Aren't you supposed to be at rehearsal, Caro?" She grabbed her spare ballet slippers and pointe shoes from the locker and dropped them inside her bag.

"You've no right to audition."

Elena tried not to sigh. She knew better than to engage with Caroline Wainwright. It was useless, especially with an embittered woman. Caroline's own fault, really. Elena would have warned her five years ago about Justin's supreme philandering and opportunistic tendencies, of how he discarded women like torn tights, especially if same woman could not advance his career. Then again, why should she have? Caroline had been the main culprit in Elena's breakup with Justin. Now, after five years, karma had been foisted on Caroline as Justin *grand jetéd* his way away from her and *châinéd* over to fawn over the up-and-coming darling of the company, Martina Brzinsky. Winner of the Lausanne Grand Prix three years prior, Vaganova trained, and lured from the Royal Ballet with the promise of prima status at Terpsichore, critics and directors had her as the new Osipova or Guillem.

And Justin wanted to be her partner, professionally, so the rumor said. And, what better way to achieve that than as Martina's real-life partner?

"She has every right," Anne Ruskin interrupted, stopping by her locker and opening it. "Derek asked her."

"Well, if it isn't our supreme leader's personal oracle."

"Bitchiness doesn't suit you, dear," Anne said with her usual phlegm. "I just thought to warn you Derek and Brod have been waiting for you for over ten minutes. They're not pleased. So, they're rehearsing Martina."

Caroline made the quickest exit Elena had ever seen.

"Welcome back." Anne grinned and opened her arms.

"And on my terms," Elena said and hugged the woman who'd guided her as a green corps de ballet member. Who'd sat with her after the Justin debacle to dry her tears, who'd told her a few deserved truths about some men, and who'd guided Elena's career in general. The pros and cons of staying, or not, in the company. Her pointers about expanding her horizons.

And after much introspection, Elena had taken Anne's advice and had quit Terpsichore a month later.

"You're looking well."

Anne scoffed. "The calendar disagrees, dear. Time is merciless, as you well know."

Only too well. Elena was barely twenty-eight and her muscles protested more often than not, her extensions suffered if she skipped class for one day, and her stamina was a bit off, not by much, but enough for her to notice. She could imagine how it was for Anne, who'd just celebrated her forty-seventh birthday. If she hadn't been Derek's lover, or had been in another ballet company, Anne would have been put out to pasture—demoted slowly to either an extra in big ballet productions, where her only role would have been to sit and nod as the Queen Mother in Sleeping Beauty or walk in agitation behind Giselle before she croaked. Or maybe as répétiteur. Or as teacher. And it was well known by all in the company that Anne hated teaching.

Anne lived to dance.

"Are you auditioning?" Elena asked.

"Derek wants me to," she said and rummaged inside her locker. "More as a courtesy to my status in the company, rather than anything else. Waste of time and effort, I say. I don't have what it takes to be the lead in this one, or any other ballet. Now, where is that stupid darning kit?"

Elena glanced at Anne's ballet bag, open on the bench next to her.

"Isn't that it?" She pointed and was about to reach for it when

Anne's hand captured the open bag. She dropped it by her feet and rummaged inside the locker once more.

"Good grief. If my head weren't attached to my body... Oh, and word of warning. There's a klepto in the company. So, keep your belongings close and your locker locked. Derek would have placed security cameras here when it first started, but that's way illegal. Here we go." Anne dropped two new pointe shoes inside the bag and banged the locker door shut.

"Come on," she said, hooking her bag over one shoulder. "Let's go see the rehearsal and nitpick every mistake Caro makes. We'll gloat over them over a glass of wine tonight."

Laughing like two teenagers, they scooted to the back of the rehearsal hall, its perimeter filled with dancers in an oxymoron of activity and sloth. Some lounged, eating snacks on the floor, others texted, read, or played games on their smartphones, while others leaned against the barres, stretching. Some mentally ticked routines with hand gestures and steps. A few, memorizing the sequence just seen, repeated the moves in their small space, hoping to be noticed for understudy work, just in case. Most didn't miss a single moment of praise or criticism given by Analisse.

"You staying at Roberto's?" Anne asked as they reached the corner where Francesca was mopping up her sweat and getting her breathing under control. Analisse was reviewing Martina's movements and suggesting minor changes.

"How's he doing?" Francesca whispered, with the usual touch of whimsy whenever Elena's brother's name came up. She'd had a soft spot for him ever since she was twelve.

"As far as I know he's fine. I'm apartment sitting while he's in LA."

"Another film score?" Anne asked.

Elena nodded, studying Martina as she repeated one of Lise's variations for *La fille mal gardée*. She'd added Analisse's previous suggestions to her movements. Truth be told, the woman was impeccable in technique. Elena watched as she held a *relevé développé* for a ridiculous moment. Seamless transition into *coupé, pas de bourrée,* and pirouettes. Incredible.

After the usual words of praise for a job well done, Caro and Mario took center stage. Elena took the moment to grab a banana and yogurt from her insulated polka-dot lunch bag and watched their rehearsal.

"How was your session?" she whispered to Francesca.

"Could have been better," Francesca admitted. "Justin was a bit off."

Anne chuckled. "Elena's presence, no doubt."

Francesca leaned forward. "He definitely acted weird during your rehearsal, especially during the kiss scene."

"That would have discombobulated him, definitely," Anne said. Her lips quirked into a smirk. "He's a tad possessive, even of ex-lovers."

"Oh, shush, both of you."

Elena's eyes roamed from the rehearsing dancers over to Broderick, who sat next to Derek, who, in turn, was engaged in conversation with Jake Forrester during another pause.

She poked Anne, who had started to darn the platform of her new toe shoe.

"Who is that next to Mr. Derek?"

"That's Jake Forrester," Anne said after a quick glance.

Elena swallowed more yogurt. "I know his name is Jake Forrester," she said a bit irritated. "What's he doing here?"

"He's the company's insurance underwriter."

"Haven't convinced him to insure my legs, yet," Francesca said, and executed a beautiful *développé*. "I mean, come on. Even Taylor Swift insures her legs. Aren't mine better?"

"You are already covered under the company's umbrella policy," Anne said. "And you couldn't afford the premiums on such frivolity."

Francesca chuckled. "There is that. Still."

"Is he always at rehearsals?" Elena asked.

Anne stopped darning, studied her, then resumed prepping her toe shoes.

"There seems to be an issue with who owns the rights to *Black Rhapsody*. When the company reached out to René Fauchier's estate to get permission to stage it, they bumped into the Gordian knot of legalese. And without permission to stage, Jake won't underwrite the ballet. And without insurance, no ballet. Very tiresome."

"So why audition now?" Elena asked.

"Broderick is dead set on finishing the piece," Anne said. "Getting ahead of the game. And Derek is an eternal optimist. He's given Jake carte blanche to do what's necessary to get those permissions."

"And Jake is a terrier at heart," Francesca said. "Do you have another yogurt in there? I'm starving."

Elena slid her lunch bag over to her friend's eager hands and bit into her banana, all the while studying Broderick Newsom, who was in earnest conversation with Derck and Forrester.

Black Rhapsody was, by all accounts, and especially stated by those who had been present at the rare rehearsals more than ten years ago, a brilliant, choreographic tour de force likened to such influential greats as Balanchine, Ashton, MacMillan, Cranko, and Robbins. But it had been left unfinished because of the untimely death of its aging creator, master choreographer René Fauchier.

During the first year after Fauchier's death, there had been multiple attempts to finish and stage the choreography, but all had ended in failure...whether through injuries, lack of permissions, bankruptcy, or absence of funds. That, ultimately, had catapulted the ballet into the realms of myth, baptizing it as jinxed.

Or cursed.

Take your pick.

Ballet dancers, after all, were a superstitious lot.

In the end, for ten years, *Black Rhapsody* had remained unfinished and unstaged, like Michelangelo's nonfinito-style sculptures. What people didn't know was that the ballet *had* been finished.

And Elena knew the truth of it all.

Enter Broderick Newsom into the picture.

Terpsichore's current artistic director and resident choreographer, a mediocre dancer, somewhat talented in choreography, and incredibly ambitious, had decided the ballet should be completed and performed. Period. This year. Why should such a magnificent piece be left gathering dust in the catacombs of ballet history? Hadn't books and movies been finished after the death of their creators, only to gather success and accolades in generations beyond? Broderick had convinced Derek the staging would be the crowning glory to the ballet company, which was dedicated to Fauchier's legacy.

Of course, Elena thought, nobody mentioned the financial bonanza it would garner. And Elena was certain those two were moved more by the possibility of new fame and glory rather than by the rumors of possible catastrophe.

Well, here I am. Possible catastrophe in the flesh.

Her attention turned to Jake Forrester, who was listening patiently to Derek's attempt at persuasion. Elena watched as he respectfully waited for Derek to finish his say, but, from his serious expression, Elena doubted his response would be the answer Derek wished to hear.

Interesting to see, once she had her say, to what lengths Derek, Broderick, and Jake Forrester would go in order to obtain those permissions.

"He is a hunk," Francesca whispered.

"Stop that."

"And quite a catch," Anne added. "Not at all like Justin."

"Good grief. Listen to you two." Elena huffed. "First, I'm not that desperate. And, second, I'm not looking."

"Actually, what you look is a bit uptight," Anne said with her usual flair for reading Elena's moods. "A good romp in the hay would do wonders, especially with that specimen." She grabbed one end of her precut elastic bands and began sewing it by the side seam of her toe shoe. "And it seems you've caught his attention. Jake's eyes wander your way every chance he gets."

"Yeah, right." Elena stood. Jake's eyes pivoted toward her and he smiled. Elena blushed.

"See?" Anne said.

"What I need is to talk to Mr. Derek before the audition starts, not a dating service."

"Ooh, you sound so mysterious," Francesca said, her fingers moving like a witch casting a spell. "What gives?"

"You'll have to wait for it." *Not for long, anyway.*

"Elena," Anne warned. "Derek hates interruptions, you know that." She glanced at the wall clock. "And we're already an hour behind schedule. Why don't you wait till dinner tonight?" Anne suggested.

"This can't wait."

"Why not?"

"It just can't," Elena said.

"Stop, stop, *stop*."

Analisse's aggravated tone of voice halted all whisperings in the room.

"What on earth is wrong with you today?"

Caro, bent over, mumbled a breathless apology.

"Your balance is off, your *piqué arabesques* are wobbly, and Mario," she turned to Caro's partner. "What on earth are you doing in the *allongés*? Grab Caro like you mean it."

Caro wiped sweat with her forearm. "You know," she looked around the room, her eyes full of annoyance and disdain. "If the rehearsal room were less of a cackling chicken coop, I'd be less distracted." She strode to the doors. "I need some water. Be right back." And with that, she marched out of the rehearsal room.

"Martina..." Analisse turned, glancing around the room. "Now, where on earth did that girl go to?"

Someone shouted she'd gone to the locker room. Another to the bathroom.

"I'm sorry, Derek," Analisse apologized. "I'll rehearse these two later."

Derek pointed to the back of the room. "Why don't you use Elena over there to help Mario with his partnering?"

Analisse pointed to Elena and then to the floor next to her. "Center stage, please."

Oh hell. This would not look good to Caro. Another excuse to dislike Elena.

Elena's reluctance showed in her hesitant steps toward Mario. He mouthed his thanks. A cute man, with a boyish face, perfect technique, who'd been recently promoted to soloist, he was at that stage where he was still eager to please and learn, not dismissive because of his new status.

Analisse turned to Mario.

"Fauchier," explained Analisse. "Wanted this to be a moment of beauty, not prowess. An instant of pure form in the adagio, akin to still life." Analisse grabbed Elena's hand, pulled her forward, and settled her in place.

"Elena, please, *piqué arabesque*. Mario, hip to thigh."

Analisse moved Mario's hand from her waist to her hip. "This is the first mistake. If you hold her by the hip, she stabilizes better. Now, *allongé*. Bring her with you slowly. She and your leg are one. Hold. Hold. See the difference?" She pointed to the mirror.

They both looked. Arms, bodies, and legs created a beautiful pattern.

"Now deepen your *allongé* a bit and make believe your hands stretch to infinity. Yes, that's it. Bring her back upright. Perfect. Did you see that, Caro?"

Caroline, who was now standing behind Mario, nodded.

"Ok. Let's see that." Analisse turned and sat. "Thank you, Elena."

"Making me look bad already?" Caro muttered, bumping her shoulder out of the way.

Elena simply looked at her. "Oh, give up."

She went back to her friends.

"Well, she's not in a great mood," Francesca said.

"You are way too nice." Elena opened a small Tupperware from her lunch bag, dug out an apple slice, and munched.

"Come on, Elena. She's going through a rough patch. It's not her fault Justin dumped her."

"I must admit," Anne mumbled as she cut thread with her teeth. "She was heavy duty into Justin. Rumors had them marrying by year's end."

"Enter Brzinsky," Francesca said. "Talented, ambitious, the sky's the limit in opportunities here."

"And *young*," Anne added. "More years added to Justin's career if they become partners."

"I'm positive she's not balking at his attention," Elena said, picking another apple slice. "He is an established dancer, with a worldwide reputation. Especially in dramatic roles."

Anne chuckled. "Bullseye, dear. She's been after Derek for weeks to dance Manon next season."

No wonder Caroline Wainwright was touchy.

Fred's hip bumped her before she could eat another apple slice.

"Stop eating." He snatched the remaining two from inside the container.

"Hey, get your own snacks."

He grinned. The food disappeared with impressive speed. "How ungrateful. I'm only helping, or I won't be able to lift you."

Elena snapped the lid into place just as enthusiastic claps marked the end of Caro and Mario's rehearsal.

"Wait till we get home," she hip bumped Fred. "I'm telling."

They smirked at each other.

"Ok, everyone," Analisse said. "Thank you. Excellent, excellent work today. Let's take ten and return for the audition. And make sure you check rehearsal schedules downstairs," she added, raising her voice for the benefit of those taking advantage of the break. "There are a few changes in it, so don't say I didn't warn you."

"I'd better grab Mr. Derek before the hordes come back."

Elena mentally crossed herself, grabbed a USB thumb drive from her ballet bag, breathed deeply, and ambled over to where Derek Michaels held court with Jake Forrester, Broderick, and now Analisse.

Silver haired, three years shy of seventy-five summers, the founder of Terpsichore was a force to reckon with. Principal dancer at American Theater for fifteen years, he'd shared the stage with such greats as Baryshnikov, Dowell, and a young Corella; had partnered with Ferri, Guillem, among others; and had danced classic choreographies, as well as modern ones, including his best friend's, Fauchier's. Then a hip labral tear injury forced his retirement. But Derek Michaels was nothing if not incredibly shrewd, or a lucky bastard as many viper tongues remarked. He'd refocused his energies and ambitions as impresario, and, together with Fauchier, had founded the Terpsichore Ballet, and its complementary ballet school, twenty years ago. Hard work and vision had propelled the initial ragtag group of ten dancers into a world-renowned and respected school of dance and company of more than one hundred and sixty. It hadn't hurt he'd married a rich New York socialite, ten years his senior, who'd been after his heart and body for several years. Now, with an inexhaustible hand on the money pot, he'd placed his dreams on hold in order to give prominence to others' dreams. At least, that was the marketing slogan he sprouted to the media and to patrons alike.

"I don't know if it's a runaround or sincerity," Jake was saying as she approached the group. "Said he'd get back to me as soon as possible."

"This is bull," Broderick said. "That lawyer is screwing with you."

Jake shrugged. "Maybe, or not. He did say the rights owner was overseas on a business trip."

"We'll just have to wait until that person returns to get an answer," Derek said. "Just stay on top of it."

"Remember what we decided this morning," Broderick told Derek. "We need..."

"Mr. Derek?"

"Elena, dear." The pleasure in Derek Michaels's voice was heartfelt.

"So good to see you, sir." Even though her family had known him from before she could execute a *changement,* she never addressed him as anything else but Mr. Derek or "sir." A sign of respect.

"Welcome home," he said. "This is a real treat."

"You're only saying that because you're plotting to get your hands on my *Concerto.*"

He chuckled. "How long have you known me?"

"Too many years to count, sir."

He turned to Jake Forrester. "Diplomacy at its best. I've known this beautiful young lady and her family for more years than I can count and she never mentions my age." He grinned. "Have you two met?"

"Told her she's a sight better looking than you," Jake said.

Elena blushed.

"How're Stef and Roberto?" Derek asked.

"Stefanía is loving Chicago. And Roberto sent his love before waltzing off to compose another film score."

"Wait." Jake's surprise was evident. "Roberto del Carral? Isn't that..."

"Your ringtone," Elena told Jake.

"Your brother?" The killer smile turned deadlier. "Wow. Now I definitely have to get to know you better."

Broderick Newsom, who possibly considered he'd been ignored for far too long, extended his hand.

"We haven't formally met." He shook hands with Elena. "Thank you for accepting our invitation to the gala. It's an honor to have you and Boelens dance with us. And, congratulations, by the way. That was a piece of luck with *Concerto*. The buzz has started."

Elena saw that eyes and words did not convey the same message.

And you are one jealous SOB, aren't you?

Derek's eyebrow arched. "That wasn't luck. That was talent. Isn't that right, dear?"

"I'd like to think so," Elena smiled. She hoped that by baring her canines, Broderick Newsom would get the message she could bite and hold her own.

"As to your *Concerto*, we'll talk later. Tomorrow, maybe. You know I like to keep the company fresh, exciting. A rich repertoire makes for happy dancers, audiences, and..."

"Patrons," she finished.

"Precisely."

"As a matter of fact, Mr. Derek, I wondered if we could have a word..."

"Mr. Michaels." Harriet Madison, Derek's personal assistant for fifteen years, approached, her rapid staccato taps accenting an urgency reflected in her expression. And that was unusual in itself, Elena thought, because it took a lot to perturb Harriet Madison.

"I'm so sorry," she waved several sheets of paper in her hand. "But there's a hiccup with the schedules that needs fixing immediately. And," she lowered her voice. "Nina Walsh from *Dance America* is on hold. Wants to confirm rumors about certain *incidents* before the taping tomorrow. Told her you're in the middle of rehearsals, but she's adamant. Won't take no for an answer."

"Be right back," Derek said to Broderick, who took the interruption as his excuse to join Martina, Caro, and Justin at the far corner of the room. Annalisse followed suit seconds later.

"What was all that about?" Francesca asked, giving Jake an enthusiastic hug. Fred and Anne were not far behind.

"Something about the schedules," Elena said.

Anne shook her head. "Derek usually doesn't look exasperated about a schedule screwup."

"Nina Walsh's journalistic nose must be itching," Jake said. "Wants clarification about certain rumors. Sorry, but I need to find out what's going on."

"Oh dear," said Anne.

"What rumors?" Fred asked.

"Not rumors. Facts. There have been petty thefts recently. Nothing too critical," Anne said, her eyes on the exit door.

"What about the vandalism?" Francesca asked. "That's a bit more critical."

"What vandalism?" Elena was surprised at her friend's worried expression.

"Toe shoes ruined," Francesca began.

Elena chuckled. "Come on, Frannie. We're sadists with our toe shoes. We mutilate, break, scar, and cut them up all the time." She herself cut part of her shank toward the heel and beat the box practically to extinction when she had a role where her jumps on stage needed to be silent.

"It is when stitches holding ribbons in place are cut deliberately, or when an entire bottle of instant Jet glue is poured inside the box, ruining the toe shoe."

"Nothing's been proven, Frannie, according to the powers that be," Anne said.

"Tell that to Angelique," Francesca replied, "who's crying every day because her ankle is a mess." She looked at Elena. "Someone sabotaged both her ribbons and elastic, which snapped just as she was practicing *fouettés*. She's young corps, but extremely talented, and rising quickly up the ranks. When they checked what happened, Derek and Broderick could see the dental floss and thread she'd used were cut, not torn."

"Are you serious?" Elena couldn't quite believe it.

"Sounds like someone is targeting the women in the company," Fred said.

"Unfortunately," Francesca answered.

"But not entirely true," Anne continued. "Justin's dance belt was tampered with."

"How can you tamper with a dance cup?" Fred asked.

"Someone rubbed itching powder on the inside," Anne said. "After he put it on..."

"Ouch," Fred said and crossed his legs in a protective move.

"And don't forget the thumb tack hidden under the insole of Tess's toe shoe," Francesca added. "It did a number on her heel. She couldn't dance for two days."

"Who's Tess?" Elena asked.

"One of our principal dancers," Anne clarified and pointed to a petite dancer by the door. She was flexing a resistance band with a foot, exercising ankle, arch, and toes.

"I've heard this type of thing sometimes happens in the big dance schools in Russia," Fred said. "It's a way of taking out the competition."

Everyone turned to stare at Martina Brzinsky.

"Oh, stop that," Elena said. "How long has this been going on?"

"About six months now," Anne answered.

"All I know is that very little is being done," Francesca said.

"That's because most of the incidents can be pigeonholed as accidents," Anne said. "After all, similar things have happened to all of us."

"Who's investigating these incidents?" Elena asked.

"Jake," Anne said. "But it's slow going."

Elena was surprised. "I thought he was an insurance underwriter."

"He is, but his actual job at the insurance company is as fraud investigator," Anne said. "Makes sure his employer underwrites the right people, right events, not scams and all that."

Elena wanted to find out more, especially about this man whom she found a bit too fascinating, but further conversation was interrupted by Derek's return.

"Okay, everyone," Derek said. "Gather round me, please."

Elena followed Anne and Francesca at a slower pace, remaining at the periphery of the group, where Fred stood. Jake, who'd followed Derek into the room, joined her.

"What's going on?" she whispered. Jake simply shook his head.

"I've just hung up with Nina Walsh from *Dance America*," Derek began. "To put it mildly, not only was I surprised by what she hinted at, but I was particularly dismayed our internal issues are being broadcast to outsiders. Now, I don't know if anyone here has directly spoken to Nina about these pranks, as she euphemistically referred to them..."

"Are you seriously suggesting we've blabbed to the press?" Justin interrupted.

"Sure looks that way," Caroline added.

"Now, Caroline, Justin, I'm not pointing fingers," Derek answered. "No names were dropped. However, Nina was well informed about the issue. Need I warn everyone here that a comment to friends or family, who later turn around and post things online, is a potential breach of contract?"

Disgruntlement abounded. Heads shook in denial. Others kept mum and fidgeted. They knew better than to oppose, or disagree, with the founder of the company.

"From now on, I hope there are no more rumors reaching Nina's ears. I also expect professional behavior during the *Dance America* taping tomorrow, is that understood? Nina is a journalist, and she's already chomping at the bit at what she suspects is a juicy story."

"But, Derek," one of the dancers interrupted. "What if we're asked point-blank?"

Martina scoffed loud enough to be heard. "Never speak to press," she stated. "They're all pir... What is that fish that bites in Amazon?"

"The word you want is piranha, dear," Anne supplied. "Piranha." She glanced at Elena and rolled her eyes.

"Enough, Anne," Derek said.

Anne lowered her eyes.

Elena watched her friend's discomfiture at the reprimand and tried to keep pity from showing in her eyes. Derek and Anne had been lovers for close to fifteen years. True love, according to some. But Elena couldn't reconcile the definition of true love with the many moments of desertion by Derek whenever he had to attend functions, vacations, or whatever else he had to do with his wife; nor could she reconcile the duplicity of keeping Anne on a perennial hook of possibility—there, but not there. A perpetual blister in Anne's life, which she'd accepted stoically like a true dancer—dismissing the constant pain and enduring it as part of her circumstances.

Elena wished Anne would retaliate somehow, but knew it wouldn't happen. These public reprimands had occurred before. Elena had witnessed many when she'd worked at Terpsichore. And she didn't like them. It was not right.

"Rest assured that Broderick, Analisse and myself will intervene and referee any uncomfortable questions during the taping, if they occur, Tess," Derek answered. "Your job is to dance and not comment on internal Terpsichore issues, even if asked point-blank. Does everyone understand?" His gaze, bordering on displeasure, fell on every member of the group.

"Good," Derek said, satisfied. "Now, before we start, I'd like for everyone to welcome Elena and Fred from Ballet Etudes."

Smiles and applause, some enthusiastic, some anemic, reverberated around the room. Never one to miss a curtain call, and knowing it would raise the bile meter of Justin and Caroline, Elena took Fred's hand and dipped into a deep *reverence* that rivaled any curtsy given to a queen. Fred bowed to acknowledge the accolades.

Francesca and Anne whooped. Jake smiled.

"The old troupers here already know Elena. But our newer members may not know she was Terpsichore raised and trained from the very day René and I founded this wonderful ballet school and company. Her mother, Amalia del Carral, God rest her soul, was our talented Head of Costume Design and Wardrobe before retiring and handing the bolt, so to speak, to Maricela."

At the mention of her mother, Elena's eyes misted. She was grateful Derek had mentioned the woman who had sacrificed and contributed so much to the company as well.

"Elena's also turning into quite a choreographer, as you've heard," Derek continued. "Her debut work, *Concerto in D*, received multiple accolades in Europe and would have made my dear friend and cofounder, René Fauchier, so very proud. Elena, kudos my dear."

Elena's cheeks exploded with heat. Jake, next to her, clapped in tandem with Fred, Francesca, and Anne.

"So, that's why you invited her," someone from the group said.

Whoops of laughter erupted.

"Now, Randy..."

"Secret's out," Anne said and turned to Elena. "Make sure Derek grovels properly and gives you exactly what you want, dear."

"Ah, come on, Anne," Analisse complained.

"Ah, come on, Analisse," she retorted.

"Stop it, you two," Derek said. "We're already behind schedule and we have an important announcement to make. Broderick?"

Broderick took center stage. Elena didn't like the bowl-of-cream smile on his face. Something was up. She would bet her toe shoes on it.

"Are you all right?" Jake whispered. "You tensed up."

"I'm fine."

"No, you're tense."

"I promise I'll make this short," Broderick began.

"You never make anything short," Francesca quipped.

Broderick laughed. "Ok, busted. But this will be quick, I promise. We have a very busy day tomorrow and it starts early. So, first things first. Many of you know we've been in negotiations with The Royal Ballet to stage *Manon*. I'm happy to announce that they've agreed and their creative producer will be handling the project. Due to her prior commitments to the company, however, things won't happen until the end of next season."

Groans and boos erupted around the room. Elena glanced over to where Martina, Justin, and Caroline were. Expressions alternated from disappointment, to delight, to impatience.

"I understand your frustrations, believe me, but we've had to juggle a nightmare in scheduling on both sides. That was the best we could do. Secondly, I had a long conversation with Derek this morning and we came to a decision not to hold auditions for *Black Rhapsody*. Instead, we'll start staging it immediately. Sorry to those who were looking forward for the chance, but Derek agreed with my recommendations and gave me the green light. Text messages will go out later this evening to let those I've chosen know what roles they'll be dancing."

Elena turned on Jake.

"Did you know about this?" The fierce whisper of disapproval appeared to take him by surprise.

"No, I didn't," he said, not looking pleased either. "Why wasn't I consulted?" Jake asked.

"Because it doesn't affect your job," Derek said, dismissing his concern.

"Mr. Derek," Elena interrupted. "A word in private, please?"

"Later, dear."

"Rehearsals begin tomorrow at eleven sharp," Broderick continued.

"Mr. Derek..." Louder.

"I reviewed the tape of the last *Black Rhapsody* rehearsal yesterday," Broderick continued from his faux pedestal. "So many ideas flowed that I can't wait to get on with it. I'll add a more modern twist and challenging choreography to expand on Fauchier's theme while preserving his style, of course."

Elena was getting more furious by the minute. Her hand fisted, the metal of the USB connector of her thumb drive biting into her palm. This would not do.

"*Mr. Derek*..." Emphatic.

Anne and Francesca heard the note of vexed urgency in her tone and were now curiously watching her. So was the entire group.

Jake placed his hand over her fisted one. "What is going on?"

"Elena, I never knew you to be rude, dear," Derek reprimanded softly.

"Stop this, please," Elena pleaded.

"Don't mind her, Broderick," Caroline's voice chimed in. "She's probably angry she can't audition for the ballet."

Elena faced Caroline. "Ignorant people should stay quiet and out of it."

Derek was not pleased. "Elena, remember where you are and that you are a guest here. This is no place for a scene or petty jealousies."

"That's okay, Derek," Broderick said. "I understand..."

"No, you don't." Elena itched to slap the fatuous smile from his face.

"Please," Broderick said. "Spare us your artistic temperament. I juggle plenty as artistic director here." He turned to the group, dismissing her. "As I was saying, tomorrow, I'll continue adding..."

"No, you won't," Elena said.

Derek was now livid. "Elena. My office. Now."

"Why not?" Anne's calm question, thrown into the heat of things, demanded sudden clarification.

Elena turned to her.

Anne's expression changed from curiosity to caution. "Oh my."

She needed to leave. Now. Before she lost her cool. Before her wayward mouth blurted what was on the tip of her tongue in front of most of the company. What she had to divulge needed to be said in private. The revelation was not for everyone's ear. At least not at the initial reveal.

She needed to leave. Go somewhere quiet. Anyplace to gather her wits. Talk to Derek privately. He deserved to know first.

Elena picked up her ballet bag.

Jake stopped her.

"Elena, what is going on?"

"Yes, Ms. del Carral, please," Broderick said. "Enlighten us."

It was the snarky tone that did her in. She slowly disengaged her hand from Jake's. With as regal a stare as she could manage, she first glanced at Broderick, then at Derek, and zeroed in on Jake.

"You won't stage a damn thing because it's *my* permission you need, *my* ballet, and *my* ending." She waved the thumb drive in front of Jake's face. "And here's my proof."

To say that the fracas which erupted was worthy of a volcanic erup-tion was the understatement of the season.

"You're the rights holder." More an affirmation rather than a query. And more scrutiny than she cared for, as well. Elena realized at that instant that Jake was more observant and perceptive than he let on. She'd need to be careful around him.

"Your ballet," Jake continued.

"Yes."

"She's lying," Broderick said, closing in on her like a shark sniffing prey, Derek not far behind. Both men had identical expressions: indig-nation mixed with a dose of incredulity and distrust.

"No. I'm not." She didn't bother with them. She simply looked at Jake.

"Are we just going to take her word for this, Derek?" Caroline asked. She, Justin, Analisse, and Martina had closed ranks behind Derek. Her friends gathered close to her. The rest of the company huddled in small groups, some talking in whispers, the rest listening to every word.

"I never thought you'd take credit for somebody else's work," Derek told her, disappointment and hurt tainting his voice. "And definitely not Fauchier's."

"Let's not jump to conclusions," Anne said, ever the arbiter. "Why don't we hear what she has to say?"

Jake, in the meantime, hadn't said a word. He kept studying her.

"But why she claiming *Black Rhapsody* is hers?" Martina asked. "Does anyone know?"

"Maybe her new stardom has turned her brain," Justin told Martina.

"Not cool, Justin," Francesca said. "Not cool at all."

Elena ignored everyone. She turned Jake's hand and pressed the flash drive into his palm.

"This is the original video copy, not what has been circulated for years," Elena said, and pointed to Broderick. "Definitely not what he has."

"What a load of crap." Broderick, now somewhat desperate, turned to Derek. "Well? When are you going to put a stop to this ridiculous nonsense? It's evident what she's doing."

Derek, however, had turned unexpectedly cautious, sensing the tables might be about to turn on them.

"Does anyone here have a laptop I can borrow?" Jake asked.

Analisse rushed over to her things. "Here," she said, setting it up on top of the piano.

Jake extended the flash drive to her. Analisse set up the computer in record time, while the whole group gathered around to watch the small screen.

Elena knew what was coming.

She didn't bother to stay. As Fauchier's voice introduced Elena, recommending to a panel of judges to accept her choreography of *Black Rhapsody* for consideration at the International Choreographic Competition in Hanover, she left the room.

There was a whole lot of satisfaction in the funereal silence, as the music to *Black Rhapsody* began.

Chapter Two

ELENA PUNCHED OPEN THE DOOR TO THE EMPTY REHEARSAL studio.

Let's face it, she was fed up. And because she was fed up, she needed to expend the anger and the frustration she felt. Choreographing was the only thing that worked for her. Or a class. But since this was the dead zone in Terpsichore, with no classes to be had or rehearsals due to lunch break, she couldn't release her emotions with jumps, turns, or kicks.

She was doubly fed up because she'd roller coasted through a grueling, emotion-packed two hours since her disclosure. Unnecessary drama, if someone had bothered to ask her. The simplest part of those hours had been notifying her lawyers about denying Terpsichore permission to stage her work. The harder had been getting away from everyone. Derek had wanted immediate explanations for the deception, going on for close to forty minutes in his office about Fauchier's betrayal and her downright stabbing him in the back. Broderick would occasionally surface from his funk with minor interruptions, repeating his incredulity about *Black Rhapsody* truly being hers. Jake, in the meantime, had been in constant communication with Elena's lawyers, trying to corroborate her statement, her video, and other important details while ignoring the barrage of interruptions and flare-ups from the angry, disillusioned men in the room.

After the umpteenth abuse and complaint, she'd had enough. She'd made a quick exit, avoiding as many people as she could, only to bump into Caroline as she'd been exiting the locker room. Elena had braced for a confrontation, or the cold shoulder, but what she did get was a look that had disturbed her, if she were honest about it.

If looks could kill, Elena thought, she'd be on her way to an early grave.

Not that she didn't understand Caroline's behavior. Caroline had accurately surmised Elena would never use her as principal in *Black Rhapsody*. Francesca, being her best friend and the better dancer, would be Elena's first choice. And Justin...

Justin.

He'd corralled her the moment after he'd pulled her into an empty classroom. Had turned all loving and persuasive, presuming she'd use him as principal for *Black Rhapsody* for old times' sake. The moment he'd realized she wasn't biting and was disgusted by his pretense, he'd turned nasty, yelling all kinds of things as she left him standing there, the pièce de résistance being his comment of her being "a nasty, selfish, opportunistic whore," which had been witnessed by the many Terpsichore dancers in the vicinity and in the hallway. So had been her angry comeback about Justin being a "washed out, has-been Lothario, whom she'd be caught dead using in any of her works, ever."

Something clattered across the floor.

What the heck?

Elena stared as a small cylindrical, orange object rolled to a standstill a couple of inches from her toe shoe.

Curious, she picked it up.

That was when she realized she wasn't alone in the room.

Saw it.

No, not it. A he.

"I'm so sorry," she said, backing up a bit, not wanting to disturb the person resting there. "I thought the room was empty."

She was about to turn when something about the position of the prone figure didn't make sense. Neither did the darkish stain by the head.

"Are you all right?" she asked, and approached cautiously.

Then it hit her.

The prone figure wasn't resting. It was the body of Justin, unconscious, his blood spreading around his head like a halo of spilled paint.

Elena rushed to her bag, grabbed her phone, and tried dialing 911.

"Help," she yelled at the top of her lungs.

She punched 911, but got 912, her trembling fingers not cooperating.

"Come on, come on, come on," she punched and deleted until she got the right combination. She ran back to the door, opened it.

"Somebody, help," she screamed again at the top of her lungs. Several dancers rushed over, alarmed. "Get Mr. Derek, Jake, anybody." She rushed back inside.

She finally heard a male dispatcher ask how to direct her emergency.

"Yes, 911? Someone's hurt badly. Please, please help."

And in between giving information to the dispatcher, she kept screaming like a banshee for Jake, Derek, or anyone to come help.

ELENA SAT ON A CHAIR, like a punished child, awaiting the pleasure of the detectives who had taken over the scene.

She blinked, as if that could erase the reality of the horror she'd witnessed.

Nope. The blood stain was still there, unlike the body, which had been rushed to the hospital in hopes of saving Justin's life.

She looked to her left. Yep. The uniform remained guarding the door, ascertaining no one entered the now-empty rehearsal hall, although she suspected it was more so she wouldn't go anywhere.

She almost giggled.

Nerves. Get ahold of yourself.

Check.

Elena, however, still wished Jake, Francesca, Anne, or Fred had been granted permission to stay with her. Unfortunately, the two detectives who'd arrived about fifteen minutes ago and had introduced themselves as Detectives Harris and Murdock, had herded everyone out of the rehearsal hall, ordered her to stay, and proceeded to blatantly ignore her. They were currently focused on examining the cordoned-off area, on collecting evidence, all the while talking sotto voce, with the tech taking photos and samples around the section by the piano.

Not for the first time, she wondered whether the police would deign to question her about what she'd stumbled on. Maybe they'd forgotten she was there?

Not likely.

Double-check.

Elena glanced at the uniform. The man looked uncomfortable and bored. She looked over the policeman's head to the peek windows in the entrance swing doors of the rehearsal hall, and saw myriad faces, like bobbing balloons, jockeying for position and not wanting to miss anything going on inside. She shifted her eyes to the viewing room windows on the upper floor. More faces, this time like colorful lollipop sticks, silently watching in various degrees of concern, curiosity, and dismay. Elena was certain speculation in the company ran rampant. So were the questions she was sure the police were thinking. Had it been an unfortunate accident? Or had it been assault? Had Justin slipped and fallen, headfirst, hitting the piano on the way down? Or had Elena, in a fit of peeve, pushed hard enough for him to stumble and fall against the edge of the piano? After all, the detectives would be told Justin had been her ex-lover. That they'd had an acrimonious breakup. They'd been seen arguing earlier this afternoon. And she was the one who'd found the body barely an hour ago.

Don't call it body. He's not dead yet.

That you know of.

Oh God.

Maybe she should create an Elena del Carral *This is Your Life* TV moment: beware the day that starts innocuously...it will bite you in your well-muscled behind.

She shivered.

Elena stood and faced the detectives.

"Listen, is this going to take any longer?"

"What's the rush, Ms. Carral?"

"del Carral," she corrected.

Detective Harris acknowledged the correction with a nod. "Please be patient. We're almost done here."

"Would you mind, then, if I do some stretching over on that side?" She pointed to the opposite end of the room, near the blocked door. "I need to stay warm for rehearsals."

The detective's partner didn't hide his surprise. "Rehearsal? After this?" He pointed to the blood.

Elena swallowed. Such thoughtfulness.

"I'm sure you've heard the show must go on." She grabbed her bag, realized she was still clutching the empty medicine bottle she'd kicked and picked up on entering the rehearsal hall. She paused. This small, translucent, orange, plastic tube had been the reason she'd not seen Justin lying by the piano at first. Wasn't even sure if she'd kicked it or if the door had rolled it away from her as she entered. She stared at it. The prescription label had been mostly torn off, possibly ripped in impatience. Only a few bar-code lines were visible, and the letters *c iz* were discernible.

But worse... her prints were all over it.

Great.

She walked over to the detectives. "Here." She gave Detective Harris the bottle. "I found it on the floor by the door. Don't know if it's important, or whose it is."

She left them to their task and made her way to the corner.

"Ms. del Carral...wait."

Well, that was one way to force an interview. She dropped her bag under the barre and turned.

"Why didn't you give this to us immediately?" asked Detective Harris.

"Honestly?"

"Always helps."

"I forgot. It's all been a blur."

"Where did you find it?" asked Murdock.

She pointed to the floor a couple of feet from the uniform. "There. When I came in, I heard a rattle. I checked the floor, and there it was."

She cleared her throat several times before looking at Harris in the eye. "That's why I didn't see Justin lying..." She waved her hand in the direction of the crime tape.

"Exactly where did you pick it up?"

She measured and calculated, and walked to the area. "Somewhere here," she said. "I was wondering what the heck it was when, out of the corner of my eye, I saw Justin." She faced the detectives. "I didn't recognize him, at first. Thought it was one of the dancers resting. You know, we do that a lot."

"What exactly?" asked Murdock.

"Search for a quiet place to rest between rehearsals or classes. Some call it a power nap, but it's just relaxation. Ballet dancers are, well, tight people."

Detective Harris's lips twitched a smidge.

"Did you see anything else?" he asked. "Find anything else?"

Elena shook her head no.

"Was this empty when you found it?"

"Yes, Detective," Elena answered. "It was empty."

Detective Harris opened the bottle, sniffed, and sealed it.

"There's some residue inside," he said to his partner and handed the bottle to the tech he'd called over. "Catalog and take pictures, here and here. And let's rush this to the lab. Find out what it is."

Detective Harris opened his notebook and asked, "When you found your colleague, did you move him? Touch him?"

"Hell, no. I'd never move another dancer after a nasty fall. Either the injured party gets up by themselves, or else I call for medical assistance. Unless..." She shrugged. "Unless, of course, it's an inconsequential drop, like falling on your behind. Or tripping. Then I help."

He wrote something on his notepad.

"What exactly did you do, then, when you saw your colleague injured?"

Elena swallowed. "I walked over." She closed her eyes. "Called out to him, but he didn't respond. Saw the blood." She omitted the part where she'd screamed like a bloody lunatic until Jake had appeared.

"Did anyone else touch him?"

"Only Jake. Mr. Derek didn't allow anyone near Justin."

"Mr. Derek, the director of the dance company?" interrupted Murdock.

"Yes."

"And who is this, Jake, you say?" Harris asked.

"Jake Forrester. He underwrites the ballets for the company. He checked for a pulse, but that's all. The EMTs did the rest."

"Let's go over your day, if you don't mind. You arrived... when?"

"A little before company class ended, around ten-ish. Went to the rehearsal Studio 4, warmed up. Rehearsed." She skipped over the debacle of her revelation.

"Did you speak with Mr. Bakare any time afterward?"

"After." She left it at that.

But the lead detective must have heard the nervousness in her voice. He waited.

"Justin cornered me earlier. Wanted me to cast him as lead in my new ballet, for old times' sake. We..." She was about to blurt *argued*, but changed it to "disagreed. He was miffed."

"Was there a history between you? *Old times' sake* is usually code for intimacy."

Elena blushed. "That was a long time ago, Detective Harris. I've moved on. So has he. And I no longer work for Terpsichore. I'm here only because I've been invited to dance at their gala fund raiser."

"But you worked here before."

"Yes. Five years ago, to be exact. I'm currently employed as a principal dancer at Ballet Etudes in Monaco."

"Really?" said Murdoch.

"Yes."

"Nice."

"Is Mr. Bakare, as far as you know, in a relationship?" Harris asked.

The ruckus that exploded outside the doors caught everyone by surprise, including the uniform guarding the door.

"Where IS she?"

Oh God. Caroline.

"Miss, you can't come in here." The policeman pointed to the door. "You have to..."

"You bitch."

Normal people underestimate the speed and strength of a petite dancer, who looks like the softest wind could topple her over. But they are all deceived. Female dancers are strong. Everywhere. Arms, legs, feet, even toes. And the bundle of fury that had just entered the rehearsal hall was no exception. Hurt, rage, and fear, had created a dangerous dynamo, one the poor policeman wasn't able to stop. Caroline pushed him aside with such force, the man bumped against the barre. Shouts of "Stop," "Don't go in there," "What are you doing?" from Derek, Broderick, and Jake, mingled with those of the two detectives warning Caroline to cease and desist. She ignored all, rounding on Elena with impressive speed.

"It's all your fault." Caroline raged, crying. "*Your* fault he's in a coma, you bitch."

"Caro..."

Heat and pain erupted on Elena's cheek, followed by a throbbing that resounded in her ears like a furious heartbeat. The whiplash that accompanied the slap was severe, enough for her neck muscles to protest the wallop.

Caroline was about to whack her once more, when Jake practically tackled Caroline from behind.

Elena nursed her burning cheek, her eyes promising retaliation.

"Elena..." Jake warned.

"How the hell is this my fault? I just found him."

"Why aren't you arresting her?" Caroline turned her blotchy, teary face to Detective Harris. The woman, in full emotional meltdown, was impressive to see. Not a pretty sight.

"Miss..."

"You should never have come back," she yelled at Elena from the handcuff of Jake's hands. "We were happy before you barged in."

Elena thought she'd be spit on next and sidestepped behind Detective Harris, who was not doing anything to stop the barrage.

"Arriving with your high and mighty airs, your superiority. Lying to everyone. You manipulative bitch."

Jake seemed to have had enough drama. "Get ahold of yourself," he said and handed her over to Broderick, who had been standing behind him, wringing his hands. Caroline collapsed against the choreographer and cried in earnest.

Anne took over. She cradled Caroline's shoulder, prying her away gently. "Come on, my dear." She glanced at Derek. "Is it okay if I take her to your office?"

Derek nodded, his face inscrutable.

"Would that be all right, Detective?" Anne asked.

"For the moment, yes." Detective Harris considered. "If you could stay with her for a bit? We'll need a statement from both of you later. Shouldn't be long."

Anne nodded and led the pliable, weeping Caroline outside.

"I'm the founder and director of the company," Derek said, advancing with stretched hand. "Derek Michaels." He shook the detectives' hands, turned and pointed, first to Broderick, then to Jake. "Broderick Newsom, artistic director and choreographer for the company, and Jake Forrester, our insurance underwriter and fraud investigator."

"Gentlemen," Detective Harris nodded. "Who was the dancer who assaulted Ms. del Carral?"

"Assaulted?" Broderick's expression went beyond shocked.

"That would be one of our principals," Derek answered. "Caroline Wainwright."

"Justin Bakare's significant other," Jake supplied.

"Married?" asked Murdock.

"Planning to," Derek answered. "At least, that was the rumor. They've been living together for the past five years."

Detective Harris glanced at Elena. Her cheeks exploded with another kind of heat. She planted herself inches behind Jake.

"You can't charge her with assault, Detective." Broderick was outraged. "She's beyond upset. She didn't mean it."

Oh, yes, she did, but Elena stayed mum.

Detective Harris consulted his scribbled notes. "Well, Mr. Newsom. It depends on whether Ms. del Carral wants to press charges." He looked at Elena. "Do you?"

Elena shook her head.

"Well, then. Where were you, gentlemen, when the incident with Mr. Bakare occurred?"

Jake made an inclusive circle encompassing Derek and Broderick with his hand. "We were in Mr. Michaels's office, discussing pending issues when we heard Elena scream."

Scream was kindly put, Elena thought. It was more like continued shrieks in between answering questions from the 911 dispatcher.

"We rushed here, thinking Elena was in distress..."

She huffed.

"We thought you'd had an accident," Jake told her.

"When we arrived, we realized what was really happening," Derek said.

"I approached Justin," Jake said. "Saw the blood, checked for a pulse, and made sure no one disturbed the body or the area around him."

"Besides Ms. del Carral, and you gentlemen, did anyone else come into this room before the EMTs arrived?" Murdock asked.

"Anne, I believe." Jake looked at Derek for confirmation, which he got. "Francesca, Martina, Fred, Caro. Those are the ones I saw and remember. There were others, probably, but you'll have to ask."

"We will interview everyone, don't worry," Detective Harris said and called over one of the techs. He whispered something and waited. The man returned with the plastic bottle neatly sealed in a clear evidence bag. Detective Harris lifted it for them to see.

"Do any of you recognize this?"

Broderick reached for it, but was gently rebuffed.

"Please," Detective Harris said. "No touching. Chain of custody and all that."

A brief scrutiny resulted in denials from the men.

Elena felt Jake's eyes on her.

"Whose is it?" Broderick asked, followed by the simultaneous questions of where was it found from Jake and Derek.

"We would like to set up a neutral place where we can do our interviews," Detective Harris said and returned the bag to the tech. "This room, however, will be sealed until further notice. I'm sorry if this disrupts your routine, but it is necessary."

Derek sighed. Suddenly he looked older than his age. "Do we have a choice?"

Harris shook his head.

"We'll make do."

"But what happened to Justin?" Broderick asked.

"Your dancer seems to have hit his head against the corner of that piano," Harris said. "We won't know if he aggravated the wound by banging his head against the floor, or if the former was enough to render him unconscious. The hospital will check and confirm. Whether he slipped or was pushed, that is another matter."

"Pushed?" Jake asked.

"There is always that possibility, Mr. Forrester. For the moment, we're treating it as a questionable accident. Normal procedure in these circumstances." Harris turned to Derek. "Where can we set up?"

Derek gestured to the door. Everyone in the room followed silently. Once outside, Elena watched as the tech adhered a yellow "no entry" tape to the swinging doors of the rehearsal hall. The policeman reprised his role as bouncer by the door, a determined expression on his face. Elena was sure Caroline had changed the man's opinion on delicate female dancers.

It was all so vile.

"Are you all right?"

"How can she be all right, Jake?" the outraged sputter came from Francesca as she squeezed Elena's shoulder in commiseration. "Awful thing to stumble on. And that B. I. T. C. H. should be prosecuted for what she did to you."

"How's your cheek?" Fred asked.

"Throbbing. Did everyone... I mean..."

"Yeah, we know what you mean," Jake said. "And yes. Everyone saw."

"And speaking of everyone," Francesca added. "Derek's called an emergency meeting in Room 2. We'll be late."

"What about the police?" Elena asked.

"Harriet escorted them downstairs."

"Think they'll continue rehearsals today?" Fred asked.

"Probably," Francesca told him. "The gala is almost here, and we have to be prepared. Costumes fitted. Dress rehearsals."

"Despite," Elena said.

"Despite," Jake answered and opened the door to Room 2.

Immediate silence.

Elena felt like a prisoner walking the last mile to his demise, while Jake led her by the hand to where Anne stood.

Cautious murmurings resumed seconds later.

"I thought you were with Caroline," Elena whispered as soon as they reached Anne.

"The police are interviewing her," she whispered back. "Company doctor gave her a sedative and suggested she go home." She sighed. "I doubt she will. How's your cheek? That was a hell of a punch."

"I'll survive."

"Ladies and gentlemen." Derek walked to the center of the room. "As you well know, Justin has had an accident. And although I would like to cancel rehearsals for the day..."

Moans and complaints erupted. Derek raised a hand for silence.

"We can't afford to," Derek finished. "Not with the gala only days away."

Someone in the room asked what exactly had happened, because no one had been forthcoming. Another asked why the police presence. It was making everyone nervous.

"To answer the first question, Justin seems to have had a serious fall while rehearsing," Derek said. "He must have slipped, or miscalculated the distance between himself and the piano while executing one of his jumps. You all know how he strives to jump higher and leap the farthest. He struck his head and is unconscious. He may have a concussion. The hospital promised to keep us informed on his condition."

"But why are the police here?"

Elena, and everyone else, turned to Martina Brzinsky. It was the third time Elena had heard the woman speak.

"It is normal procedure after an accident," Derek answered. "They've asked for our cooperation and are requesting interviews from all. I'm asking everyone to be as patient and as helpful as possible. Harriet is setting up police interviews in her office to accommodate the officers in charge and will fetch whoever is needed from wherever. If you need to leave the premises, let Harriet know as well."

"Will the *Dance America* interview be cancelled tomorrow?" Mario Llanos asked.

"No," Derek said. "We need the publicity. But I'll let Nina Walsh know there's been a change in the program due to a serious injury." He scanned everyone's face. "And that is all Nina, or anyone, needs to know about what happened to Justin. I'll issue a press release about what happened later."

"Who's the understudy for Justin?" asked Mario Llanos.

"We haven't discussed that yet," Derek said, pointing to Broderick and himself. "I'll make the final decision tomorrow, once I get an update on Justin's condition. Another thing, and I don't want to hear complaints. Some rehearsals will be downstairs and definitely short on space. We've lost the use of Rehearsal Hall 1 until further notice. Now, Analisse has printed out a revised schedule of rehearsals and fittings. Please review."

Elena understood the groans that followed. The original studios downstairs were narrow and small, made for a starting ballet company with much fewer members. She remembered the rehearsals of *Giselle* there, and the corps having to limit their moves to a postage stamp square, elbows rubbing against torsos, arms barely extending, and not enough room to kneel and stand because one could topple the dancer who was barely an inch away in front. It had been a blessing when the upper floor of the building had been vacated, and Derek had built the two beautiful, and spacious, rehearsal halls. The theater's stage, where Terpsichore performed every season, was now smaller, in comparison.

"I'll be speaking with the theater today to see if the company can rehearse there earlier than planned," Analisse said while handing out the schedules. "That should help a lot. Read through the changes and expect to be interrupted if the police require it. I'll let you know if there are any further substitutions."

People began dispersing, all checking the schedules.

"Elena, a word, please?" Derek said.

Francesca and Fred looked at her, worried. She shooed them away.

"Sure?" Francesca whispered.

"Yes."

Her friends left. Broderick nodded her way and exited with

Analisse, who was waiting for him by the doorway. Jake, however, did not budge. Silence gripped the room once more.

She faced Derek.

"This is obviously not the moment," he said, with an underlying sadness in his gaze. "The video you showed us after rehearsal, I must say..." He closed his eyes for a moment. "An eye-opener."

Despite what had happened earlier, a surge of pity welled in her heart. Derek Michaels and René Fauchier had been friends for close to forty years, first as dancers and then as collaborators. It must have pained him that Fauchier, before his untimely death, had not confided in him about *Black Rhapsody*. Secrets revealed, unfortunately, always made you wonder how well you knew the person you called an inseparable friend.

"Did you ever present it?"

"No."

"Because of Fauchier," Derek stated.

Elena nodded. Fauchier had died soon after.

"I must apologize for our previous behavior. And we should have waited, like Jake said."

Despite his silence, Jake's expression was a glaring one of I told you so.

"Anyway, I hope you don't hold past sins against me, my dear," Derek said.

By way of an apology, that statement from Derek came close to it.

"We still need to talk about quite a few things after the gala. Do you have to rush back to Monaco?"

"Not immediately. I can stay for a couple more days."

"Good. Good." Derek patted her shoulder and left.

She turned and found Jake looking at her intensely. His sudden feathery touch on her cheek startled her.

"Does it hurt much?" he asked.

"Can we talk about something else, please?"

Jake sighed.

It felt weird the moment his fingers left her face.

Bereft of human touch.

Jeez. How archaic. And yet, it had felt good. It even had relieved the throbbing for a moment. Maybe it was a simple reaction, an automatic response to the empathy and regret she'd seen in his eyes.

"It's been a hell of a welcome back for you, hasn't it?"

"You could say that."

His sudden smile was a relief.

"I must admit, it was touch and go there for a minute. From the look in your eye after Caroline belted you, I would have sworn you were about to wallop her with a harder one had I not held her back."

She started laughing. She couldn't help it. Maybe it was a form of hysteria. But it felt good to release the tension she'd been holding back.

"You're something else."

"Will you be okay?" he asked.

"Trust me. Caro is a wimp in comparison to the blows I've gotten from arms and legs in rehearsals and performances." It was a hazard of the trade. She'd almost broken the nose of a dancer once when he wasn't paying attention and got too close to her *cloche*. "This is nothing."

"What were you doing alone with Justin in that room?"

The tension rushed back into her body. She retrieved her bag from the floor.

"Is this your way of asking if I did that to him?"

"Elena, many saw you arguing with Justin earlier. It's all over the company."

"Well, they can say or think what they want. Justin was already injured when I arrived." She was sure her eyes reflected the pain she felt. "You think I did it."

"Never. I'm just trying to piece everything together. The police will want to know."

"They already know. I told them." She paused. "You're worried. Why?"

"I'm sure Caroline is not giving a complimentary view of things, nor of you. And with everything that's been going on recently..."

"You mean the thefts?"

"The vandalism. It's been escalating."

"You're worried."

He nodded. "The thefts don't concern me as much. The vandalism now... Those underscore a profuse amount of bottled anger. Add to that what just happened to Justin..."

"But that was an accident. Surely."

He took her shoulders.

"Elena, what was all that about with the plastic bottle Detective Harris showed us? It looked like a medicine bottle. You said you found it?"

"It was in the room when I got there."

"Is it Justin's?"

"I have no idea. There was nothing on it to identify whose it was, except some gibberish."

"Like?"

"It had a *c* and *iz* printed on it. The rest of the label, as you saw, was ripped."

"Apart from Justin and this bottle, you saw nothing else? No one else?"

"No."

"Are you through for the day?"

Elena studied him for a minute, then scanned the schedule Analisse had given her.

"I have nothing except the taping of *Dance America* tomorrow and a fitting."

"Good. Go home. Stay there."

"Why?"

"Because my gut tells me you might be targeted."

She almost blurted out he was being ridiculous, until she saw his expression.

She stared.

"You think *Black Rhapsody*, and the fact everyone now knows it's mine, will make me a bullseye for someone?"

"Especially because of *Black Rhapsody*," he said, quite serious.

"But, why?"

"Because you hold all control of it—the staging, the dancers who'll participate. And someone here is trying to derail things."

Chapter Three

LATER IN THE AFTERNOON, AND AGAINST JAKE'S ADVICE TO stay put at her apartment, Elena had agreed to meet her friends for dinner at a new French bistro close to Fred's hotel. They wanted to hear all about the debacle with *Black Rhapsody,* her finding Justin, and discuss the chaotic day they'd had, overall. Elena also wanted to talk about the day, surrounded by people she loved and trusted. Get their perspectives, even advice on how to proceed.

And it would be a welcome change to talk about *Black Rhapsody* freely. It had been her guarded secret for far too long.

The restaurant was super busy. Patiently, she stood behind the many who waited to be seated, the hostess taking down names, while another handed out electronic beepers.

"Fancy seeing you here."

The whisper, from a familiar voice, caught her by surprise. She turned. Jake Forrester, in the flesh, stood behind her, looking impressive despite the casual black jacket covering a teal t-shirt.

"What on earth are you doing here?" she asked, suspicion mixed with frustration.

"Frannie mentioned you were meeting here tonight," he said. "And since you seem to ignore advice, and I need answers to a few questions, I invited myself. Anne approved."

"Nervy of you."

"Nosy, more like."

"What makes you think I'll answer any?"

"I thought an informal chat, away from all the drama, stress, and misery of the day, would clarify a few things. My experience with lawyers is that they don't divulge all. I prefer to tap primary sources on issues."

He nodded to a corner, near the takeout section of the room.

"Let's go hang out over there," he said, and raised an electronic beeper in his hand. "They'll notify me when the table is ready."

She sat on the only available space on the bench while he hovered.

"On another, and a very personal note, I must say you are looking exceptionally lovely tonight."

"Mr. Forrester..."

"Are we back to formality?"

"Are you hitting on me?"

"Is it working?"

She inspected him, in turn. He truly was a beautiful specimen of man.

Her senses tingled.

"Maybe."

"I'll work harder... for a definite."

Elena smiled. Jake Forrester was turning into a delightful possibility, despite her not entirely trusting him.

"Don't waste much time, huh?"

"Not much of a procrastinator." He leaned forward. Vibrations played with her nerve endings as he whispered in her ear, "I think it's worth a try."

She stood and asked for a menu from a server. Distance was definitely needed. "Francesca said the food here is scrumptious, her words. But I'm not familiar with the place."

"Chicken."

She studied him for a minute, then the menu.

"I prefer to live my life as an adagio, you know," she said, attempting to read the choices. She gave up after a few seconds. "That way you don't miss much."

"Ah, but scherzos are so much more fun."

She just couldn't help it. She laughed.

"So, indulge me. Why did you really leave Terpsichore?"

"Is this part of the nosy you?"

"You bet. Ever since you accepted the invite for the gala, Francesca and Anne have been your greatest enthusiasts, recounting your bio to anyone who wants to hear. So does my youngest sister, by the way."

She stared. Somehow Jake Forrester surrounded by siblings did not correspond with the mental image she'd supplied.

His grin widened.

"Three sisters, to be exact. Jackie, the oldest; then me; then Jodie; and last, the little ballerina of the family, Jenna. And before you ask, my mother believed once she started using a letter of the alphabet for names, she'd stick with it. At least, she didn't name us all George, like George Foreman did with all his sons. What about you? Apart from your brother, who I'll hound you to introduce me to, by the way, I'm that much of a fan. Any other siblings?"

"My sister, Stefanía, after the youngest princess of Monaco's name, but in Spanish. Who'd have thought I'd eventually end up there."

"So why did you?"

"You mean my friends haven't told you? I thought they were enthusiasts."

"Let's say Francesca is loyal and loves to embellish, while Anne is devoted to Derek and abridges information. My sister spouts off only what she reads about you online. I prefer to know the truth."

Elena was silent for a moment. Wow. He'd nailed the essence of her friends in two seconds flat. And it could be a risk to open herself up to his scrutiny. Then again, he'd witnessed the acrimonious interchange between her and Justin this morning, so learning the truth didn't require too much guessing on his part.

"Justin had something to do with my leaving," she admitted.

His sardonic expression said it all.

"Okay," she said. "A bit more than something. But Anne showed me that I'd hit a plateau in my career. At least within Terpsichore."

"No advancement because of Justin?"

"That, in a sense. I was a very inexperienced first soloist and, because of my tiff with Justin, Mr. Derek would never have paired us, especially when the animosity was beginning to show at rehearsals. And since Justin danced the most coveted roles in the bigger productions..."

"It would take many years to dance what you wanted."

She nodded. "But Anne also made me realize that I had other ambitions, beside doing the traditional ballets. I was chomping at the bit to choreograph. To innovate. To branch out and dance less traditional roles. Experiment."

"And you wouldn't have been able to do that here?"

"Not as I would have liked. Mr. Derek is a wonderful teacher and director of the company, but he's also very much conservative and heavy into status. I had not yet acquired sufficient prestige and ranking in the ballet world to allow for that. Anne helped me see the pros and cons of remaining with Terpsichore, and after a heavy-duty discussion with my family, it seemed the best fit for my aspirations was in Europe, especially in younger ballet companies that were eager for established talent and still offered a myriad possibilities. So, I auditioned in different places and, voilà, as the French say."

"And you got your wish—reputation and choreography."

She tilted her head in acknowledgment.

His beeper went off. At the same time Frannie called out her name, waving at them from the entrance of the restaurant. Jake raised his hand in acknowledgment to her and they walked over, Jake to the hostess, and she to her friends.

"I could strangle you," Elena said by way of greeting. She turned to Anne. "You too."

"What for?" Francesca was at a loss.

"Frannie," Anne said, nodding to where Jake was handing over his flashing beeper. "You really have to get with the program."

"You mean Jake?"

"Who the hell else?" Elena said, irritated.

"But he's a friend, Elena," Frannie said. "You can trust him."

Maybe Frannie could, Elena thought. But, could she?

They were seated with surprising efficiency, their drink orders dispatched quickly, and their server, Frank, food order in hand, left them to attend other diners.

During the meal that followed, conversation was light, with Jake asking Fred about his life and his wife. Frannie occasionally asked about Ballet Etudes, and Anne was content to hear Elena and Fred entertain them with stories about the company, their colleagues, and the beautiful area where they lived.

Drinking her coffee after a satisfying dinner, Elena sighed in pleasure. This was what they'd needed after a day from hell. What she'd needed. But she also knew, by a subtle shift in Jake's mood, that the contentment would end soon.

And, as if on cue, Jake leaned back to study Elena, his coffee untouched.

"So, I'll be the bad guy and broach the subject no one wants to bring up," he said, a touch of deprecating humor in his eyes. "The *Black Rhapsody* disclosure was a hell of a bombshell, Elena. If I were the suspicious kind, I'd say it was the fib to end all fibs. But it wasn't."

"Lovely word *fib*," Elena said. "Very charitable."

"Oh, lots of choice words have been bandied about all day, dear, including liar, malicious, witch, pathetic, even envious bitch," Anne told Elena. "And then there was the slap heard around the whole company." She took a satisfying sip of the cappuccino she'd ordered.

"Gee, Anne. Thanks for reminding me."

Fred lifted his espresso and saluted her. "Never thought this trip would be so exciting. And so tragic. Wait till I tell Amèlie." His eyes opened wider. "Wait till Ballet Etudes hears you're the choreographer of *Black Rhapsody*. Wow."

Wow did not cover it, Elena thought. Once the rumor mill started, she would have a monster in her hands. The bidding war would begin in earnest and the pressure to be the first to stage *Black Rhapsody* would be intense, especially since she was under contract with Ballet Etudes. Derek Michaels would be livid. He always had dibs on Fauchier's premiere ballets.

Then again, *Black Rhapsody* hadn't been Fauchier's to dib.

"And that is precisely what I'd like clarified," Jake said. "How did

Black Rhapsody become attached to Fauchier and not to you? The lawyers were not forthcoming."

"René never said it was his work," Elena said.

"And, secondly," Jake added, some annoyance showing. "Why didn't you come clean earlier? Why the subterfuge?"

"It wasn't subterfuge. It was consideration. I wanted to tell Mr. Derek privately, but that didn't happen because Broderick forced my hand."

"Really?" Some humor underscored his voice.

"Yeah, well. I'm susceptible to snarky comments..."

"I can confirm that," Anne interrupted.

So could Jake. She shrugged. "Broderick's lucky I didn't slap the sarcasm out of him."

"Oh, forget about Broderick," Francesca said with impatience. "Spill."

"From the top, my dear," Anne urged.

"Well, I had been working on *Black Rhapsody* for a while when I learned several choreography competitions in Europe opened up for submissions. So I applied to several."

"No way," said Fred. "Even the CICC?"

"Yes," Elena said.

"But you never presented it," Jake said, remembering her remark to Derek.

"No. Never."

Anne squeezed Elena's hand. "Because of Fauchier." She was completing the puzzle.

"What do you mean because of Fauchier?" Fred looked confused.

"A few days before the competition deadlines, Fauchier died. My family, especially my mother, was devastated. I missed the dates to present. And, honestly, I didn't have the heart to showcase it. Not then. Later that year I was accepted as corps in Terpsichore and life took over."

"So, *Rhapsody* remained on the back burner," Anne said.

Elena nodded. "Until now."

"Excuse me, but I'm totally confused..."

"Join the club, Frannie," Jake said. "How on earth did Fauchier get credit for *Rhapsody's* creation?"

"Ah, that is another story."

Elena's prolonged silence irritated Francesca. She huffed. "Well?"

"You know my dad died when I was eight, right?"

Everyone but Jake and Fred nodded.

"One reason why Derek brought her mom over to Terpsichore from American Theater," Anne explained.

"And my siblings and I will be forever grateful to him. Newly widowed, with three small children, and living in New York, my mom would have really struggled if she'd stayed at American. Derek offered not only the control of the costume design and wardrobe department at Terpsichore, but also provided a very generous salary increase. And as the company flourished, so did my mom's reputation and paycheck."

"Derek always loved your mom's work," Anne said. "She had a gift for simplicity and style that won her quite a few awards."

"Fauchier called her the Edith Head of the ballet world." Elena smiled at the memory.

"We're still wearing many of her beautiful creations," Francesca told Jake.

"I've heard," said Jake. "But...can we get back to you, Fauchier, and *Rhapsody*?"

"Fauchier and my mom, because of their close collaboration at Terpsichore, got very close..."

"How close?"

"Really, Frannie. Do I need to spell it out?"

"Sorry."

"Anyway, after my mom started working at Terpsichore, René spent more and more time with mom, as well as with the family. During that time, I was not only taking lessons at Terpsichore School, but also with our friends, Rick and Nat. They have a ballet school on Broadway and they lease out rehearsal space for those who want to practice after hours, or rehearse, or choreograph. And because of my other obsession, choreography..."

Francesca laughed. "I can vouch for that. After class or rehearsals, you'd always find her in an empty room, listening to some orchestral piece that had caught her fancy, and contorting or jumping to her own creations."

"Used you often enough in my, ahem, masterpieces."

"Or anyone you could con into dancing them."

Elena smiled. "Well, I was at Rick and Nat's working on my entry when mom showed up. It was late, and she didn't want me to ride the subway alone at that hour of the night. René came with her."

"Puh-lease," Francesca said. "You've been riding subways alone since you were twelve."

"Yeah, but you know how she was."

"That part of Broadway is a tad desolate at night," Anne said. "Can't blame her for being protective. What did Fauchier say, by the way?"

"He loved the piece, the music. Asked all sorts of questions. Started showing up during my rehearsals of the piece. Guided me. We spent hours in our living room talking ensemble formation, effective pas de deux, lifts, choreographic styles, you name it."

"Is that why people thought the piece was Fauchier's? He being there watching as you choreographed and rehearsed?" Jake asked.

"Partly. Remember Raymond Berend, Frannie?"

"Sure. One of Rick's best protégés."

"Isn't he one of the principals at the Royal Danish?" asked Fred.

Elena nodded. "He volunteered as my guinea pig. So did Rick and Nat's daughter."

"Ha," Anne scoffed. "I smell hidden agenda in their offer."

"Wasn't hidden. That year Berend was gunning to audition for the Royal Danish. Had been training with Rick for years."

"God, don't remind me. Rick's classes are brutal," Francesca said. "My calves require pampering after his itsy-bitty-shitty *difficult* Bournonville routines."

"Well, I agreed Berend could use a video minute of my pas de deux and of the solo variation in his application. A friend of my brother's came to record the session. Fauchier was there. Word got around we were rehearsing a special piece, and, well, the ball got rolling that it was a new ballet and Fauchier wanted it kept secret. It didn't help that a pirate video of Berend dancing my choreography showed Fauchier looking on, giving advice. Word spread like wildfire. René got a kick out of it. Said people would be absolutely shocked when they knew the truth."

"That sounds like Fauchier," Anne said.

"Anyway, my lawyers contacted me about *Black Rhapsody* just as I received the invitation to appear at the gala. I thought it would be the perfect time to clear the air. Until Broderick forced my hand by grandiosely announcing he'd stage *Black Rhapsody* and finish choreographing it, without my permission. The gall."

"No one knew it required *your* permission," said Anne.

"Does it matter?" Elena's look said it all. "Legally, they shouldn't have been able to breathe the name of the ballet without consent from the owner."

Jake's head tilted in acknowledgment. "Touché. And I did warn Derek about it. The trust lawyers were very explicit on that one issue."

"It was a nice gesture on Fauchier's part, though, that he took the necessary legal steps so no one could take ownership of *Black Rhapsody* away from you," Anne added.

"The lawyers made that clear when I spoke to them today," Jake said.

"Yes. René was very generous and protective of us, especially after mom and he got married."

It was as if a shock grenade had been thrown in the middle of their table. No one moved a muscle or said anything for several seconds.

"Oh dear. Oh dear. Oh dear," Anne drained the rest of the cappuccino in one gulp.

"What's the problem?" Elena asked.

"Why the hell didn't you say something about this before?" Jake said.

"OMG, Elena, and I'm supposed to be your best friend," Francesca said, recovering from her surprise. "You *never* told me, my parents."

"No one knew. René and mom didn't want a media circus. We were sworn to secrecy until they announced it. Besides, it was personal and private."

Jake looked at Anne. "I don't think she realizes the ramifications of what she just said. And Derek has no clue. I'll have to tell him."

"Derek will be flabbergasted to say the least," Anne replied.

"What on earth are you both talking about?" Elena asked.

"The business consequences to this are exponential," Jake added, still addressing Anne and ignoring her.

"Oh dear. Oh dear. Oh dear."

"Can I ask when this happened?" Jake asked.

"A month before René flew to Europe. They had a quiet ceremony at the City Clerk's office, with the family as witnesses. They planned to announce their union once René returned. Thought they had all the time in the world. Then he died."

"I always wondered at the air of sadness your mom couldn't dispel." Anne's voice caught.

"Then my mom died." Elena said, her eyes watering.

Francesca took her hands and squeezed. No words were needed. They'd both shared in the grief and the loss over Elena's mom.

"Do you have proof of marriage? Exact dates?" Jake asked.

"Yes. My lawyers have a copy of everything, including their wills. The originals are in my brother's safe deposit box."

"Well, you have certainly been a bundle of surprises today," he said and called the waiter to pay the bill.

"Will you skip company class tomorrow?" Francesca asked.

"No. I'll be there."

"Risky business," Anne said.

"Afraid I'll get kicked, pushed, or tripped?" She said it as a joke, but Anne and Jake didn't smile as Fred and Francesca did.

"Petty jealousies have been known to escalate in a blink," Jake said. "And when this added info comes out, you'll definitely be targeted."

"Are you seriously suggesting what I think you are?" Elena asked.

He ticked off his mental list on his fingers.

"The vandalism. The targeting of dancers with pranks that can seriously hurt a dancer. The reveal *Black Rhapsody* is yours. Your fight denying Justin a role in that ballet, which was witnessed by many. Justin's attack. You, discovering his body. The marriage, not to mention, wills? This is a catastrophe of major proportions for Terpsichore and all its members." He took out his phone and dialed quickly.

"Of that I'm now certain," he told her and left the restaurant, phone to ear.

Chapter Four

"I STILL THINK JAKE IS LOSING HIS MIND," FRANCESCA whispered next morning, watching as he entered the rehearsal room with Derek and Broderick.

Elena adjusted the romantic rehearsal tutu Maricela Fuentes, the wardrobe mistress, had so graciously lent her for this video shoot, thinking she agreed with her best friend. Jake's reasoning behind his statements last night were, well, totally ridiculous. The situation she'd stumbled onto yesterday afternoon with Justin was equally absurd. She was convinced, more now than ever, that Justin had had an accident. At least that was what she tried to tell herself. God knows the idiot was always off by himself practicing turns and jumps, all in the name of perfection. He'd done that for years. Everybody in the company knew that to be so too. Elena suspected Justin had been rehearsing his variation to keep up with the competition, as had been suggested. The new gamut of dancers hired by the company were getting more and more prodigious in their technique and range and, to Elena, the world of ballet was becoming more like the repository of outrageous gymnastic feats rather than pure dancing. Circus Maximus material, definitely, she thought. Wanting to make the audience ooh and aah by holding an *arabesque on pointe* for five seconds longer than normal, or by jumping one foot higher in *jetés*, or by adding double and triple pirouettes to already difficult *fouettés* simply to build on the dizzying pleasure of the masses. More and more performing feats and weird contortions and lifts, all replacing intricate steps, musicality of movement, or variations requiring real skill to perform. It was murder on a dancer's skeletal frame.

And Justin was getting up there in age. An older body could only do so much without risking injury and massive harm.

But what if, a little voice kept repeating in the back of her mind, someone had crept in and given Justin a little shove, just enough to screw up his landing?

"And I concur," Anne said, interrupting her train of thought. "Just because you found Justin unconscious, or that you are the rights owner to *Black Rhapsody*, doesn't mean someone is out to get you."

Elena watched as Caroline arrived. She'd regained some of her composure, and although Elena suspected she'd applied cold compresses to her face before her makeup, Caroline hadn't quite camouflaged all the ravages of her grief. As the woman spoke with her dance partner, Mario Llanos, Elena saw the slight tremor as she fixed hair that was perfectly coiffed in a ballerina's bun. Elena's heart went out to her, wanting to tell her how very sorry she felt for what had happened to Justin. But Elena knew Caroline would not appreciate her sympathy. And she certainly didn't want a repeat slap performance. Her cheek throbbed just thinking about it.

"Have you two been interviewed by the police yet?" Although separate from the other groups, Elena lowered her voice to a bare minimum. She didn't want the journalistic ears in the room to catch this conversation.

"No," Francesca said, sotto voce herself. "I heard from one of the dancers that the detectives are concentrating interviews on the corps first."

"Ha," Anne said. "It's more like Harriet and Derek don't want those over there to know what's going on." She pointed with her chin toward the crew from *Dance America* setting up for the video recording. "They'll make sure the detectives interview us last. And, by the way, what was all that about a medicine bottle?" Anne asked.

"No clue," Elena said. "I don't know if Justin dropped it or if it fell from someone else's bag. I mean, it could have been there before yesterday."

"Improbable." Anne made small touches to her makeup. "Cleaning crew is here every night."

"What do you think is in it?" Francesca asked.

"Was. It was empty. And there was no label. It had been ripped off."

"Well, that is neither here nor there, Elena. I use those to store my quarters for the laundry room in my building." Anne bent, reached into her purse and took one out. She shook it, jingling its metallic sound.

"You still use those?" Francesca was amused. "A bit antiquated."

"My apartment building's management is cheap. No techno cards for us yet."

"What if it's medicine?" Elena asked, a bit uneasy. "Is Justin healthy?"

"Yes. That we know of," Anne replied.

"No flu, infections, muscle relaxants, or anything else?"

"What? Playing doctor now? Maybe it's for STDs." At Elena's horrified gasp, Anne turned serious. "You of all people know what he's like. Although, until Martina arrived, I would have sworn Justin had reformed his ways."

"Why is everyone so serious?"

"You're late," Anne told Fred as he rushed to their side. "Almost."

"Any theories from Jake?" Francesca asked. "I mean, apart from that ridiculous statement."

"What I believe," Anne said after stretching. "Is that Jake'll use whatever excuse there is to be with Elena."

"There is definitely a strong vibe between you both," Francesca agreed. "Electric."

"He looks at you the same way I look at Amèlie," Fred added.

"With love?" Elena chuckled at the outrageous comment.

"With hunger," Fred said, quite serious.

"Nailed it. That man definitely wants to jump your bones."

"Really, Anne." Elena huffed, but couldn't help glancing at Jake. His eyes were on her. And there it was...that killer smile.

If Elena hadn't had her back against the barre, she'd have tried to quantum leap behind the wall.

Anne hip bumped her. "See what I mean?"

"Oh, shush," Elena said, her cheeks exploding with heat.

"Oh, oh. Get ready." Francesca warned.

Elena turned. Martina Brzinsky, with a saccharine smile you knew was fake, was approaching their group, hand extended.

"Elena. May I call you Elena? I know, no proper introduction yet. Mistake," She shook Elena's hand and ignored everyone else. "Had to meet you. Still wonderful ballerina. Great choreography. *Concerto in D... Black Rhapsody.*" She gestured, like a chef giving his approval on a succulent dish. "Incredible."

Elena studied this woman, who wasn't even twenty-one yet. Maybe even younger. Nineteen? Justin always had had a predilection for young flesh.

"Thank you, Ms. Brzinsky. Glad you liked them both."

"Martina, please. And yes. But much prefer *Concerto*, must admit," she said. "*Rhapsody* is..." Martina glanced at the ceiling, as if it could give her the answer. "Childish? Is that not the English word? You know, lack of maturity?"

"Really..." Francesca sputtered, but Elena smiled at her friend, a slight shake telling her to stop.

Martina's hand covered her heart. "You must excuse my lack of knowledge in language. Still learning."

I bet.

"You'll be staging both here, no?"

That had been one of several bones of contention Justin had thrown at her face when arguing yesterday: her silence about it being her work, her refusal to give permission to stage it, and, worse, that she'd used someone else to dance the choreography rather than using him, her lover at the time.

"Haven't decided. For the moment, though, no."

Martina's shock was replaced in nanoseconds by eagerness. This time it wasn't faked. The woman grabbed Elena's hands and squeezed. "Must give me opportunity to dance *Rhapsody* and *Concerto*. Anne, you convince Derek he must bring ballets to Terpsichore."

Anne chuckled. "You're crediting me with much more influence over Derek than what I have."

"But you're his mistress," Martina said, surprised with Anne. "Mistresses hold a lot of power."

"That is beyond rude," Francesca said, insulted.

"Why rude?" Her confusion was real. "It's not truth?"

Thankfully, Analisse came into the room before things got out of hand, beelining it to Francesca with a young dancer in tow. Elena remembered seeing him in class today.

"Fran, Randy is partnering you for the gala. Derek just ordered the change so the programs could go out for printing. He already knows the variation."

Randy Dimmig greeted everyone with an orthodontic, perfect smile and hugged Francesca. Elena saw the substitution in partners pleased her friend. It would have been horrible if, for expediency's sake, Francesca had been partnered with someone she didn't like or with whom she didn't work well. Or worse: her friend being scrapped from the gala altogether.

"Derek, the eternal pragmatist." The mockery in the whisper surprised Elena.

"Come on, Anne," she whispered back, knowing Anne's comment had more to do with what Martina had blurted out before than derision against Derek. Or did it? A little of both, maybe? "Even if Justin recovers today, it would be unconscionable to let him perform so soon after that injury."

"Good afternoon, everyone," Derek interrupted from the middle of the room. "I want to thank you all for being the professionals you are, as well as for your total commitment to this company, especially today. I, and all our staff, are extremely grateful to you, and to those that couldn't make it today." He didn't elaborate, because all knew he meant Justin. Besides, they'd been warned yesterday—no mention of the incident unless asked point-blank. And not even then.

"First off, let's give a big round of applause for Nina Walsh and her *Dance America* crew."

Derek waited for the applause to wind down.

"On behalf of the company and myself, Nina, thank you for the years you've dedicated in interviewing world class dancers and documenting ballets for the masses. It is indeed a privilege to have you here today. And, before I get too maudlin, I'll cede the floor to you."

"Thank you, Mr. Michaels. It is a treat to be here." She turned to the room at large and faux clapped all around. "I can't start without admitting I'm a huge fan of Terpsichore and of what Mr. Michaels has done with the company throughout his years of directorship. I've never had this open access to your company before. This is a real privilege." She went on to introduce her assistant and the two videographers, acknowledged Terpsichore's own video guru, and finished by pointing to the chairs set in a semicircle a few feet from the mirror.

"We'll be doing our informal interviews of the principals and guest artists first. Afterward, we'll record you rehearsing parts of your pieces. Finally, we'll record a few minutes of your corps rehearsing the gala's end performance of *Giselle*, act 2. We'll conclude with all the information about the event and where tickets can be purchased. If you would so kindly take your places?" She pointed to her assistant. "Andrea will direct you to your seats."

Once seated, the interview began. Overall, it was quick, cordial, informative for the viewer, and particularly, held no journalistic traps or embarrassing questions. Smiles and bonhomie all around. No surprises that could get your beautiful behind thrown out of the company quicker than a *fouetté*. Frankly, Elena wondered how Derek had pulled things off, muzzling Nina's curiosity. The woman had not once made a reference to pranks, Justin, his accident, or the detectives underfoot.

Twenty minutes later, the interviews were over and the seats rearranged against the mirrors, facing the room. The videographers were now busy adjusting their tripods in new positions, setting the best angles for the rehearsal's recording. While waiting to be called, Elena and Fred, along with all the other principals, had taken over their own small fiefdoms around the room, marking their variations while waiting to be called. Derek and Broderick were conferring with Nina Walsh and her assistant, with Broderick's occasional gestures indicating the best vantage points so that Nina's team could record the best angles. The company's videographer was already familiar with all things Terpsichore, so there was no need to direct him.

"Before we begin, listen up." Analisse took center stage. "I just received a text from the theater indicating they will accommodate us earlier. However, it won't be until the day after tomorrow. Be warned: we'll have to work around light crews, stage riggers, and sound engineers since they're updating equipment and revamping props for the gala this Friday night. So, be patient and pay close attention to debris and anything else. Company class is at ten tomorrow, here. Rehearsals will be divided between this rehearsal hall and Studio 3."

Groans ensued.

"Get over it. Schedules will be posted outside later today. Fittings will take place at the theater. Maricela should finish relocating all costumes there by tomorrow." She looked at Francesca and Randy. "Let's go over your variation. Just mark it. I want to see a few things."

Five minutes later, they received their one-minute warning and Nina's assistant requested for all to clear the area. Jake scooted to the chair next to where Elena waited her turn.

"Francesca seems to work well with Dimmig," Jake commented.

"She's a professional."

"Yeah, but isn't partnering a symbiosis of sorts? If you don't like, it shows?"

"Definitely, but you fake it. Frannie, however, is a beautiful dancer and soul. She can't *not* work well with anyone. And, from what I just saw, they've partnered before and have the variation down pat."

She looked at her friend and Dimmig, who were listening attentively to some last tips from Analisse. "Derek made a good choice."

"With all the mess that's surrounding us, I'm surprised he's had the head for it, and doing the substitution so quickly."

Elena grinned at Jake. "We dancers think very fast on our feet."

"Cute."

"Any word on Justin?"

Jake shook his head. "Still in ICU," he whispered. "Derek is getting updates every hour."

"What hospital?"

"Mt. Sinai, over at Tenth."

Elena lowered her voice to the barest whisper. "Are they, you know, still here?"

Another nod.

"Have they interviewed you?"

"Not yet."

Nina's assistant announced recording on three. Broderick, as artistic director of the company, took center stage with Nina. He would introduce each dancer, gloss a bit about the piece to be rehearsed, and then rehearsal would start.

Martina, first up on the roster schedule, stood quietly next to Broderick, that fake smile once more plastered on her face. She replied to one or two questions and took center stage. The instant the intro music began, the transformation of this young woman was beyond words. Incredible could not even define her performance. Not only that, Martina knew she was awesome and flaunted it with every posture, every pause, every flourish, her eyes expressing a braggadocio that was not an empty boast.

Martina Brzinksy knew she was beyond good—she was great.

And everyone who would view this video would agree the woman was phenomenal.

Elena watched her in awe.

But arrogance, up to a point, had its demerits. True, dancers who reached soloist level, and then principal in a company, took every advantage to boast and show off all their years of training, hard work, and sacrifice, including herself. She remembered when she'd overflowed with pride and spite, including an arrogance not dissimilar from Martina's. Many moons ago, one particular dancer always got on her nerves, always trying to upstage Elena, in class, auditions, rehearsals. A particularly annoying habit had been the woman crowding Elena out of her place on stage. But karma always had a tendency to circle back. In an important audition, Elena had held back until the woman was already in position, the usual smirk on her face. Elena had then done exactly what had been done to her often. And since Elena was taller and with a wider reach of arm and leg, she'd overshadowed her on every move.

That afternoon, Elena had gotten the role and been asked to join the company. The other woman hadn't.

But not every dancer fit a part or did it well either. Elena thought back to what Martina had asked, to dance Elena's choreography. She honestly didn't know if Brzinsky would be a good choice. Not that Martina's technique wasn't perfect. The problem was that, oftentimes, the more gifted dancers were the more difficult to work with. Would Martina be flexible enough to carry out Elena's choreographic vision of *Concerto in D* and stick with it, dancing for the pure joy of combinations, or would she interpret it as she pleased, getting bratty and diva-ish? Elena wasn't sure. Besides, she had always envisioned Francesca dancing *Concerto*.

Something to consider.

"That was perfect, my dear," Broderick said. Martina waved in a cutesy manner to the invisible audience, reached for her bag, and walked off to the changing rooms, her arm up in a final farewell.

"Elena. Fred. You're next."

Jake caressed her hand. "Make-believe."

"What?"

Another fleeting caress. "Make-believe. I will."

Good grief. This man was on a mission. And she kept wondering why. Was it because he was truly interested in her? Or was it to lower her guard, his goal still to get permission for Derek to stage her ballet at Terpsichore? Or was his reason as innocuous as he'd said before: to stay close to her so he could meet her brother?

Something to think about later.

After a small introduction, and one or two questions about how long they'd been dancing this ballet, and its difficulties, Broderick gave instructions to the pianist to intro into the balcony scene's manège. "And we'll stop after the third lift from your knees, Fred."

Nina complained they would miss the best part, the kiss. Broderick reminded her, with a laugh, that that part was reserved for the theatergoers.

Elena had always been aware of her surroundings in rehearsals or performances, whether it was of the répétiteur, the artistic director, fellow dancers, and especially the audience. But today, darn the man, she was on fire, her awareness of him intense. He'd done it on purpose, she swore. Now, she couldn't get the image out of her head—what would it feel like if Jake were dancing with her as Romeo?

Make-believe. Jeesh.

The man was definitely dangerous.

Afterward, Elena didn't know how she made it through the rehearsal. Fred, fortunately, had been blissfully oblivious to her transformation. She was sure she had blushed a thousand times, trembled a few hundred, and had definitely immersed herself far deeper into her role than customary. Thank the dance fairies Broderick hadn't demanded the entire scene. Elena was sure her head would have exploded like a supernova if they had pretend kissed while Jake watched. She wouldn't have been able to finish the scene.

Elena grabbed her gear and, after a quick 'thank you' and 'pleased to meet you' to all the crew, she followed Fred out and headed for the locker room, where she took a long, hot shower. She was folding the romantic tutu to return it to wardrobe when Francesca came in. She looked radiant.

"I can tell it went well."

"Dimmig is wonderful." Francesca took off her toe shoes and sat on the bench in front of the lockers with a satisfied smile. "The variation went without a single snag."

"And it doesn't hurt that Randy is tall, well built, and has a Friedemann Vogel kind of vibe?"

Francesca considered, looking surprised. Friedemann Vogel was one of the most beautiful male dancers from the Stuttgart Ballet to grace the dance world. Talented, with a technique to die for, incredible body and musculature, he was the best partner a ballerina could hope to have. Not to mention, he was droolworthy.

"Yeah." Francesca took off her sweaty leotard and tights. "Yeah. A younger version, but yeah." She looked at her friend. "Speaking of, your variation was beautiful. I've never seen you dance like that before."

That's because she had never imagined a man like Jake as Romeo.

"All for the cameras, Frannie," Elena lied through her teeth. She threw dirty clothes and her towel inside her bag, zipped it with more force than necessary, and grabbed her purse and the folded rehearsal robe. "All for the cameras."

"Want to come with me to see Justin?" Francesca whispered. "Anne wants to go too."

"Let me take this to wardrobe, and I'll meet you when you're done."

"I'll text you."

Minutes later, after circumnavigating sweaty bodies, loungers eating snacks, and other dancers stretching against the walls, Elena headed down the elevator to the basement of the building.

The cement and brick-encased space that was the building's basement had been a second home to Elena, as well as a playground for her and her siblings ever since she'd started dancing at the school many years ago.

Elena hooked a right and walked in the direction of the costume design area. Unlike previous years, where the hallways were kept relatively clutter free, this time around the entire length of hallway was filled with old props and pieces of sets pressed against walls, with translucent boxes storing decorations, wigs clumped on top of those, tutu trees, and clothing racks chock-full of costumes. Usually, staff from the props/sets and costume departments would be everywhere, and so would some dancers. Hums from tools and sewing machines would be constant, as well as muted conversations.

But today, the basement was eerily quiet.

Probably everyone was at the theater, Elena thought, getting things transferred and organized for the gala. Ergo the disarray.

But for the first time the basement felt, well, strange.

With the echoes of her footsteps as her only companion, Elena walked the remaining length of the building to where Maricela Fuentes held court over the workshop. She peeked inside and paused, not so much because it was empty, but because it stood the same as when her mother had worked there. Nothing had been changed or rearranged.

The deluge of memories assaulted Elena in ways for which she wasn't prepared. So did the enveloping sadness. She hadn't realized how coming down here would affect her, even now. After all, she'd been away for five years, and her mother had passed the baton to Maricela two years before her death. But seeing the workspace untouched and her mother's painted costume designs still gracing the walls behind the desk, undid her. The ache was intense. This was where her mother had spent most of her days and nights, creating designs and bringing them to life. This was where Elena had been fitted for her first school recital. This was where she'd done her homework with her brother and sister while her mother sewed into the night. Where René and her mother had butted heads about functionality of costumes, or where they'd immersed themselves in art books for inspirations from historical dresses to use in future designs.

She walked around, reminiscing, touching tulles and taffetas, inspecting a beautiful blue tutu being constructed on the tailor mannequin, rummaging through some of the costumes hanging on the wall. She sighed and walked to the desk. Chuckled. Ever practical, Maricela had left an open milk crate on her desk with a huge note taped to the front: Drop costumes here! Elena grabbed a pen and a notepaper next to the phone and wrote a small thank-you message to Maricela. She pinned the note to the dress and dropped it in the nearly empty crate.

That was when she heard it.

A rustle and a scrape.

She poked her head out the door and looked both ways, but the hallway was empty.

"Hello?"

But her voice fell flat in the surrounding space. A bit unnerving, especially when the answering silence felt not entirely deserted.

Elena mentally shook herself. What a ridiculous notion. But the feeling did not leave her, almost as if someone were holding their breath so as not to be caught.

Time to get the heck out of Dodge.

The return trip to the elevator stretched out longer than was comfortable. It could be rats she'd heard, she tried to rationalize. But the feeling that someone was watching her, waiting, persisted. Her steps quickened. A soft scrape on her right made her heart jump and her feet move faster. She half expected someone to jump out from behind one of the props, boxes, or costume racks littering the hallway at any moment.

Another creak, this time behind.

Elena practically ran the last yards to the elevator.

She forgot how many times she pushed the Up button outside and the Close door button inside the elevator, ridiculously expecting a zombie-like hand to stop the doors from closing at the last minute. She unhooked her ballet satchel and switched it from shoulder to chest. If a stranger dared to threaten her physically, there was no better defense than throwing her cumbersome bag at their face.

Nothing happened.

She stared at the emptiness before her, her heartbeat loud in her ears.

The elevator doors moved. Closed.

Her chuckle had a nervous and relieved vibration to it, and only when she felt the jerk of the upward movement, did she breathe deeply in an effort to calm her runaway heartbeat.

No zombies, at least.

Her phone pinged.

She jumped.

Okay, Elena, get ahold of yourself. This was all Jake's fault for expressing his ridiculous concern, and Justin's, for getting himself nearly killed and, of course, hers for her discovering his body.

Stop calling it a body.

She dug into her bag for the cell and saw Francesca had texted her. Shaking off her anxiety, she got out and went to find her friend.

Chapter Five

After texting Francesca that she'd meet her and Anne in the waiting area by the entrance of the building, Elena was still waiting. From her vantage point inside the reception area, she'd seen the team of *Dance America* leave, company members rush to other rehearsals, parents of students pick up and drop off their charges, as well as the wardrobe team exiting, ladened with some of the boxes she'd seen in the basement, probably on their way to the theater.

"Where the hell are you?" she whispered, at the same time that she typed her mumble in a text. It had been fifteen minutes since she'd received a response, but both women were still nowhere to be found.

Not one to wait in one place too long, Elena swung her ballet bag and purse over her shoulder and went in search of her friends.

The street-level floor of the building was one long hallway bisected by various rooms on either side, with the elevator banks and adjacent offices at the very end. A couple of feet to her left and right, some rooms had been converted into classrooms, and others into changing rooms. At the end of the hallway, the elevator flanked the sign-in area, a room with a window in the middle with an iron grille latticing it. It had been constructed similar to an old box-office ticket window, Elena thought. There, a secretary sat answering phones, fielding questions, registering visitors, logging in members of staff and company, and issuing passes for any dancer who wanted to take advantage of the variety of professors and dance disciplines the school offered. Surrounding the entire window were bulletin boards heavy with flyers, schedules for rehearsals, classes, requests for roommates, open auditions, miscellaneous photographs from students and staff, classifieds, and professional head-shots of the current company members, staff, and directorship. On the right of that area, was Harriet's office, and immediately next to it, Derek's. All rooms had access to each other on the inside, as well as from the hallway.

She was almost to the elevator when she heard the receptionist on duty call out to her. Elena saw the door to the woman's sanctum open and a hand waving her in.

She hefted her ballet bag's strap more comfortably on her shoulder and bumped the door wider so she could fit in.

"Analisse wanted me to give you this." The receptionist flopped an envelope into her hand. "It's a revised copy of the rehearsal and call times for this week."

Elena thanked her and stuffed the envelope in her bag.

"I can't tell you how excited we all are that you're dancing in this special fundraiser gala," the woman continued. Elena remembered being introduced to her when she arrived, but she'd forgotten the woman's name. What was it? Fayelynn... Faya? The only thing Elena recalled was that the name started with an F.

"I'm looking forward to it."

"And dancing the R&J balcony scene," the woman continued. Her whole body bobbed up and down in suppressed excitement. "With Boelens! OMG. What a dreamboat." Her eyes rolled up to the ceiling and she sighed. "I can usually go and peek at some of the rehearsals," she said with a wistful tone in her voice. "But..." Here she lowered her voice to barely a whisper. "Yesterday was so awful. How are you doing? Such a shock, I'm sure. Heard you found Justin after his accident. Any news on him?"

The phone rang, interrupting the woman who, as soon as she answered, went into her spiel of identifying school, company, and how to direct the call. She raised a finger in a request for Elena to stay.

At any other time, Elena would have engaged the woman in conversation. Commiserated, even.

"Listen, I..." But her words caught when she heard the voice of Detective Harris taking his leave out in the hallway.

"We appreciate your cooperation, Mr. Michaels. We'll keep you updated."

Elena dropped her bag on the floor, turned her back to the window and open door, and made as if she were rummaging in it. If the detectives glanced inside the office, her jean-clad behind would be the only distinguishable part of her body.

"Any time, Detective."

"Harriet's office is empty," the receptionist said in a hushed whisper. "I'll give you the all clear when I see it."

"We'll continue the remaining interviews tomorrow," Detective Harris continued. "Expect us at nine."

"But detective, company class is our sacred cow," Derek complained. "If our dancers don't warm up properly, injuries can happen. Can't you delay or reschedule it for a later time? This situation has already disrupted everything as it is."

A small tap on her back and a thumbs up by her face.

"Sorry, but the quicker we find out what happened, the faster we'll be out of your hair," Detective Harris said, his voice receding.

Mr. Derek was probably herding the detectives toward the building's entrance. Time to disappear.

Elena grabbed her bag and, still crouched, headed for the connecting door.

"Please have Ms. Madison coordinate things for us tomorrow, as well."

Derek's answer was lost in the distance.

Elena waved a quick goodbye to the woman and slid into Harriet's office. She closed the door, leaned into it, sighed, and looked around.

Goodness. Harriet's office resembled a still life, without much change over the years Elena had been away. The same battered wood desk still blocked the middle of the room with now a streamline, top-of-the-line computer screen on top. In turn, everything else on it fought for space—printer, mesh office metal organizers filled with paperwork, miscellaneous office supplies, and a phone. Legal filing cabinets hugged the entire wall behind the desk, their bulk not quite disguising the different colored paint coats at the edges in an attempt to keep them looking fresh. And amid everything, scattered haphazardly, were the little personal bric-a-bracs that Harriet had collected (or been given as gifts) throughout the years: a Lladró figurine in the classic pose of the dying swan, an extra-thick, oversized pencil topped with a tutu for an eraser, a ballet-slipper stapler, a cute Precious Moments ballerina in an eternal twirling pose, and a snowball paperweight with a ballerina in classical garb inside. Elena smiled. She'd chosen that gift for Harriet as a Christmas gift several years before she'd left the company. Facing the desk, the same uncomfortable, ratty chairs had not been replaced either. She walked over and slid a finger over the metal backrest of the nearest one. Here she'd signed her first company contract. Here too, she'd signed her resignation. She glanced at the wall next to the slightly open connecting door to Mr. Derek's office and saw her headshot was still in place, including several company photos of her as soloist and as part of the corps. The rest of the space was wallpapered with photos of other company members, past and present, together with company performance shots and oldies from Mr. Derek dancing and of Fauchier's productions.

She'd forgotten the memories—too many to count.

Elena was grateful when her cell phone pinged. It stopped her from getting too maudlin.

"Well, it's about time," she mumbled, reading Frannie's text that she and Anne were finally on their way down. She texted she'd meet them by the elevators and was almost at the door when her name stopped her short.

"Elena needs to know."

Jake's voice, filtering from Derek's office, stopped her short.

"No." Adamant, with finality.

"And why not?" Jake's tone was close to belligerent.

Yeah, why not? And what the heck did they need to tell her? She inched closer to Derek's office.

"None of her business."

She stiffened. She'd never heard this tone from Derek.

"I beg to differ," Jake answered. "It became her business the moment she opened her mouth at dinner last night. And with everything that is happening..."

"Exactly my point," said Derek. "Priority has to be given to the gala. It's imperative that it goes off without a hitch."

"What about the well-being of Justin, not to mention finding the perpetrator of the other incidents?"

"That too."

"Derek, out of sight on this is not out of mind. Justin and the vandalism are one and the same. And they're escalating. Someone is targeting the company, and now the bullseye is on its members. Elena could well be in the crosshairs now that she's here and part own..."

"What utter rubbish," Derek said. "You have no proof of that as yet."

Part? Part of what?

"Are you serious? You don't believe everything is related?"

"No."

"Someone wants to ruin you and you're, what, filing it under supposition?"

"Jake."

"No, you listen to me. These attacks are connected and raising my hackles."

They're raising everyone's. Mine particularly.

"You're exaggerating."

"Don't be insulting. My gut has been flaring for months now. Yours should have too. One or two odd things can be chucked off as coincidence, pranks, mischief, even malice, but not all. Someone is very angry and is taking it out on everyone in the company. Now it has escalated to injuring one of your best dancers."

"Oh, come on. Don't be ridiculous."

"I'm not being ridiculous and you know it, Derek. Things may have started innocuously enough. But not anymore. Someone seems to have it out for you, and badly. And probably won't be satisfied unless they destroy the company as well. This attack on Justin..."

"Really. What crap. You honestly believe someone went out of their way to hurt Justin? He slipped. Fell. An unfortunate accident. You know how Justin is, going off by himself to practice at every opportunity. And the detective even said there were no signs of a struggle."

Elena sighed, trying not to make too much noise. Hearing the detective didn't suspect any foul play was a relief, especially since *she* had found him. *Although...*

"Well, you may think it's nonsense," Jake said, his voice reflecting his mounting frustration. "But let me warn you, the rumor mill here is cranked and at full speed. The gossip is someone did Justin in after he approached Elena, particularly when quite a few in the company heard her telling him to bugger off, as the Brits say. And you know why Justin approached her."

"I doubt it was to renew his past romance with her."

Ha! You weren't there, Mr. Derek. That's exactly the card he played. It just so happened I wasn't playing his game anymore.

"On that score you're right. She's way over him from what I witnessed yesterday. Nevertheless, whispers are swirling that Elena's *Rhapsody* was Justin's last ticket to fame..."

Elena smiled. It was eminently satisfying hearing someone recognizing *Rhapsody* as her*s*.

"That's unfounded, malicious hearsay," Derek interrupted.

Is it, Mr. Derek? You didn't see or hear the sweet manipulative dribble that came out of Justin's mouth when he cornered me. Nor his violent reaction when I pointed out that exact same thing.

"No, Derek. Not off the mark at all, once he found out *Rhapsody* is Elena's. Justin is on his last legs as a dancer. He injures easily now, despite therapy, Pilates, and weight training. You know it. He knows it. His only future now is to teach or choreograph and he isn't good at either. I've heard your complaints every time he replaces Analisse as répétiteur or does a stint as ballet master. He'll be depending more and more on Caroline's support and whatever he's saved or invested. And you know how that's going to go with his ego."

Yeah. He would hate that. Nice observation, Jake.

"Not to mention that, financially, the company has been struggling to stay afloat for several years now due to this horrible economic downturn," Jake said.

Now that was news. By all appearances, the company seemed to be doing well. The salary to borrow her and Boelens from Ballet Etudes for this gala was a pretty penny. Not to mention the cost of the gala itself. What had happened to Mr. Derek's wife's financial backing? Was that what Jake was referring to?

"It's been brutal," Derek admitted.

"And the news Elena is the choreographer of *Black Rhapsody*, not to mention the bombshell about her mother being married to Fauchier, a possible will, well, that makes things..."

"Untenable."

"Difficult," Jake finished.

Elena was baffled. What on earth had her mother's marriage to Fauchier have to do with anything? She understood, and had known, the complications and ramifications of her being the choreographer of *Black Rhapsody*, but her mom? What on earth were they talking about?

A cell phone rang and her heart stopped. But she realized it wasn't hers.

Time to exit, stage left.

As quietly as she could, she opened the door into the hallway and strode to the elevators as quickly as she could. But as she waved to her friends, she knew she had to have a very serious conversation with killer smile Forrester.

Something, somehow, was not right in Terpsichore. And she might have landed in the center of it all.

AFTER A QUICK TRAIN ride over to Tenth, Elena and her friends arrived at the hospital. There, they'd been IDed, photographed, and plastic-labeled badged through. It was worse than an airport. When they finally reached intensive care, more waiting ensued before they'd be allowed to see Justin. Not that this would be a regular visit, the nurse had explained. Justin was still comatose and his condition had not changed since he'd been brought in. The nurse, with her no-nonsense, efficient manner, had encouraged them to speak to him. Coma patients often responded to outside stimuli, especially to family and close friends or colleagues. So, they'd decided Anne would go first, then Francesca, and lastly, Elena. Five minutes each. Thankfully, Anne had been ushered in a few minutes ago.

But it still felt like they'd been waiting for hours.

"God, hospitals are so depressing, aren't they?"

Elena didn't answer. What could she say?

"Do you think he'll recover?"

"I don't know, Frannie. I really, really hope so."

"This is so freaking messed up."

"It sure is."

"What if he doesn't come out of his coma soon?" Frannie stood, restlessness taking hold. She paced until Elena thought she'd go dizzy in the small room.

"I'm sure he will, Frannie. We all hope so," Elena said, but didn't add what she was really thinking.

God, what a mess.

"Poor Caroline," Frannie said.

"Yes." And Elena left it at that.

Five minutes later, Anne joined them. Elena could tell she'd been crying. Frannie took her turn next, disappearing through the silent slide doors.

"This was a waste," Anne said after a minute or so. "And very depressing. He's just there, tubes and monitors replacing life. God."

"Did the nurses say anything?"

"Apart from he is like a vegetable?" Tears began to overflow.

Elena hugged her and Annie leaned into her, weeping.

"I am so, so sorry this happened."

"It's just not fair," Anne's voice came from somewhere in Elena's chest. "He's young. Vibrant still. It's old farts like me that should have the health problems. Not him."

"So, you're an old fart, huh?" Elena's chuckle brought Anne out of her funk.

"You know what I mean." Anne grabbed a couple of tissues from the box on the table and wiped her eyes. "It's expected, normal, even, that anyone over fifty in our careers will have issues with tendons, ligaments, even bones. We can't keep abusing our bodies day in and day out without consequences in the future. Heck, even the present. But this…" Anne's sigh was hiccupy. "We never think of accidents."

Jake doesn't believe it was one, and I'm not sure I do either. Not after what I heard back at Harriet's office.

"Even though we constantly land on the floor tripping over ourselves, or overshooting a lift?"

Anne smiled. "Yeah. Even though."

"Listen, we have to be optimistic about this," Elena said. "I'm certain he'll recover."

"What the hell are you doing here?"

Elena and Anne started.

Framed in the doorway, Caroline Wainwright looked like an avenging Queen of the Wilis ready to zap Elena out of existence—or drive her to her death. "Get out. You have no business being here."

"Caroline."

"It's all your fault…"

"How can it be my fault?" Elena said, incensed. "I was nowhere near him when this happened."

"Now, dear," said Anne, forever the arbitrator. "You are being unfair."

"Oh, Anne." Caroline crumbled under the weight of her distress. "What am I going to do without him?"

Anne rushed to cradle Caroline as she broke down. Elena watched in pity.

"You can't think that way," Anne chided, guiding her to the sofa. "He'll recover. He's strong."

"I'm so scared, especially with everything that's been happening…" Caroline blew into a tissue, and calmed a bit. "It feels like we all have targets on our backs."

That was a strange comment, Elena thought. When Caroline didn't expand on it, Elena turned to Anne. Maybe she could shed a bit of light on what was going on in Terpsichore. "What on earth does she mean. What is happening now?"

Anne sighed. "The company's been bleeding soloists from its ranks for a bit, and we couldn't understand the why."

"Isn't that normal? I mean, every company loses dancers when contracts aren't renewed."

"But that is the point," said Caroline. Her anger brought life back to her face. "I received a letter yesterday that Derek wasn't renewing my contract."

"And that," said Anne, "is a lie."

Caroline rummaged into her bag and shoved a rumpled letter toward Elena. She scanned the letter quickly and saw the sentences that would have incensed any dancer, aside from not having their contract renewed:

"... your dancing lately is subpar and lacking luster. Because of that, and your increasing age, we can no longer see fit to offer you a position with Terpsichore. We are looking elsewhere for an influx of younger and more talented dancers."

Elena saw Derek's stamped signature at the bottom. Good Lord. This was sabotage. Mr. Derek would never, ever address a dancer in such derogatory terms, would he? He'd definitely be more diplomatic than this. And he would never rubber-stamp a letter that was so personal.

"Was this the incident Jake referred to yesterday?" Elena asked. "The one that had Harriet and Mr. Derek in a tizzy, apart from the Nina Walsh call?"

Anne nodded. "Someone took stationery and envelopes from the office and typed those to ten of our principal dancers who were expected to renew contracts. It seems this has been happening under the radar for several weeks now. Suffice it to say that some did not take it too well." Anne pointed to Caroline.

"If I hadn't demanded from Harriet an explanation for this, this..." She pointed to the letter in Elena's possession. "This outrage, Harriet and Derek would not be the wiser until too late."

"Derek, Broderick, and Harriet spent the entire afternoon yesterday trying to track down the people affected before an even greater catastrophe happened."

"So, these weren't mailed?"

"They were left in our designated inboxes at reception," Caroline said. "Justin received one too." She turned to Anne. "Do you think that's why he…" She burst into tears.

"Oh dear." Anne patted Caroline's back in an effort to console.

Could that be the reason Justin ended up like he did? Had he been trying to outperform himself in practice so much so that he'd caused his own accident? Elena thought back at what she'd overheard earlier this afternoon. Jake had mentioned Justin had been suffering from injuries more often than not, lately. Could he have pushed himself so far because he'd read a fake letter that said Derek thought him useless and too old to renew a contract? God. She hoped not. But if that weren't the case, then the other possibility would be even worse.

Elena shivered.

"Elena, you can go…" Frannie stopped short at the room's entrance. "Oh."

"Listen," Elena said to Caroline after an awkward silence. "I don't have to be there. Why don't you go in instead?"

"He needs you," Frannie said, always the generous soul. "You have to be strong for him."

"She's right," Anne echoed. "Go."

Caroline looked at them with the teary, wide-eyed wonder of the characters in the anime shows Elena's brother used to watch.

But Elena turned wary and didn't know whether to run or stay as Caroline approached her.

"I'm sorry I slapped you," she said. "It wasn't fair taking my anxiety out on you. Will you forgive me?"

At that moment, years of antipathy for this woman slipped away, like a rapid change of costumes, and was replaced by pity at having to face a possible horrific loss. Elena had nothing to lose by being kind and charitable. Time enough later, once Justin was back in form, to get the professional competition and animosity back to normal levels. Now wasn't the time.

"There's nothing to forgive," she said, hoping she wouldn't regret it later.

Caroline nodded in acknowledgment and was almost at the automatic doors when she turned. "Why don't you come in with me? You can say hello."

Elena hesitated.

"Up to two people can be with him," Frannie said out loud and pushed her forward. "The nurse told me."

Leave it to Francesca to know that, Elena thought.

Feeling like she had no choice now but to go, Elena followed Caroline into the ICU.

To say that this section was even more depressing than the waiting room was an understatement. And it wasn't because of the actual setting, no, Elena thought. In this section of the hospital, everything seemed state of the art. The rooms she passed? Roomy, with what seemed the latest monitors and equipment. It was the ambience of the place: hushed, expectant of tragedy, with constant mechanical beeps, whirrs, artificially induced breaths, whispered pain, and tragic faces of dear ones reflecting patience, regret, inevitability, even hopelessness for those being taken care of inside the cubicles. And as Elena walked by, the feeling of gratitude grew, albeit coated with a good layer of guilt, for her state of good health.

They entered Justin's room as if it were a holy place. Elena shuddered on seeing him, remembering the first moment of discovery at the studio. Prostrate, but with no blood halo, Justin was still unmoving, so, so weak and pale, his usual energetic aura was practically nonexistent and replaced by tubes supporting life and giving breath. Elena's pity tripled. It didn't matter if he'd been a self-centered, unfaithful SOB while they'd been together five years ago, this shouldn't have happened.

"Oh, Justin," Elena whispered. "Of all the stupid things to do."

Caroline brushed his hair back and kissed his forehead.

"He's always doing that, you know?" At Elena's raised eyebrow, she answered. "Going off by himself. Practicing."

Elena stared at Justin. Was it really that?

"We're always off practicing somewhere by ourselves, Caroline," Elena said. "It's the nature of our beast. I do it. You do it."

"Not any more, I don't. But lately, with him, it's been obsessive. He has to outdo the competition at all costs." Caroline caressed his hand. "I warned him, but he doesn't listen. He just wants to dance, dance, dance, and be damned to the consequences. And he'd do anything to keep top billing." A tear fell on Justin's arm. "He didn't even consider options.

No. Everything his way. No consideration for us, for me. Nothing. Whatever it takes."

Elena didn't like the way this conversation was going. One thing was to feel sorry for the dancer, the artist, but another was to air their dirty laundry to someone who was too keenly aware of this man's faults and shortcomings. And, at this moment, Elena didn't want to blurt out anything that spoke ill of a man who couldn't defend himself. Besides, it was none of her business what had been going on behind the scenes in their relationship.

Time to exit.

"I have to go," Elena said. "I need to practice something and work out a few kinks on my choreography. Want to update a few things, change others. You know how it is."

"*Black Rhapsody*?"

It was a statement of fact.

"Yes."

Caroline nodded, without breaking her gaze on Justin.

"I heard you were not considering him for it." She turned to look at Elena for confirmation.

Elena nodded. "Yes." There was regret in her voice. "I probably won't stage it here either. I'm sorry."

Without saying a word, Caroline sat on the nearest chair next to the bed's railing. Took Justin's hand. Ignored her completely.

Elena could see she was in another world already. She walked to the opposite side of the bed, leaned in, and whispered, "Get well soon, please. Fight this."

And as she got to the doorway, she heard Caroline whisper, "You shouldn't have, Justin. You shouldn't have."

Chapter Six

THE RIDE BACK TO TERPSICHORE WAS DONE IN SILENCE, while the subway car rumbled, screeched, dinged, swayed, and disgorged passengers on its daily reruns up and down Broadway. Not even when they got off at Columbus Circle did they speak, Elena and the others mired in a funk of their own. It wasn't until her stomach growled that she realized she hadn't eaten lunch, and it was going on close to six o'clock now. She nixed going back to her brother's apartment because if she went there, she wouldn't come out until tomorrow. And she had things she wanted to do before going back to her temporary home.

"I don't know about you," Elena said. "But I'm starving."

Anne stopped and looked at her watch. "Good grief. Is that really the time?"

Francesca shifted her shoulder bag a bit more comfortably. "Nothing too heavy, please. I have a Pilates class at eight."

Elena looked across the roundabout toward Fifty-Eighth street on Broadway and pointed. "Is the French bistro over there still open?"

Francesca nodded.

Fifteen minutes later, seated and served, Elena blurted, "What on earth is going on in Terpsichore? And don't tell me it's nothing."

"I could tell you it's none of your business, since you're no longer a member of the company," Anne said. "But that changed yesterday."

"You know, this is pissing me off. What changed yesterday? It's like I'm a pariah now, and not because I choreographed *Black Rhapsody*. And, why would Jake Forrester mention my mom's marriage to Fauchier as important? Keep harping about wills? What the hell is going on?" And Elena dug into her mushroom quiche as if to skewer it.

"Seriously?" asked Anne. "You have no idea why your mother tying the knot with Fauchier would be a problem?"

Elena stared at Anne. "Maybe you do because you have Mr. Derek's ear. But, no, I don't. And that is not the issue." She made a mental note to hash it out with scherzo Forrester later. He knew what was going on better than anyone. "After these problems started, why is it taking this long to find the culprit?"

"It's not as simple as when we caught Tina Martin," Anne said.

"Oh goodness," Francesca choked on her salad trying not to laugh. "Talk about the mother from hell. She gave *Dance Moms* a run for their money in nasty."

"Reminded me of the pompom mom in the eighties, except Tina Martin was doing the dirty deeds herself," Anne said. "I never really understood this derangement syndrome in some mothers."

"In all fairness, Magaly wasn't that good, but wanted, beyond all costs, to be a prima ballerina," Elena said. "I can understand her mom wanting that for her."

"Bah. With what? She was a good dancer, but not prima quality. Soloist, tops. There were dozens of other dancers with extraordinary talent surrounding her. That mother was sick and obsessed. Delusions of grandeur, if you ask me, instead of anchored in reality." Anne swallowed some mint lemonade. "But she was laser focused on her daughter getting the part of Giselle. As if that would have lifted her to prima ballerina status. Laughable. The woman went so far as to leave the chit alone with Derek at the theater one evening for a bit of skin-to-skin rubbing. He packed her out into a taxi lickety-split as soon as he realized what was going on."

"My mother was livid when Tina actually messed up one of her costumes," Elena said. "Which brings me back to what you've said about what's been going on. Those things are very similar to the sabotage Tina perpetrated back then," Elena said, remembering how the woman had ruined toe shoes, changed critical audition times to benefit her daughter, and added licorice to drinks to give her targets the runs. The woman even went so far as to add chili oil to the liquid eyeliner of a dancer her daughter was the understudy of so that she could replace the woman on the performing roster.

Someone could be taking a page from that awful woman's book, Elena thought. If so, that meant it was one of the original members of Terpsichore who was doing these things. Only those who were present during Tina's reign of destruction would remember what she'd done.

However, Tina Martin had been targeting specific quarry. The incidents now seemed to be random, more in the vein of destroying Mr. Derek and the company. Why? And how could it be related with what had occurred to Justin?

"But, really, this had nothing to do with Justin's accident," Francesca said, placing her fork next to her half-eaten grilled-chicken salad, as if she'd lost her appetite completely. "His *was* an accident, surely?"

"The police are not letting that one go," Elena said. "Heard they'll be back interviewing more people tomorrow, early. Even taking people out of class."

Frannie grabbed Elena's hand and squeezed. "Elena, be careful. That detective, Harris, asked me all kinds of questions about you, where you were, and your relationship with Justin. If you could be vindictive, jealous even."

Elena stared at her best friend. "You can't think that I... that I would...?"

Frannie was insulted. "I would never..."

"Don't be ridiculous," Anne interrupted in a huff. "We don't think that at all. However, it's unfortunate that you found him, and that half the company heard him dissing you off, and you dissing him." She sighed and pushed her half-eaten plate away from her. "What a mess."

"I bet that medicine bottle holds the clue to all this," Elena said.

"To what specifically?" Anne waved away Elena's notion with a hand. "You're grasping here."

"But, think about it. Could Justin have seen someone, the one who's doing all this, confronted them in the studio, and that person dropped it?"

"But that means he would have been hurt on purpose," Francesca said a bit horrified. "That is way out there."

"Well, it's a possibility."

"Or maybe it was Justin taking something he shouldn't have, like a codeine-laced ibuprofen pill for pain that made him dizzy. Or we're morbidly speculating on something that was, and still is, an unfortunate accident," Anne suggested. "It's not like it hasn't happened before. There was that dancer in Nicosia months back who banged his head in a fall and died suddenly. In Justin's case it could be the same. Nobody knows exactly what happened. It's up to the hospital to find out and for the police to reveal what they know."

"If they reveal anything," Elena said.

"Well, everyone will know for sure one way or another if the police arrest or don't arrest someone."

Elena was still unconvinced. The letters left on the ripped label kept flashing in her mind. Those letters had been in a weird combination, one that did not coincide with Justin's name or any analgesic he may have ingested. At least, any analgesic known to her, she thought, being honest. So, why believe Justin hadn't had an accident? What proof did she have? Gut feelings were not evidence, just a reaction to the distasteful events happening. And why should she continue in this vein, when, after the gala performance, she and Fred would be out of New York and back to their somewhat sane ballet world in Monaco.

It shouldn't worry her at all.

But it did.

"What if they arrest an innocent person?"

Francesca's sudden whisper brought Elena back to reality. For a few nanoseconds, they stared at each other, and then down at their half-eaten food. On cue and without prompting, they finished eating in silence, more out of habit than hunger. It was a calorie thing, Elena knew, and they needed theirs in order to keep their bodies performing well. All the while they avoided saying what Elena was sure they were all thinking.

Ten minutes later, they left the restaurant in different directions. No further mention of Justin or the events happening in the company were broached.

Elena cut across Fifty-Ninth and walked down Broadway to Terpsichore. Without acknowledging anyone, she took the elevator to the locker rooms, changed back into her leotard and tights and went in search of any advanced class she could take.

She needed to get back into her groove, so to speak. And a class was the best way to center her.

"There you are." Fred joined her a few minutes after class had ended. "I sometimes forget the advanced classes can be a real workout."

"Which one did you take?"

"Men's jumps. Broderick was on a roll. Or blowing off steam. The poor kids were exhausted."

"Kids, huh?"

"Don't smirk. It doesn't become you." He mopped up his sweat. "Some of those boys can't be more than fifteen. Need to grow into their jumping muscles."

"In a few years' time they'll be out-jumping you."

"Tell me about it. Saw some of them already applying Daniil Simkin's strength exercises before class. Anyway, where the hell have you been? I've been looking all over for you after the video shoot."

"Went to see Justin at the hospital."

Fred paused in zipping his bag. "Any improvement?"

Elena shook her head, but her expression said it all. "Where are you off to?"

"Hotel. Shower. Dinner. Bed. In that order."

"Do you mind if I borrow you for a bit? Want to try out something new."

Fred, bless him, was always ready to please.

Elena explained the new move and lift she had envisioned and they spent the next half hour executing it, tweaking it, perfecting it. Satisfied for the moment, Elena told Fred to scoot and get some rest. But instead of leaving, Fred held her shoulders. He turned serious.

"I don't know what is going on here," he said. "But I don't like it."

"Have you heard anything?"

He shook his head. "Nothing substantial, but everyone is nervous, jumpy. In the locker room, I did overhear Dimmig say to another dancer that the infighting between director and upper management was escalating, and that this latest thing with Justin... well, they shut up the moment they realized I was nearby."

"Francesca is nervous as well. Anne, I'm not sure of. She thinks what happened was an accident, just that. But I know she's disturbed about the other incidents going on. But she's not opening up."

"I have a feeling we landed in the middle of a very nasty quarrel. We need to steer away, go to class, rehearsal, hotel, gala, and nothing more. Promise?"

She nodded.

"We'll leave them to their disputes and, come Saturday, we're back home." He gave her a quick peck on the cheek. "Don't stay here. Go to your brother's now." With those parting words he was gone before she could blink.

Elena sighed and bent to untie her toe shoe. Fred was right. It was not their squabble.

"We really have to stop meeting this way."

At the familiar voice, Elena looked between her legs at Jake Forrester, whose smile held more than simple pleasure at seeing her.

The rascal. But Elena remembered she had a bone to pick with this man and all her fear, anger, and frustrations of the day effervesced.

"You." She forgot about untying her toe shoe and strode over to plant herself just inches from his nose.

The smile transformed into perplexity.

"What the hell is your game in all this? Huh? Tell me."

His look turned cautious. "What on earth are you talking about?"

"Don't play the innocent with me. I heard you this afternoon." She pushed a finger into his chest. "What is it that I need to know that Mr. Derek refuses to tell me? Well? I'm here now." She planted both fists on her waist à la Wonder Woman and waited. "I'm here. Tell."

"Have I told you, you look formidable when angry?"

"*Do...not...*change the subject," she said, leaning forward. "I have landed in a maelstrom not of my doing..." She paused, reconsidered. "Well, some of it is my doing. But, for the rest I'm steering blind against an unknown. So, what on earth has my mother's marriage to Fauchier have to do with anything?"

"My, my," Jake said, stepping back. "Pretty little ears have been truly busy today."

"So what? I didn't eavesdrop on purpose."

"Didn't you?"

"No." She studied him for a moment and strode back to her ballet bag. "Fine. Be that way." She shoved her sweaty towel and drinking bottle inside, and zipped it shut with force. She wasn't going to get any answers from him by the look of things.

"Elena."

She hefted the bag on her shoulder, turned, and tried to brush past him. She came to a halt when he grabbed her forearm, stopping her with an ease that surprised her.

"Listen, it's not for me to say..."

"Oh, right," she scoffed. "The conventional excuse. Let go."

The sigh she heard was deep and heartfelt.

"If you really heard our *private* conversation," he began, "you also heard that I want Derek to come clean."

"Good grief. Clean about what? The only thing that was tangled up in secrecy and legalese was the permission to stage *Black Rhapsody*."

And that was revealed with a bang.

"Not the only thing."

She stared. He watched her as if trying to impart a telepathic message. Or at least something she should have realized beforehand.

Jake sighed, even more deeply, if that were even possible. He released her and began to pace.

"I told Derek yesterday that things changed with your revelation. That you need to know, because it will affect you." He looked at her. "Does affect you."

"Doesn't it affect him more? I mean I can give or withdraw permission for *Black Rhapsody* at any given moment. But other than upsetting him personally, I don't see what that has to do with anything."

Jake laughed, more in exasperation than in humor.

"This has nothing to do with *Black Rhapsody* but with Fauchier."

"I don't understand."

"I know you don't." He stepped back toward her and held her shoulders softly. "Do you know anything about Fauchier's will?"

Elena shrugged a bit. "Not really, except what everyone knows, that he willed all his choreographic estate to Terpsichore."

"If he died single."

Elena stared, at first confused, and then with dawning comprehension. "You can't mean. No. That's ridiculous."

"Fauchier was very clear. If he died single, his fifty percent of the company and all his choreographic works, together with all proceeds from revenues, commissions, permissions, and staging would revert back to his partner, Derek Michaels. Which is what happened. But, in case Fauchier married, all his shares and choreographic works would revert to his wife and, at her death, to whomever she willed it to."

The enormity of what Jake was telling her was too much to process, but when she did, the only thing that she could utter was a soft "Oh Lord."

"And that sums it up succinctly. Yes," Jake said.

For a moment both said nothing. The air conditioner blasted air and noise into the room. Somewhere Elena heard a squeak and a bump, and the hum of a vacuum cleaner a good way off.

"Terpsichore, to give you some background, like many ballet companies recently, especially those which are not subsidized by the government, have been struggling financially," Jake said. "Some have gone under. Derek has been somewhat immune to the trend because of his wife's backing, but it's been difficult. However, months ago, word got out that the golden goose that buoyed up Terpsichore couldn't anymore. The economic downturn, together with the shutdowns of biblical proportions of a year ago, diminished a lot of wealth, including Derek's wife's. Even the school has suffered."

Jake didn't elaborate further. Elena understood. The arts were the first thing that got affected by economic downturns. It was considered a luxury (which it was) and the choice between spending the money on food or on ballet classes, well, groceries won. And after the hysteria and the ridiculous draconian measures some countries had taken with what had happened worldwide, well, it had been difficult for all.

"Many of our principals and soloists wanted to leave for Europe, whose major companies are subsidized by the government and did not bleed too much money, but Derek had them in unbreakable contracts. But those contracts started expiring six months ago. Some dancers have been lucky to be offered positions in opera houses and other smaller companies worldwide, but employment possibilities at the level they've achieved are few and far between. Then these things began to happen. It's as if someone has it out for Derek."

"Or doing away with competition."

"A possibility. But, financially, things began improving for Terpsichore at the same time, especially after Derek announced the revival of *Black Rhapsody*. And then..."

"I happened," she interrupted.

"Yes." He smiled, the wattage still there but with a touch of concern.

"Ok. I understand now why my mother's marriage to Fauchier was important. I am at a loss, however, as to what you're hinting at and still not saying, though."

"You don't get it?" Jake said a bit exasperated. "You are in charge of *all* Fauchier's works. You could be the ruin or salvation of the company, and not just by giving permission to stage his works."

There was a loud bang somewhere outside the corridor, as if someone had slammed a door closed or thrown something on the floor.

Jake stilled. Elena jumped. He didn't move for a bit, while Elena strained to hear movement. The only thing she heard was the hum of a vacuum cleaner droning somewhere far off.

She relaxed. Jake not so much.

"Sorry, but you've lost me," she said, wanting to return to the previous conversation.

"Elena, if you exercise your rights as the beneficiary of Fauchier's will, Derek Michaels will have no choice but to give you years' worth of the monetary gain he's received from every single work he's staged in Fauchier's name. He'll be forced to cough up half of all the profits he's received from the school and from all the performances of the company since Fauchier's death."

"You're serious?"

"Deadly."

Not the choice of words she would have preferred.

"I think you're exaggerating," she scoffed. "What can the returns be? In the tens of thousands?"

Jake's laugh held no humor.

"Millions, my dear. Millions. Whether you want it or not, you are currently half owner of Terpsichore and all its assets, including the school, and your *yea* or *nay* to getting the arrears will affect the future of all its dancers. You now have the power to recruit and fire any dancer you wish. And, judging by the way you reacted to Justin's suggestion about *Black Rhapsody*, and the fact that you're not a member of Terpsichore, and have no stake in its success, everybody else will realize that you can make or break them when all this comes out. Only you can stop or release the financial spigot that will bleed Terpsichore dry. And because the company is now barely recovering, this will be its ruin."

Elena was horrified. What the hell had she landed in? Maelstrom wouldn't cover it.

"Who knows about the stipulations of Fauchier's will?" she asked. She still was in shock.

"Derek, Anne, Harriet, Analisse, Broderick. By extension, their partners, or whoever they've mentioned this to. You. Me."

The lights went out. Instant, absolute blackness.

Elena froze. Jake spouted hushed curses near her.

"Stay here," he ordered. "Don't move."

Interesting how, in the absolute darkness, you still could feel the pressure of a body's presence. Elena knew the instant Jake was no longer near her. A second later, the reed-thin light from Jake's flashlight app on his phone was almost blinding.

With unusual care, he opened the door into the hallway. Same darkness. Not even the red neon glare of the exit signs above the stairwell doors on their right were visible.

The drone of the vacuum cleaner had died. So had the air conditioner.

"It's probably the fuse box that tripped. It's been happening more often lately. Do you have everything with you? Purse, phone?" His voice, even in whispers held an urgency that raised the hairs on her neck.

"Yes." She'd kept her purse together with her ballet bag ever since coming in from the French bistro. She'd left nothing in the locker room. "Could the cleaning crew have tripped it?"

"Anything is possible. Building is old. The electrical system needs revamping. I'll have to go check the breaker box. It's in the basement. Come."

Elena shook her head. "You go," she said. She wasn't going anywhere, especially not that basement, she thought. In such complete darkness, it would be even more creepy than when she had visited it today.

"Wait for me here, then, and keep your phone handy." Jake was already behind the door. "Lock this thing. Do not, and I mean do not open it to anyone, except me. I'll be right back."

She rummaged in her purse more by feel than sight. Got her flashlight app working and peered around the door. Jake was nowhere in sight.

She heard the stair doors bang shut on the opposite end of the hallway at the same time she pressed the locking mechanism on the side of the door and closed it.

Might as well get out of these clothes.

Elena sat on the floor, phone light toward the ceiling and spread what she wanted around her. Good grief. She'd need to purge her bag soon. So much crap in it, no wonder it weighed a ton. It also had all her dirty clothes she'd collected from the locker when she went to change for class. Tonight, she thanked her brother's prescience to get a built-in washer and dryer in the apartment. If not, she'd have to lug everything to the laundry room five floors down, spend a ton of money for the washer and dryer, and lug everything back, wasting time and trips up and down. That brought to mind poor Fred, stuck in the hotel, hand washing and littering the bathroom with all his things hanging from whatever hook or rod, table or chair he could use. She dropped her brush next to her thigh. One way or another, they'd all had to do that when on the road, and many times the tights and leotards they'd had to use in class the next day were still damp. She made a mental note to offer him her brother's machines tomorrow. Made life easier. She hated to hand wash anything or wear damp clothing. She knew Fred didn't like it either.

Not getting up, and with quick efficiency, Elena slipped sweatpants over her tights, replaced toe shoes with sneakers, and undid her hair from the tight bun. She was brushing her hair, relieving the tightness in her skull, when she heard the doorknob rattle.

She grabbed her phone and pointed the light toward the solid door. "Jake?"

An unnatural stillness seemed to permeate her entire surroundings. A waiting. The sense of unease gripped her in a quick visc and she held her breath for a moment. Leaving her phone on the floor because it dissipated the shadows of the enclosed room well, she approached the door as quietly as she could. Pressed her ear to it. Silence, and yet, something else also. A vague sense of breath, as if someone was trying to control their breathing, doing exactly what she was doing, listening, waiting.

Oh hell. This can't be good.

"Jake? Is that you?' she whispered.

And, as if in answer, the door handle moved downward in slow motion, paused, and reverted to its original position.

No way that was Jake.

For a second, nothing else happened.

Then the banging and rattling on the door exploded in a deafening roar.

Elena jumped back a foot.

Desperation, anger, madness—Elena could describe all three driving the actions of whoever wanted in. If things weren't so out of hand and menacing, she would be laughing, thinking she was the protagonist of those zombie movies her siblings loved, where the undead forced their way in by hook or by crook in order to consume her.

Elena ran to her bag and desperately searched inside for her hairspray. Her phone was useless, unless she dialed 911. But, at least, it gave off light. She couldn't call or warn Jake because she didn't have his damn number. How could she be so stupid as to have him leave without getting it? She fisted her hand around the cold aluminum canister, shook it to make sure there were still contents in it, snapped the cap off, and threw the latter on the floor. She picked up her hairbrush too. If anyone came in through that door, they'd get a jet of stinging hairspray in their eyes, and another wallop from the brick-hard plastic of the hairbrush.

Hell. She wasn't going down without a fight.

Elena stood her ground, despite the awful racket, and the sudden thought that she might have to defend herself, when everything went quiet.

If that maniac thought she'd open the door for a quick peek, he had another thing coming. She'd seen enough horror movies not to become a TSTL character—one too stupid to live.

She waited. Inched her way to the door. Waited. Inched further on. Waited.

Nothing.

She must have stood there for what seemed like an eternity, but probably was only a few minutes, when she was startled into dropping her hairbrush by a loud knock.

"Elena, open up. It's Jake."

The voice was muffled and low.

"How do I know it's you?"

A pause. "Are you serious?"

"Deadly." To use his phrase.

After a lengthier pause. "I have your brother's movie score as my ringtone."

And at that precise moment the lights came on.

Elena closed her eyes, blinded. She didn't move.

"What the hell is the matter with you?" Jake banged on the door once more. "Open up."

When she still didn't move, she heard Jake say something to another person, heard a key slide into the cylinder, and the lock click open.

Jake found her standing in the middle of the room, hairspray can at the ready, a hand over her eyes, covering the glare of the lights.

"What the hell?"

There was a janitor, overalls and all, next to Jake, staring at her as if she had two heads. A walkie-talkie was in his hand next to his open mouth. Elena knew she looked ridiculous, but she didn't change her stance.

"Thanks, Manolo," Jake said. "We're good."

Said Manolo turned, squawking to an Ileana into the two-way radio that the lights were finally on.

Elena realized she really looked ridiculous and turned to put everything away. She was searching for the hairspray can's lid when Jake lifted it into her line of sight. "Is this what you are looking for?"

She grabbed it, snapped it back into place, dropped everything inside her ballet tote, and lifted an imperious finger at Jake, who had just opened his mouth to say something.

Jake paused, his expression at once curious, mixed in with a big dose of concern.

She zipped everything inside, including her purse and phone, scanned the surroundings for anything else she may have missed that was personal, and turned to face him.

"Take me out of here, please, before I implode. Preferably to a place that can furnish a big, big stiff drink."

Without saying a word, Jake grabbed her hand and pulled her out of the room.

Chapter Seven

NEXT MORNING, ELENA FINISHED CLASS MORE EXHAUSTED than usual. She blamed it on the four margaritas she'd downed in less than an hour after leaving the room from hell last night, and the small amount of food she'd consumed at the restaurant Jake had taken her to. Add to that the few hours of sleep she'd had, and her muscles had protested, no, screamed the abuse. And because she'd been consuming excessive amounts of water this morning, she was drowning in a sea of perspiration, leaving sweat imprints, as if created by a manic drunkard, all over the classroom floor.

And God, had she been tipsy yesterday. Just barely this side of drunk. She remembered Jake grabbing a taxi, which had driven them to a Mexican restaurant of Jake's choice, where he had dutifully ordered their drinks, and listened with quiet intensity to her account of events. In the meantime, she'd emptied margarita after margarita, snacking without pause on the *queso derretido* appetizer with the chips he'd ordered, and ignoring his warning to take it easy on the tequila. By the third drink, things had blurred quite satisfactorily. At least, her fear had dissipated with an alcohol-induced bonhomie and been replaced with complaints whenever Jake shooed away the accommodating waiter who wanted to refill her drink order indefinitely. And, somewhere in between all that, he'd ordered a chicken quesadilla to share, and made sure she at least ate half of it. Things were a bit fuzzy after that. She vaguely registered the taxi drive back to her brother's apartment due to her contented, sleepy haze. By then, Jake had basically taken over, navigated her wobbly self to the right floor, opened the apartment door, dropped all her things next to it, given her a kiss that melted her muscles to her toes, and didn't leave the hallway until he heard her lock the apartment door.

Mr. Scherzo had transformed into Mr. Gallantry last night. Not what she'd expected. At least not what she'd desired after that kiss. Chivalry to the core on his part hadn't been on her agenda last night.

Oh well.

She pressed the towel to her face, not so much to mop up the sweat there but to hide the idiotic smile the thought of Jake brought on.

A good man never takes advantage of a drunk woman. At least, that's what Roberto always said, especially if her brother liked said woman.

She rubbed her face hard and placed the damp towel on the lower barre to air. Her brother also said it never hurt not to be around said woman when the drunkenness disappeared and the projectile vomiting began.

Very pragmatic, her brother. Probably Jake was as pragmatic too.

However, she could have told him she never hurled, despite the level of alcohol in her system.

Speaking of. Elena drank some more water and scanned the schedule for her rehearsal times. According to this, she also had a fitting at the theater around three o'clock. If she timed things right, she might be able to take a class afterward at Rick and Nat's studio and maybe even get some choreography done there, as well.

She almost jumped out of her skin when Francesca's heavy tote collided with the wall behind her with a big thump.

"Freaking A, Frannie."

"What?"

You wouldn't be asking that question if what took place last night had happened to you.

Elena suppressed the manic laugh bubbling up. Despite the fact activities today rolled along normally, she couldn't help but feel that it was anything but. It was as if she were waiting for the literal other shoe to drop, with the added disadvantage of not knowing where it would hit and when. Stupid feeling, but, after last night, she wasn't so sure it was without merit. Jake was nervous too, especially after she conveyed, and he understood, the intensity behind that attack on the locked door. And her suspicion all was not normal was not that far out there after he told her the janitor had discovered the breaker had been shut down on purpose. When she'd asked how on earth he was so positive about that, he explained that, when a breaker trips, it stays in the middle. The thing was firmly in the off position. That only happened when done deliberately.

Anne strode to where Francesca and Elena were, perusing her own schedule.

"Your fitting is about the same time as mine," Anne said. "Want to share a taxi?"

Fred glided toward them from his sitting position by the door. He pushed his bag next to Francesca's and placed his own sweaty towel on the barre next to Elena's.

"I get a 'one size fits all' romantic shirt," he said with a gleeful smirk. "Last worn by Julio Bocca no less." He took out his phone and showed them the photo he'd captured of the label inside the shirt. "Amèlie is over the moon."

"Be grateful it was his and not a shorter principal of the company," Anne said, chuckling.

"Well, I'm thrilled and relieved. That way I can rest this afternoon while you all get poked and squeezed."

"I'll share a cab," Elena told Anne and turned to Fred. "Don't smirk. Be grateful you're dancing the balcony scene from R&J, if not, you'd be rigid with corsets and whalebones."

Anne laughed. "Now, that's archaic."

Elena chuckled. "Mom's favorite phrase. She would have loved using them for some costumes too."

"Thank Diaghilev for the change to freer and more romantic garb," Francesca said, who was a bit of a snob about the history of ballet.

"Thank God for elastane," said Fred. "Imagine how restrictive those costumes would make you. Difficult to dance in. Seams stretched to max. Costume failures galore."

"Everyone has the newest rehearsal schedules, right?" Analisse interrupted, stepping into the room, clapping to get everyone's attention.

Nods and yeas answered her. "The police are here," she continued, "and they guaranteed Mr. Derek they'd finish the remaining interviews today."

That bit of news spoiled everyone's mood, particularly Elena's.

Someone at the other extreme of the room asked, "What's the news on Justin?"

"Broderick called the hospital this morning and nothing has changed." Analisse shook her head. "I'll keep you informed as I receive news." She clapped once more. "Okay, people. Let's roll."

The exodus out of the room was swift, except for the gala soloists who were scheduled to rehearse there.

"Heads up," whispered Anne.

And indeed, Caroline and Randy were approaching, involved in a friendly conversation, while Analisse and Tadana discussed rehearsal music on their way to the piano. Martina was also beelining it to where Elena and her friends stood, eyes set on Elena as if pinned to a quarry.

The woman looked like she was going on a mission.

Just the choice of words she needed.

"Would you teach me that lift? The routine?"

No good mornings. No hey, theres. Martina didn't seem to believe in the niceties of good manners.

"Pardon me?" Elena asked.

"Last night. You rehearsed dance routine and lift with Boelens. Saw you on my way to change room." She sat next to Fred and squirmed in such a manner as to dislodge him a bit. She took Elena's hand and placed her other on Fred's knee. She glanced from one to the other, her expression eager. Hungry.

Elena was momentarily fascinated. This woman was definitely driven to get what she wanted.

"This is for *Black Rhapsody,* yes? The routine, lift?" Martina continued. "It was—what is the word—moving."

Everyone's eyes were on Elena now, with different degrees of curiosity.

"Yes. It's for *Black Rhapsody*." Grudging acknowledgment.

"Please. I'll do anything. I'll be your, what is it that you say..." She struggled for a bit. "Your Guinea Pig."

"Her what?" Francesca began to chuckle.

"Isn't that what you say? A person you *montage* with, experiment your choreography with?"

"Martina," Elena began.

"Please. Would love for you to use me for setting up choreography. To improve or change *Black Rhapsody*. I love what I saw."

"Well, you can forget about it," Caroline's voice interrupted the harangue. "Elena told Justin in no uncertain terms that she won't stage *Black Rhapsody* here. As a matter of fact, won't use anyone from Terpsichore for it."

"Caroline. Really," said Anne.

"Everyone heard when she dissed him," Caroline answered, a catch in her voice. Elena wasn't sure if it was because she was miffed, or if it had brought memories of the injured Justin. "And at the hospital yesterday, she confirmed she probably won't stage *Black Rhapsody* here, if at all."

"But it is so beautiful," Martina said. "Look," Martina stood, forcing Fred to get up by grabbing his arm and pulling. She mimicked almost exactly what Elena had choreographed yesterday.

Good grief. How long had Martina been standing outside where they'd been rehearsing, staring and absorbing all her moves? Granted, dancers had almost eidetic memories, capturing complete routines in seconds. Center work and auditions had a tendency to ingrain that quickness in you. But Martina had to have been watching them a while, because Elena had not finished the routine, in its entirety, until well into the half hour she and Fred had been practicing.

And why hadn't she seen her? Could she have been the person outside the door last night? Then again, wouldn't Martina have identified herself when asked?

Grudgingly, Elena had to admit the choreography did look beautiful, especially when executed by a gifted dancer such as Martina, despite the fact she'd gotten the lead into the lift wrong. It was a treat to watch.

Usually, she didn't view the steps, moves, ensemble, positions, and music residing in her head until executed later, after she'd begun staging it.

"Wow, Elena," Francesca said. "You came up with that?"

"It's beautiful, isn't it?" Martina insisted.

"Show off, more like," Caroline said. "Both of you. And if I were you, Martina, I wouldn't lay my hopes on someone whom you may never see again except as a guest artist." She strode toward Analisse, her words of "when are we starting rehearsal?" trailing after her.

"Well, I not care," Martina cut in. "I'll go to where Elena is. Get into company. I must dance this."

Good Lord.

"Must I remind you, dear, that you've signed a contract with *this* company?" Anne said.

Francesca leaned over. "That won't settle well with Mr. Derek," she whispered.

Oh, Frannie, you have no idea what is really going to hit the fan.

But rehearsal cut into any further conversation. Caroline and Mario went first. Elena watched and thought Caroline had recovered well from the fiasco of two days ago. She looked strong, sure, and the corrections Analisse had given her and Mario were executed flawlessly today. Fauchier would have been proud.

Elena and Fred took center stage next. They were in the middle of their R&J routine when, out of the corner of her eye, she saw Jake step into the room and pause by the door. Eyes met for an instant. No welcoming smile.

Oh-oh.

She almost missed her musical cue for the *piqué attitude derrière* turns. She slapped herself mentally. Distractions at the moment wouldn't do, so she ignored as best she could Jake's presence in the room.

They finished, as usual, out of breath and exhausted, especially Fred. It was an infernal variation for the man in particular, so much so that, in the full-length ballet, she'd seen Fred throw up in the wings from the nonstop dancing between scenes in act 1. MacMillan's choreography, though exquisite, was brutal.

"That was nicely done, you two," Analisse told them, as they both tried to catch their breath holding their knees. "Elena, you were a few beats out of sync with the music on your pique turns. Fix that. Fred, remember you're slipping her skirt through your fingers, smelling her perfume. A delicate wonder for you. It looked like you were mopping sweat from your face instead of adoring every bit of your lover."

Amid the laughter that followed, Jake asked, "Are you done with Elena and Fred, Analisse? Can I borrow her for a few?"

Analisse answered by shooing them his way. "Francesca, Randy. You're up."

Elena grabbed her stuff and headed for the door.

"That was beautifully done," Caroline admitted from the floor, where she was drinking from her mug.

"So were you," she said, pausing on her way to meet Jake. "You've got Fauchier down to perfection." She meant every word.

Caroline shrugged.

"Will you see Justin today?"

"Derek told me I could take off after rehearsal."

"Give him a hug from me," she said.

"Elena." Jake sounded impatient.

The moment she neared, Jake grabbed her forearm and guided her into the hallway and in the elevator's direction. At the last moment, however, Jake swung her into the stairwell instead.

"The police want to see you," he whispered by way of greeting, once they were secure from prying eyes and eager ears.

She stopped on the landing. "What on earth for?"

"I mentioned last night, what happened."

"Why on earth would you do that?"

"They needed to know. I also told Derek. He wants to see you right after. He's not pleased at all."

"Sounds ominous."

They continued downstairs but Jake stopped before opening the door at ground level.

"Let me know exactly where you'll be today at all times, please," he said. "Any plans, other than your fitting at the theater, before you go home?"

"You've been looking at my schedule," she said a bit peeved. "I really don't need a babysitter, you know."

"Elena, when are you going to trust me?" he said. "I'm really on your side."

Elena stared at her feet, considering. If she were honest about it, and examined everything he'd said and done, there was no reason not to trust him, especially after yesterday.

"I may walk over to Rick and Nat's this afternoon," she admitted, capitulating. She really needed someone like Jake on her side. "It's a couple of blocks from the theater. I can take a class. Create more choreography, if they have an empty room."

He was about to contradict her, she was sure, when she saw he thought better of it. At that time of day, the city was buzzing and full of people, so there shouldn't be any chance for her to get mugged or attacked in the middle of the street. Well, sort of. This was New York City she was talking about. Both could happen anywhere.

"Text me the address. You have my numbers, right?"

"Yes," she said, her tone half amusement, half exasperation. "Even I remember you grabbing my phone last night and entering all your info into my contacts. Including adding them to my favorites."

For the first time, his beautiful smile twitched his lips upward.

"Surprised you remember anything." His eyes danced with mirth. "You, my dear, were smashed."

"Lightly inebriated," she contradicted.

"Remember anything else?" He surprised her by running his thumb over her lips, ever so slow and soft.

Her face exploded with heat.

"Hm. Wouldn't have wanted to be the only one who remembered."

He bent and kissed her in delicious exploration. Her legs began to tremble.

Jake opened the door and guided her the short distance to Harriet's office.

"You're a dangerous man, Mr. Scherzo," she said, while he knocked on the door. How on earth could she face the police feeling this way? Her mind was mush. Maybe he'd done it on purpose.

At the permission to enter, he opened the door, a very male and satisfied smile on his face. "I'll see you in Derek's office after you're done here," he said and left.

"Good morning, Ms. del Carral. Have a seat." Detective Harris didn't seem enthused about this interview. Well, neither was she.

She saw they'd left only one chair in front of their seats of power behind the desk. She sat and waited.

"Why is it that certain events in this investigation..." The pause was extended as Harris studied her in minute detail. "...gravitate exclusively around you?"

Elena kept her mouth shut.

"Mr. Forrester came to us with an interesting story." Harris looked at his partner. "A theory, wouldn't you say, Murdock?"

"Flimsy one, at best, I think," replied the second in command.

"Said you'd had a nasty encounter with an unknown person, or persons, of possible interest to us." He doodled into his open notepad, trying to look nonchalant. But Elena knew he was anything but. Definitely on the lookout for what exactly? Whatever it was, she wasn't going to play. She kept quiet.

"Of course," the detective continued, "according to Mr. Forrester, neither he, nor you for that matter, were able to identify whoever wanted to break into a bolted room to, what was it that Mr. Forrester said, Murdock?"

"Brain you," his partner supplied, a sort of cynic humor pouring out with the words.

"Yes. That was the correct phrase." Harris locked eyes with her, a give-no-quarter expression on his face. "Now you must understand my skepticism here, Ms. del Carral. 'Brain you' attributes intent on the part of the person trying to get into the room. And you have no clue, according to Mr. Forrester, as well, about who that person could be. Now, why would anyone, especially a stranger, want to do that to you?"

She shrugged and offered no response.

Detective Harris sighed. "Okay. Let's have the story."

Elena explained, without the details of what she'd done to protect herself, to the detective. If she had, she was positive they'd get a good chuckle out of her attempts at defending herself with a hairspray can. A meager weapon, she realized now under the light of cold logic. Possibly not even a very effective weapon against a deranged person. But she was a ballerina and she had a few good kicks under her belt that would bring down a horse.

And she'd had the hairbrush too.

"I don't know, Detective Harris, if there was animosity on anyone's part behind the crazy attempt to get into that room last night," Elena said in all honesty. "At least, by the sound of it, there was total desperation in breaking down the door. But... For all I know the person had left something personal and important in there and was frantic to retrieve it. However, after what happened to Justin, and the sudden loss of electricity to that room and the entire hall, I was really scared. Jake was cautious too. You must admit, I may have had some due cause for concern."

"But, Ms. del Carral, that is what baffles me," Detective Harris said. "Why?"

Why, indeed.

She shrugged again, not giving him further information, and definitely not the particulars she was now co-owner of Terpsichore and everything in between. Because of that, Jake suspected she could be a target for whoever was trying to mess up Terpsichore.

She didn't mention either, there had been a noise before the lights went out which may have been someone listening in to Jake's and her conversation. She didn't add that they may have put a bullseye on her, especially after all the reckless attacks perpetrated for months on dancers and founder alike.

She didn't mention either, Martina's loitering outside the room. She'd been there for God knows how long, watching and memorizing her variation. Could she have been the one trying to enter the room last night?

Somehow, Elena doubted it. There had been a ferocity about it that belied any casual interest in talking to her about her choreography. And, the bit about turning the electricity off? She didn't think Martina would think about that, let alone know where the breaker box was.

"Again, Ms. del Carral, could you answer the why?"

The man was insistent.

"No idea, Detective Harris," she said. "All I know is Fred and I..."

"Fred?" asked Murdock.

"My partner, Fredrik Boelens. We landed in a feud of some sort, with all kinds of mishaps happening within the company. Has Mr. Derek said anything?"

"He has. But he believes it's an internal squabble and unimportant. Down to egos, he said. Nothing to investigate there and soon resolved."

"And what happened to Justin?"

"Open to interpretation yet," Detective Harris said. "But you, Ms. del Carral, tick off all my question boxes—found the victim, fingerprints all over a bottle with prescription drug residue, raise the animosity of a few of the company members..."

"What?" *The nerve of some people.*

"Were in a relationship with said victim..."

"But that was ages ago," she sputtered.

"Had a very public fight with said victim, was heard dissing the victim, and, last night, had someone who may have (or may not have) wanted to attack you. Aside from all that, I believe you are hiding something."

"Well, I think that is super unfair," she said, her frustration turning to anger. "If you can't recall, I'll remind you, respectfully so, that my partner and I arrived on a plane less than a week ago, and that I just came here to dance. Dance. I resent everything else that you've thrown at me. How the heck can this be my fault? It's what you're implying."

"I rarely imply, Ms. del Carral," Detective Harris said. "But I will say this, although I'm sure everyone knows it's a cliché, but it's not, really: don't leave town unless I give you leave."

"But I'm due back home to work next week." She almost shouted it.

The connecting door to Derek's office opened abruptly. Jake appeared.

"Is anything wrong?"

Detective Harris gave Elena a knowing smirk.

Oh, go *grand jeté* somewhere in the Hudson, she thought.

"No," Harris said. "We're done here."

Elena stood, grabbed all her stuff and exited stage right, like an offended grande dame of the theater.

Chapter Eight

ELENA WAS FURIOUS.

And it showed.

It showed in the way she slammed the connecting door between Harriet's office and Mr. Derek's; it showed in the way she threw her ballet tote across the floor so that it skidded over the floor and bumped on the wall; it showed in her furious pacing and the 'do not touch me' attitude every time Jake tried to hold her in place.

"I can't believe that that, that *detective*, could even suggest that I may have had something to do with Justin's accident," she told Jake in a furious whisper. "That everything somehow revolves around me."

"Elena..." Jake tried to catch her again, but she was having none of it.

She turned on him. "Do you know what he said? What that man said?"

Jake humored her. "Not a clue."

She made a face. "He warned me not to leave the city without his permission, that's what. The damn *nerve*."

"Elena, calm down."

She stopped her pacing to stare open-mouthed. "Calm down? *Calm down?*"

He held her in place to make his point.

"This is exactly what Detective Harris wants." His words were low but emphatic. "You losing control. Getting mad and upset. It makes for mistakes, unintended statements, revelations. That's how the police work. How I work when on a fraud case."

"Really?"

"Really."

"It's so awful," she whispered.

"Come here," he said. He must have caught the catch in her voice because he pulled her into his arms, and she burrowed into the temporary safety he offered.

"Stop worrying. You know you had nothing to do with what's been happening. I know it. Derek knows it. Even Detective Harris knows it."

"He said the bottle I found definitely had prescription drug residue."

"Did he, now?"

"But not what kind." She looked at him. "Was Justin sick? Was he taking medicine that could have caused his fall?"

"Not that we know of." He considered. "I may be able to dig into that. What were those letters you said you saw on the ripped label?"

Elena blurted them.

"I'll ask my assistant to check on search engines if any medicines fit those letters."

"You have an assistant?"

His smile went up by a megawatt. "And staff too."

"And here I only have a volunteer Guinea Pig."

"A what?"

"Martina's words, not mine." And she explained what Martina had said.

Hilarity ensued on both their parts. But it did help defuse some of her tension.

"Mastery of the English language is not one of her virtues," Jake said. "Poor woman."

"Funny, though. What's not so funny is her obsession to dance *Black Rhapsody* and her plans. Everyone heard. It'll soon be in Mr. Derek's ear, either through the rumor mill, or definitely through Anne."

She stopped, at that instant realizing in what office they were standing.

"Relax. He went to get Broderick," he said, reading her mind.

She sank into the plush leather armchair facing Mr. Derek's desk and tried to relax. "Have you any idea what he wants to discuss? I mean, apart from the obvious."

"About that…"

Whatever else he would have said was cut short by the entrance of Derek and Broderick.

"Good," Derek said, sitting in what Elena called his throne: a swivel leather wing chair centered behind an impressive mahogany desk which, in turn, was in front of an oversized oleo portrait of him executing one of his double *cabrioles*. It had been commissioned and copied from an old photograph of Derek dancing Don Quijote.

Derek's throne room. Daunting and impressive, and meant to be that way.

Broderick stood slightly to his side, the ever-faithful lapdog.

"Seems things have come to a head," Derek began. "Unexpectedly so. I just wish your mother, first, and you, later, had approached me…"

"I tried…"

"Years ago," Derek interrupted. "I can't understand the reasons behind Rene's secrecy about his attachment to your mother…"

"He died," she said with a bluntness to her tone unlike the usual when addressing him, a man whom not only she'd known most of her life, but also whom she'd admired and considered a friend. At that time, he'd been so busy riding the prosperity train, enjoying the success he and Fauchier had garnered in the ballet world, adding to the company's legacy of internationally renowned dancers, doing the cocktail and donor party circuit with his wife, and enjoying Anne, that he'd hardly been around to notice. Besides, Fauchier and her mother had worked so closely, for so many years, no one would have put two and two together. It had only been the family who'd seen the progression from colleague, to friend, to lover, and finally to husband.

"And they weren't hiding."

Derek dismissed that with a wave of his hand.

"Regardless, I contacted the company's lawyers today. There's simply no other option. On my orders, they'll be filing papers with the court contesting Fauchier's and your mother's most recent wills."

Elena didn't know if her mother had drafted a will, but she'd have to talk to her brother about it. He was the one who had handled everything after their mother's death.

"Don't get me wrong. I understand that *Black Rhapsody* is yours. The proof you presented was irrefutable. And, believe it or not, I'm very happy for you. But as for the rest of Fauchier's works, well, I hate to disabuse you..."

"Mr. Derek..."

"They are Terpsichore property," he said, emphasizing every word. Anger was bubbling up to the surface. "Those works were created *here*, for *this* company, for *its* dancers, and have been since the company's inception. And they will stay that way."

"Mr..."

"I don't know what's in your head, or your plans," he continued. "I can't risk the future of the company on personal whims, vendettas, or avarice."

Vendettas? Good grief. Where did that come from?

"Derek," Jake interrupted. "That is unfair and uncalled for."

"I'm sorry," Derek said with a touch of disdain. "But did I ask for your input, Jake? Remember who pays your salary."

Jake's expression changed. Up to that moment, Elena had seen him preoccupied, concerned, playful, sensual, seductive, impatient, and serious. Now, something dangerous flashed there.

"This is a friendly warning." Derek ignored Jake and concentrated on Elena. "So, pay attention. I will do everything in my power to stop you getting those works, from getting half of Terpsichore, and I'm getting things rolling with lawsuits and counterlawsuits, hoping that drowns you in legalese and legal expenses for years."

Talk about, "Will the real Derek Michaels please stand up?"

Wow, she thought. So that was the way he wanted to play. No friendly discussions, or serious negotiations between friends. Lawyers versus lawyers, and a battle to the death. She should have guessed that when it came to his baby, Terpsichore, and Fauchier's works, Derek would become a ruthless adversary.

What a disappointment. And how sad.

"And if I may interject," Broderick said, a bit of arrogant scorn underscoring his words. "We would appreciate it if you didn't incite our dancers to defect."

"Broderick, you'd better stop right now," Jake said.

But the man ignored the warning in Jake's words.

"We heard that you're enticing Martina away from the company by baiting her with the lure of dancing *Black Rhapsody*. But you won't get away with that. She has a binding contract with the company." He turned to Derek. "Maybe this woman here is the one behind those letters. I wouldn't put it past her."

A deep cold invaded Elena's body. Was it anger? Or was it fear? Definitely incredulousness.

Jake's icy rage, on the other hand, lowered his voice to a level that surprised her.

"Elena, this meeting is over."

"Good idea." She stood.

"I always took you for a fool," Jake told Broderick, ignoring his outraged sputters. "But, not you, Derek. Ms. del Carral, your only obligation at the moment is to fulfill your contract to dance in the gala and nothing else. From now on, any further discussions will be exclusively through your lawyers."

Elena gathered her things. In the silence that ensued, he guided Elena to the door.

"And, by the way, Derek, you don't pay my salary. My employer does. You'll hear from our lawyers soon too."

He ushered Elena out of the room and didn't stop until they were in the main entrance's vestibule.

"I meant what I said in there, Elena, and I hate to sound ..."

"Bossy?" she said, but with a reluctant smile.

"Guilty as charged." He wasn't sharing her humor, though. "Especially after that idiot hinted..."

"Broderick didn't hint," she contradicted.

"Agreed," he said. "You've got to promise me you'll be extra careful and aware. Don't go anywhere alone, if you can, and don't get blind-sided into discussions with those two without your lawyer present."

"Okay."

"I mean it," he said and, with a quickness she was beginning to expect, he cupped her face and kissed her.

Mr. Scherzo strikes again.

"I've got to go. Sort a few things out. There's more to this than what I've been told, I bet my job on it. And with them blind to anything that crawls near them," Jake said with disgust, "they won't consider anything else. Bet my next lunch they're scared too. Of what, I can only guess. It's unfortunate a convenient scapegoat just so happened to arrive to solve their temporary problems."

"Me," she said.

"Sorry, but yes. Tag. You're it."

THE SHARED taxi ride to the theater was a silent one.

The easy camaraderie they'd always shared was muted, and the silence felt heavy with untold secrets. Or was it just reticence? Elena knew Anne knew what had transpired in the office. Or at least, what Derek had wanted to discuss. Would Anne take sides? She had always excelled at remaining neutral except...well, if Elena were honest, Anne remained neutral except when it came to Derek. Loyal to the end, regardless.

The silence stretched, long enough to be uncomfortable. The taxi zipped up Central Park West on its way to the theater, streaking through traffic, avoiding cyclists, jaywalkers, buses, and delivery vehicles. She'd forgotten the smells, sounds, and tastes of this city, which assaulted her anew every time she stepped outdoors. It was like, poof, she'd never left five years ago.

"Derek and I are splitting." Matter-of-fact and unemotional. "No longer an item. *Kaput.*"

It took a couple of seconds for the meaning to sink in.

"You're what?"

Anne chuckled after seeing Elena's shocked expression. "My dear, don't look so surprised. You don't think it's about time?"

Elena stared.

Anne watched the periphery of Central Park slide past the taxi windows. The only true green therapy found in the city.

"Elena, remember our conversation before you decided to leave Terpsichore?"

Elena nodded, still dumbfounded.

"Why do you think I was so blunt, speaking about relationships and about some men in our chosen careers? It was experience talking, dear. And because I knew you were not like me, or Caroline for that matter, even Martina, I wanted to give you options. I wanted to open your eyes, because if you had stayed, it should have been because you absolutely knew what you were getting into. And your decision, your growth as a dancer, and the opportunities you would acquire were dependent on that choice. Glad to say you made the right one."

Anne's sigh was heavy with memories, regret, and inevitability. She studied Elena's expression for a moment and must have read it accurately.

"I hate to disabuse you, and everyone else for that matter, but my decision to become Derek's mistress wasn't because I fell madly in love with him. Well, a little in lust, as everyone seems to say nowadays. After all, he was a fine specimen of a man, still is, despite pushing seventy-three. But that choice was a rather bland, pragmatic one: I fervently desired the package he offered—a spot as principal, prestige, and economic stability with a good romp on the side. In return, I gave him exactly what he wanted: a body to expend his passions on, no jealousy, no strings attached. We became mutual parasites, if you want to be crude about it. Period."

Elena finally found her voice.

"Why now?"

"Why not?"

"I mean," Elena tried to get her thoughts wrapped around Anne's confession. "What changed? You and Derek's relationship appeared to be almost eternal."

Anne laughed outright.

"You and Jake have a better chance of 'eternal' as you call it than Derek and I ever did." She chuckled once more. "Don't get me wrong. I owe Derek a lot. He has my eternal loyalty and respect. Despite what it may have seemed, Derek's been a good man to me. A good partner for my career. Loyal himself, up to a point." She shrugged. "Then again, he is married, and the survival of the company depends on that marriage remaining whole." She looked at Elena. "You, my dear, have been a rather unwelcome catalyst in the drama of Terpsichore. Maybe you should create a ballet based on it."

"But...after all these years?"

"Oh, our goals have diverged for a while and, frankly, neither I nor his wife can compete with his only love: the company." She shrugged. "Let's be honest. He's a driven man—dancer, first, and entrepreneur, second. He's got that glaring vein of narcissism going but, then again, what ballet dancer doesn't? I mean, we're so into ourselves because we have to be aware of our bodies, our muscles, our positions, even our minds, and emotions. But the money spigot is drying up. As she ages, Derek's wife demands more, expects more bang for her investment."

This time she outright laughed at her own pun.

"Besides, I have to look to my future, which, as you know, is not a promising one at my age."

Elena understood that. She'd read an article once in a magazine suggesting that a dancer's career dies twice. Euphemism, maybe, but true. It dies the moment you reach a certain age and your body can't function as it should. A dancing career can end through injury, like Derek's did. Once that happens, a dancer has to scramble to reinvent himself, or change careers altogether. And if one is lucky to continue in dance in any avenue within the industry except as dancer, your career dies anew when you're forced to retire, again.

"What are you going to do?"

"Good Lord. Don't look so glum, my dear." Anne's humor had not abated. "Not shedding any tears about this. Some regret, yes, a twinge of hurt, but nothing earth-shattering. Ah, here we are."

The taxi dropped them at the curb. As Anne was paying the driver, Elena studied her friend for a few seconds. How to explain the sudden certitude that there was something else? Something had shifted in Anne's world, and there was a certain, what, glow to her? Ineffable, she knew, but she'd seen her mother's face reflect what she now observed in Anne's.

"You owe me fifteen bucks."

Elena dismissed the conversational tangent.

"You've met someone," she blurted, accusatory, as well as in affirmation.

"Touché."

Oh my God, another blow to Mr. Derek's ego, Elena thought. No wonder he was in such a bad mood.

"That is *awesome*." Elena practically screamed it, hugged her friend and started laughing. A few seconds later, Anne joined in her laughter. They began jumping up and down in their excitement amid the shouts of *pervs* and a whispered *get a room* from cars and passersby. Someone from the costume department asked them to share the joke as he opened the door to the theater and held it for them to pass in.

That sobered them up.

"Come on," Elena said, as they stepped inside. She waited until the young man disappeared through the lobby doors toward the stage.

"OK, woman, spill."

"Well, he's a banker. International vice president of a very prestigious European bank, which I'm not naming." She grabbed Elena's hands and leaned in. "One of Terpsichore's donors," she whispered.

Wow.

"Close your mouth before something flies into it," Anne said. They entered the auditorium and walked down the center aisle toward the orchestra pit.

The theater was a beehive of activity with carpenters setting up flats, a few riggers checking backcloth and curtains, fly riggers lifting or setting lights, spots, changing gels, a stage manager issuing orders, and sound engineers dabbling with the sound system.

"Listen, let's talk about this another time." They walked up the side stairs and veered left into the wings that led to the dressing rooms. "No one really knows about this, and I'd rather keep it that way for a bit."

Elena understood. This breakup, or what Elena thought had turned more into a thaw out, would rev up the rumor mill into steroid levels. And with everything that had been happening lately, it would give the impression also that things were falling apart at the company.

Too many changes all at once. And as forebodings go, not a very good one.

"Let's have dinner at my brother's tomorrow," Elena said. "After dress rehearsal."

"I'll check my social calendar."

Elena burst out laughing. "Okay. Be that way. Anyway, I was planning to invite Frannie, and Fred, and Jake. Takeout, mind you. I'm not cooking after dress rehearsal. But I thought it'd be nice just to hang out and have a quiet evening. We need food, and I'll raid the wine cooler my brother keeps. Quite good vintages, I have to say."

"You've supplied him with most of them," Anne said.

Elena chuckled as they wound their way down the flight of stairs and in the direction of the storage/workshop area, where Maricela had set up shop with the costumes.

"You don't mind them knowing, right?"

"Not really. Francesca doesn't really blab, and I'm sure Fred won't care one way or another. Doesn't affect him. As far as Jake...well, I think Jake will be pleased, although it's difficult to peg him, sometimes. He keeps things close to his vest."

"Well, if you can make it, do." Elena smiled. "We deserve a break from all this drama."

They were almost at the door, when Anne stopped her.

"I know some of what is going on, Elena," she whispered. "Be careful. Derek holds grudges. And he can be brutal in his retaliation."

Chapter Nine

"OK, STOP. STOP THE MUSIC, PLEASE," ORDERED ANALISSE from her seat in the orchestra section of the auditorium. She'd sat there to get a panoramic view of the entire stage and the ensemble rehearsing there.

Everyone was out of sorts today, Elena thought. Company class had been a mess, with everyone screwing up center work one way or another. Fred was slower than usual, claiming he had woken up at three in the morning and hadn't been able to go back to sleep. Elena suspected jet lag had struck again, or his wife had woken him up.

Caroline had also been having difficulties with her balances in class but, then again, she'd had a rough couple of days. Elena would have fared equally bad or worse, if she were honest. Martina had messed up the center variation and her pirouettes were not up to par. She was currently practicing backstage, muttering to herself.

Elena also knew why she'd been off. Her mind had been elsewhere, distracted constantly with snippets from her phone conversation with the director of Ballet Etudes, Pascal Benoit. He had woken her up at four o'clock in the morning, completely forgetting there was a six-hour difference between Monaco and New York. He'd heard from Fred's wife about the debacle in Terpsichore with Justin, and it was very sad and all that, but what really thrilled him was knowing *Black Rhapsody* was her choreography and not Fauchier's. He was already making plans for another world premiere and informed her he'd spoken to His Serene Highness's secretary and that of the Princess of Hanover's, both benefactors of the arts, especially ballet companies in the area, about staging it. And, despite what she'd explained about the demand of a certain New York City detective to stay in the city, Pascal had been dismissive and wouldn't hear about any delays, insisting on Fred's and her return immediately after the gala. He announced they'd been invited to perform the adagio of *Concerto in D* as part of another gala in Spain in two weeks. That meant she and Fred would have to rehearse that on top of their rehearsal schedules here.

The only ones who hadn't appeared affected by the current malaise were Anne and Francesca. Leave it to her friends to have no worries to screw their coordination and memories today.

Elena watched Analisse approach the orchestra pit to address the corps members, while she, Francesca, and Anne waited in the wings for their turn to rehearse. Fred lay, with his head cushioned on Elena's thigh, taking a breather. They'd set up an impromptu rehearsal downstairs in one of the rehearsal studios under the stage immediately after their routine. Caroline huddled with her variation partner across the way, stage left, with Randy speaking to the principal and soloist representing Albrecht and Hilarion, as they waited for their cue. For the life of her she couldn't remember their names at the moment.

Shame on her.

Now, however, the messes seemed to continue in a seamless flow from class into rehearsals. This time around, the twenty-six women dancing the second act of *Giselle* on stage were the focus of an exasperated Analisse.

"Ladies," Analisse told the corps, mildly chastising. "I know you're tired, but you're supposed to be ethereal spirits, not cows plodding across the stage. Try to keep in unison as well. A few of you were off."

Elena looked at her friends. They smirked. They themselves had plodded in arabesque while attempting to look ethereal across stage many times. Difficult didn't describe it.

"Let's take it from the entrances of the Wilis Moyna and Zulma, please. Places." She clapped. "Patrick, a few measures before their entrance, please."

"So, still want to get together tonight?" Elena whispered, as Adam's beautiful score echoed around the theater via the nimble fingers of Patrick Tadana on the piano. "Or do we bump it to tomorrow like dress rehearsal was."

"I'm all for a free meal today," said Fred, without opening his eyes. "Especially now that we have double rehearsal. And you promised I could use the washer and dryer in your brother's apartment."

"Cheapskate," Elena said, bumping his head upward with her thigh.

"Hey, I have to save my money for baby Boelens."

"Who is arriving in seven months," Elena countered.

"Please tell me you're ordering the fried rice and BBQ ribs from the Chinese place across the street from your brother's," said Francesca. "They are sooo good."

Elena nodded as she watched the two first soloists perform their *piqué arabesque* turns. They were a bit off. Definitely unsynchronized. "Unless you want pizza."

"Ladies," Analisse shouted to the soloists. "Together, please. Together."

"Chinese, please," Anne whispered. "More food. And tell them to go easy on the soy sauce in the rice," Anne said. "If not, I'll be bloated the day after."

"And get those fried wontons that I like so much," Francesca said.

"And the lettuce wraps," Anne said.

"*Watch the lines,*" Analisse shouted again from the orchestra section of the auditorium.

"Oh-oh," Anne said.

"Does anyone know what Jake might like?" Elena asked.

"Why don't you ask him?"

"Can't get through to him," Elena said. "Left two voicemails."

"Do you think something's going on?" Francesca asked. "Broderick was supposed to handle rehearsals today, and no one has seen him. Analisse was p-i-s-s-e-d. She had to cancel her appointment with the chiropractor today."

Elena shrugged. So many things had been happening lately that she didn't even want to contemplate another thing going wrong.

"Sorry to bother you."

The words came at the same moment Elena felt a tap on her shoulder. She turned to see Tess, the principal who was dancing Myrtha, the Queen of the Wilis at the gala, crouched next to her.

"Oh, hi."

"Listen," Tess said, looking over her shoulder so as not to miss her entrance cue. "Would you mind a lot if we swapped times with the physiotherapist today? I saw you're scheduled for two. Mine is at five this afternoon, but Maricela needs an extra fitting and can't reschedule me earlier. I wouldn't ask, but my right ankle doesn't feel right, and those *bourrées* across stage are killing me."

Oh, freaking A. She'd forgotten she'd scheduled a session at that time with Chiara Dapny, the assistant physiotherapist of the company. She had set up shop in an empty room next to the dressing rooms downstairs for just these occasions before a show. Now, because of Elena's boss, Pascal, Elena would be rehearsing for an additional one or two hours with Fred instead of getting the tense muscles on her shoulders unkinked.

"I was going to have to reschedule for another time, anyway. So go ahead."

"Oh, thank you." Her relief was palpable. "I'll tell Chiara you'll take my slot."

"Oh, don't do that. I really have to cancel. Rehearsal."

"I'll tell her when I go." Tess hugged her. "You're a doll. I owe you one." She scooted back to her position and made it in time for her cue.

"Don't worry about Chiara," Anne said. "She's used to it. We swap and cancel all the time."

Ten minutes later, Analisse ended giving her observations to the ensemble and called for a five-minute break.

Elena bumped Fred's head. "You'd better go warm up. We're up soon."

Twenty minutes later, as Elena and Fred were finishing their variation, she caught sight of Derek and Broderick entering the auditorium. Somber did not describe their expressions.

Now what?

Fred and she ended their routine and returned to their previous place stage right where they plopped down exhausted. Caroline and Mario took center stage next, but Elena saw that neither Derek nor Broderick approached, just sat with glum faces in the same row as Analisse in the auditorium.

"They look chirpy," whispered Anne, nodding toward the somber duo. "What do you think is going on?"

Elena mopped her sweat. "Not a clue. But it doesn't look good."

"Those two," Francesca pointed to the Caroline and Mario partnership. "Look good together today, don't they?"

Elena watched for a few minutes. Caroline did look in top form, unlike in class. She almost looked in symbiosis with Fauchier's beautiful adagio.

When the piece ended, everyone clapped, not only because that meant the end of rehearsal, but also as kudos to what they'd just witnessed.

"Ok, everybody. That's a wrap," Analisse said. "Let's hope dress rehearsal tomorrow is as good."

Elena smirked. She hoped the dance gods weren't listening and proved ornery at Analisse's words. Everyone knew good dress rehearsal made for so-so performances. Bad ones made for great ones.

"Go and relax," Analisse continued. "You've earned it. Tomorrow will be a very busy day. Assigned dressing rooms are posted downstairs and online."

"But before you go," Derek interrupted. "I'd like a few words." He walked up to stage level and stood facing them at the apron. He launched into his spiel about how proud he was of everyone, that the company looked wonderful, and that they were going to have one of the best gala performances in years. He finished by saying they needed to yield the stage to theater personnel, reiterated Justin's condition critical but stable this morning, and for everyone to enjoy the rest of the day.

Derek gathered Broderick and Analisse, who had been standing by him like dutiful statuettes, and left in the direction of the auditorium.

And like a light switch turned on, workers began weaving their way on stage, replacing dancers and music with the voices of riggers working on battens and counterweights, by electrical engineers futzing with foot-lights, and thumps from the stage design crew moving and placing flats according to plan. Someone near them started making a racket under the open trapdoor where Myrtha appeared and Giselle needed to disap-pear at the end of act 2.

"I'm going to hunt down the location of our dressing room," Anne said, sniffing. "Drop a few things there for tomorrow. Frannie, want to come?"

"Sure."

"We'll catch up with you downstairs," Anne said. "I want to see some of your *Concerto in D* rehearsal."

"Let's go, Fred," Elena said, following in the wake of her friends. "We have some more sweating to do."

The area in the theater under the stage went beyond the size of the theater itself. The section was built like an H, with the storage and repair rooms for stage designs located under stage right. Next to it, costuming filled a huge room. Elena had been there yesterday for her fitting. In the hall that joined the other side of the H, were several stage manager offices, a small canteen, and rehearsal areas for orchestra, choir, thespians, or dancers. At the other side, under stage left, were the dressing rooms, bathrooms, and the physiotherapist room. Each side had exit stairways that led either to the stage or the auditorium level.

Elena entered one of the smaller, empty rehearsal rooms in the connecting hallway followed by Fred. They dropped their bags on the floor and while Fred stretched, Elena scrolled through her music app until she found the adagio music for *Concerto in D*.

"Ready?"

"The sooner the better. I'm tired."

She switched the music on.

They danced through the piece without stopping, Elena making mental notes. Halfway through she messed up and Fred had to rescue her before she landed on the floor. After a second of apology, rewinding the music to the proper cue, they continued. Somewhere between that and the end of the piece, Anne and Francesca had come in, sitting out of the way by the doorway to observe the rehearsal.

After they finished, Elena went over with Fred the parts where they'd had some glitches and tempo mishaps. Fred made some observations as well, asking if they could go over one part of a difficult lift. They marked it first, then practiced it with the music.

By the time she called an end to the rehearsal, Elena saw Jake was there as well, lounging by the doorframe next to Anne. Francesca, taking the opportunity as they'd finished, went to Fred, asking him to explain one of the lifts.

"You've really outdone yourself, Elena," Anne said. "What a beautiful adagio."

"Sexy moves," Jake added and smiled.

Danger, danger, Will Robinson.

She knelt by her ballet bag and swept the sweat off her brow and neck with the towel she'd dropped on top of it. Distance was definitely needed.

"Have to pick up things at the hotel," Fred said, grabbing his gear. He turned to leave but stopped. "We are still getting together tonight, right?"

Everyone nodded.

"OK." He gave Elena's cheek a peck. "See you soon. With my laundry." He chuckled all the way out of the room.

"Gosh, Elena, I'm in love," said Francesca. "You *have* to let me dance that adagio. It's so, so…"

"Sexy," Jake supplied once more.

"Yeah."

"Listen, ladies, do you mind if I borrow Elena for a bit?" Jake asked.

"Depends what you're borrowing her for," Anne said with a knowing smile.

"Minx," he returned with humor.

Francesca chuckled.

"You know what they say about assumptions," Elena warned.

"Do I?" Jake said.

Good grief. The man was definitely a menace. A delightful menace.

"Come on, Frannie," Anne said. "They need a *room*." They left hand in hand, chuckling all the way out the door.

Elena walked to her bag, took out her clogs and jeans, and bent down to undo her toe shoes.

"So, what's going on?" she asked, looking at him from between her legs.

"Do you honestly think we can have a serious conversation while you're like that? I'm conjuring up other images, especially after seeing that adagio."

Elena dropped her toe shoes inside her bag, slipped into her jeans and clogs, and went to get her phone from the temporary perch she'd created for it.

"Did you talk to your boss?"

"He was definitely not happy with what I told him," Jake said. "Said he'd speak with Derek today. Clarify a few things."

"I spoke with my lawyers too," she said, undoing her bun and brushing her hair. She needed to air it out a bit. It was wet through and through from all her sweat. "Told me they'll handle everything from now on."

"Good." Jake said and pouted his lips in the direction of the theater upstairs. "How was rehearsal?"

"Normal, for the most part. Some hiccups in class and rehearsal, but nothing outlandish. And Mr. Derek said Justin's condition hasn't changed. How about you?"

"Put my assistant on the hunt for any drug names with those combination of letters this morning. As soon as she has something, she'll let me know. But it may take a while."

She zipped her bag shut and dropped her phone in her purse. Before she could slip her bags onto her shoulder, though, Jake took her hand and drew her in.

"Listen, I'm curious. How on earth do you do those turns without bashing your partner's gonads off?"

Of all the questions her convoluted mind could supply, that was the last one she expected.

"Very carefully."

"Show me?"

"What on earth for?"

"In case I have to give pointers to my sister. She starts Adagio and Partnering next month."

She stared, uncertain whether to laugh or take him seriously. She opted for the latter.

"I swear," she said. "You're full of surprises. Or do you do this on purpose to get brownie points?"

"No. Really. I'm honestly curious," he said, crossing his heart and hoping to die with his fingers. "I'm my sister's 'go to' guy for lifts and partnering in general, ever since she was six and wanted to execute a fish dive she'd seen."

That was sweet, she thought. And believable. Elena couldn't remember the times she'd used her own brother as her stand-in test subject, despite his bitching and moaning. He still helped, regardless, because, well, Roberto loved her, and he'd do anything for her and Stefanía, her sister.

"It's the man who needs to be careful," she said. "Your sister has to learn to move within the man's periphery without depending exclusively on his assistance."

"Show me?"

She dragged him to the center of the room, slipped off her clogs, placed his hands on her waist, and explained.

"Relax your hands but don't take them from my waist. Don't press," she warned. "Just allow my body to turn within your hands. I'll be doing most of the work."

"I like it when a woman takes charge." He leered.

"Be quiet," she chided. "OK, get ready." She slowly *bourreéd* in place in a three-hundred-and-sixty-degree turn. She felt his hands on her waist, strong, but relaxed, as he allowed her to turn.

"Not too shabby, Forrester."

The smile came back in force. "For this. You haven't done the *passé* thingy yet."

"Thingy? Good Lord." She chuckled and did a quarter turn in *passé*.

"Woah there, lady." Her knee had come perilously close to his waist. He let go. "Warn me first."

"Chicken."

He clucked.

"You are incorrigible. Now, hold me again."

"With pleasure."

Slowly she lifted her leg in another *passé*. Slowly his groin moved further back until her knee was but an inch away.

"Now, don't panic. I'm going to pirouette slowly. Don't let go. Don't stiffen either. Remember I'll be doing all the work and I'm balanced."

Slowly she prepared in fourth and did one turn. "See?"

"Wow."

"I can do one turn or several, depending on the choreography. If you've been to enough ballets, you've seen the man moving the ballerina's torso a bit. That happens if the woman falls short of a complete turn. That way her partner can move her enough so she faces the audience, or prepares her in a position to segue into whatever comes next."

"Can we give it another go? That was super cool. Wait till I tell my sister."

He resembled a little kid with candy.

"Ready?" At his nod, she added. "I'll be doing two turns now."

And she did.

"So," he said and turned her a bit. "If you finish, but don't face the audience..."

"Then it's the partner's responsibility to make it so."

He slowly turned her until she was facing him. Stepped in.

"Gotcha."

The kiss was one to end all kisses. Warm, sensual, exploratory. A discovery. A promise. And, as promises went, it didn't disappoint.

"You, lady," he said softly, after ending the kiss, "are driving me crazy."

The cry for help was sudden, loud, and so anguished, Jake was on the run a second after hearing it, with Elena running close behind.

In the hallway, Jake looked right and left in frenzy. Several people from props and costuming had stopped what they were doing, as well. "Anyone know where that came from?"

As if in answer, the cry for help reverberated around the corner, where the dressing rooms were.

A panicked woman rounded the corner, hands bloodied. Elena recognized Chiara, the physiotherapist. She'd seen the woman's headshot on the website page to book appointments.

"Please, help," she told them. "Call 911. She's really hurt."

Without waiting, Chiara pivoted and ran back where she'd come from. Jake ran close behind, speaking into his cell while someone from the theater crew spoke into his portable. Elena followed not two steps behind.

They reached a small room at the end of the hall.

"I've stopped some of the bleeding, but she's not responding," Chiara said, in tears. "I don't know what happened."

Elena took stock of the room in seconds. Saw it was bare except for a massage table pressed against the left wall. Perpendicular to that was a small portable table with what looked like a slow cooker with rocks inside. But what truly captured her attention was the woman who lay still, her head placed face down into the cradle. Blood caked part of her hair, as well as the towel Chiara pressed against a wound of some sort.

"I don't know what happened," Chiara kept saying, half sobbing, trying to staunch the flow of blood. "I left her alone five minutes, tops, and when I returned..." The last word was pitched high at close to the point of hysteria. "Where the hell are the paramedics?"

Elena grabbed Jake's arm in a vise and pulled him out of the room.

"What's wrong?" He looked back at the prone woman, then back at Elena. "Do you know her?"

"What time is it?" Elena asked, trying to hold at bay some of the terror she was feeling.

Jake, without questioning her ridiculous inquiry, looked at his watch. "It's two oh-five."

Oh my God.

She shouldn't have said everything had been normal back in the small rehearsal hall just now. As her mother used to say: Don't spit upward, because it will land right smack back on your face. Gravity had a tendency to work that way.

"That's Tess."

"One of the principal dancers?"

"Yeah," she said, starting to tremble. "But that should have been me. Tess took my spot."

Chapter Ten

"You, Ms. del Carral," said a disgusted Detective Harris, as they stood in the hallway, "are worse than the proverbial bad penny." His look did not augur any patience or tolerance toward her this time.

Elena remained mute. Here she was again, facing scrutiny from a detective who'd probably already cemented suspicion on her. And here she was again, a witness to another assault. This time around, however, she hadn't been the one to stumble onto the body.

Oh God. Here she was again referring to Tess as the body.

Elena glanced at Chiara Dapny who was being consoled by one of the theater crew members near the exit of the hallway near the physio-therapy room. The woman looked like someone had dumped a bucket full of ice over her, her eyes glazed in shock and staring into space. The paramedics who'd responded to Jake's 911 had come and gone, taking the wounded Tess to the hospital. As they'd triaged Tess, they discovered the head wound was nasty, but more nasty than serious—a wide gash that had generated beaucoup blood, as one of the paramedics had mentioned. Head wounds, he'd continued as if addressing a Paramedics 101 course, were notorious bleeders. But the blow had been hard enough to cause Tess to lose consciousness. That meant a serious concussion but, of course, that was his opinion, he qualified, based on his experience. He believed all that Tess needed were a few stitches, painkillers, and rest. They'd know more after a CAT scan, but he surmised she'd be good to go in a day or two, again based on his experience.

"Why is it every time I turn around, things seem to revolve around you?" Harris continued.

At the detective's statement, Jake's arm tightened around her shoulders.

"Are you seriously suggesting this is Elena's fault?" he whispered, incensed.

"No, Mr. Forrester," Harris answered. "All I'm saying is that ever since Ms. del Carral arrived, unpleasant things have been happening in the company. I'm just wondering why."

Why indeed? But just because bad things were happening around her, Elena thought, it didn't mean she was the proverbial portent of doom. Or did it? Maybe it did. Events had taken a life of their own the moment the routine request for permission to stage *Black Rhapsody* had arrived. And then, whammo, things had conflated into a debatable assault on Justin, a potential hostile takeover of the company's co-ownership due to her being the heir apparent to all of Fauchier's works and his portion of the company, and now the attack on Tess.

Someone knew things, had been extremely discontented about it and, now, someone was out to get her.

There was no ambiguity this time, at least not in her mind. Tess had been attacked at the appointed hour she was supposed to be at the physiotherapy session.

"Ok, let's recap," Detective Harris said, pen poised over pad to tick off things he'd written there. "You were rehearsing and heard Ms. Dapny, over there, yell for help."

Elena and Jake nodded.

"You saw the victim…"

"And Ms. Dapny trying to staunch the blood flow," Jake finished.

"You saw no one else, apart from the people here in the hallway."

Again, both Jake and Elena nodded.

"No one coming in or out from the exit at the end there? The dressing rooms?" Detective Murdock asked, speaking for the first time.

"Sorry, no," Jake said.

"Honestly, Detective," Elena added. "We were rushing to help. Not much registered at the time except for what was going on in that room."

"Okay. I'll grant you that." Detective Harris consulted his notes once more. "You said you switched appointments with Ms. Baukman. Did anyone hear your conversation?"

"Only my friends," she said. He had already asked that question and knew the answer. Elena didn't know where this line of questioning was heading.

"Do you know of anyone who may have an animosity toward Ms. Baukman? A rival, perhaps?"

Elena scoffed.

"Why the sudden derision?" Harris asked with genuine curiosity.

"You don't know much about the ballet world, do you?"

"To my regret, I'm learning a bit too much about it," Harris said.

"We're the supreme competitors, Detective. From class, to rehearsal, to performance, we wage war against ourselves and against others in a closed and challenging environment every second of every day. We're friendly with one another, but we're mortal enemies as well, some more openly belligerent than others. As far as who might wish Tess harm, I have no clue. She seemed harmless enough. Friendly from the little I had to deal with her in class. As to others in the company, I hardly know anyone here to give you an honest answer."

"Besides, that's an HR matter," Jake added. "Any problem with dancers is usually dealt with verbal warnings, removal from certain performances, or by not offering a contract for the following season. The machinery needs to be kept well-oiled and cohesive, if not, the company would not survive."

Harris wrote some more notes.

"Did you talk to anyone else about the appointment switch?" Harris asked.

"No."

"And you said that those appointment hours are available to anyone who wants to see them, both online and on that bulletin board?" Harris pointed to a small whiteboard next to the door where the physiotherapy sessions were attached with cute little toe-shoe magnets. Her name was still printed there, large as life, for the two o'clock appointment. Neither Chiara Dapny nor Tess had scratched her name out.

"Yes."

Detective Harris sighed. "OK. And..."

"Yeah, yeah," Elena said. "Don't leave town."

"I was going to say if you remember anything else, contact me immediately." It was his turn to smirk. "You have my number."

"Let's go," Jake said, the disgust in his voice palpable.

But it wasn't in the cards they would leave anytime soon.

"Elena."

Caroline's voice trembled a bit when Elena and Jake stepped out of the rehearsal room after picking up her stuff. The poor woman looked like a lost waif in the middle of the hallway.

"OMG, Elena." Caroline rushed over. "One of the crew said Tess was attacked. It's all over the theater." She looked at Jake. "When did this happen?"

"Detective Harris will fill you in soon," Jake answered.

"But this is horrible," Caroline said. "What is happening to this company? Who would do such a thing?"

Elena squeezed Caroline's hands in commiseration. "We really don't know."

"Did anyone see who it was?" Her whisper was horrified.

"We didn't see anything except..." Elena swallowed. "Except Tess injured."

"Why everyone so glum?" Martina interrupted. She had her hands full of frothy tutu, hair accessories, and overstuffed ballet bag, on her way to the dressing rooms to drop everything off for dress rehearsal tomorrow.

"Why police here?" she asked, staring at the uniform standing guard at the entrance of the hallway where the attack had taken place. Behind him, the yellow crime scene "do not cross" tape ruffled from the air-conditioning stream blowing on it. She huffed. "Don't tell me. More interrogations? Incompetent police." She finished with a few choice expletives in her native language. "This no good."

"Oh my God, Elena."

Elena turned at Francesca's voice. She and Anne were rushing to meet them, their expressions worried and horrified at once.

"We just heard from Derek someone was attacked at physiotherapy and rushed back here," Anne said. "To say he's very unsettled is an understatement."

"This is scary," Francesca said. "Especially when it could have been you..." She stopped, suddenly realizing what she was about to blurt.

Martina caught on fast. "You...what? Please finish."

But Elena and Jake were both shaking their heads.

"Tess was attacked." Caroline dismissed their protests with a wave of her hand. "They rushed her to the hospital."

"Was it bad?" Martina asked.

"Nasty gash in her skull," Jake answered.

"Concussion, definitely," Elena said. "Well, according to the paramedics."

"I need to leave this in dressing room," Martina hefted her tutu a bit more comfortably.

"I'm not sure you'll be allowed," Jake said. "They have the hallway roped off."

"My room other side of hallway." And she marched to where the police barrier blocked the path, hooked a right to the dressing rooms in that area, and disappeared.

"Well, that shows her priorities," Caroline said. "Nasty woman."

"Come on, Caro," Francesca said. "Be charitable."

"That woman has been nothing but trouble since Derek contracted her." She looked at everyone. "Hasn't anyone noticed the moment she arrived things have been going wrong?"

"What do you mean?" Jake asked.

"Petty theft begins. Vandalism." She shrugged. "Nothing like that had happened before."

Anne pooh-poohed. "You're forgetting the men Derek has hired. It's not a woman issue exclusively."

"But why?" Elena asked, truly perplexed. "She's an incredibly gifted dancer. She wouldn't need to descend to that level of pettiness."

"Why do you think the Royal let her go?"

"Enough, Caroline," Anne said. For the first time, Elena saw real anger in her friend's face. "Unfounded rumors. Don't go there."

"Well, I don't trust her."

Elena only noticed Detective Harris and Detective Murdock's approach when Jake squeezed her upper arm.

"Comparing notes?" Harris asked.

"And why would you think that?" Anne asked.

Elena didn't say anything, but she wanted to whoop, admiring the composure with which Anne always reacted.

"I need to ask your whereabouts at the time of the assault," Detective Harris said, looking at Caroline and her friends. "If you don't mind, Ms. Wainwright? We'll start with you. Why don't we go into this empty room for a chat?"

Elena loved the detective's euphemism for an interrogation.

Harris nodded to Murdock, who led Caroline to the nearest room. "Don't go anywhere, ladies." He left after the request.

"Arrogant sod, as the Brits say," Anne said.

"He's only doing his job," Jake murmured.

"I know," Anne sighed.

Francesca jabbed Elena with her elbow. "Oh boy. Here comes Derek..."

"...and his entourage," finished Jake. "And why is Harriet trailing them, I wonder?"

"This is not to be borne," Derek said by way of greeting. "What kind of deranged person would do such a thing?"

It was obviously a rhetorical question, since no one answered him.

Detective Murdock, in the meantime, had recruited two crew members to place chairs against the wall to the left of the doorway where Detective Harris was questioning Caroline. Another uniform guided possible witnesses to those chairs. Elena recognized some of those who had responded to the cry for help, including Chiara Dapny.

A complaining Martina had been dragged away from her dressing room too. The woman did not look happy. And when she saw Derek, she no longer needed guidance.

"I do not sign up for this harangue, Mr. Derek."

"Harassment," offered an unflappable Anne.

"What?"

"You mean harassment, dear, not harangue."

"Whatever," Martina said. "I will not be interrogated, third time, for something I was not here for."

Oh my God. Elena needed to flee from this increasingly ridiculous comedy of errors or she would dissolve in hysterical laughter. Or scream like a banshee.

"Please, Martina," Broderick said, holding her shoulders and turning on the commiseration. "Bear with us. This is disturbing for all of us, but especially for you with your passionate temperament and experiences."

What? OMG.

Jake gave her shoulder a squeeze, as though warning her to keep it together.

"We need to get to the bottom of this, and why they attacked another one of our dancers," Derek said, an outraged tremble in his voice.

"Well, I did suggest you hire security several weeks ago, and especially after what happened to Justin," Jake said.

Derek turned on him. "If you'd been more competent, Mr. Forrester, we wouldn't be where we're currently at. Frankly, you have been a waste of money and resources in this affair. You and your firm." His face turned a mottled red. "And once Elena arrived on the scene..."

"I'd be very, very careful with what comes out of your mouth next, Derek," Jake said. His voice was nothing short of menacing. "Very careful."

"Well, it is true, isn't it?" Broderick chimed in. "Your behavior implies favoritism, and not to the person who pays for your services."

Elena thought Jake was about to whack Broderick a good one. Not that he didn't deserve it, but things were getting out of hand. They needed to get out of there. Go to neutral ground to regroup. She was about to forcibly drag Jake out of there when Harriet, of all people, intervened.

"Gentlemen, please," Harriet addressed the men with the force of an irritated mother chiding her spoilt children. "Stop the drama. Tensions are high. Have been for a while. But don't say anything you will regret later. There are more important people, and things, at stake."

Anne agreed and added that it was a police matter now. "However," she continued, placing a hand on Derek's shoulder. "What Jake suggested is not a bad idea. Not after what happened today, dear."

Derek shrugged off Anne's hand in annoyance. But his shoulders sagged, nonetheless. In defeat, Elena thought?

"Anne is right," Jake said. "You can't self-police anymore. Too many people, distractions, and activities to keep tabs on. Not without outside help."

"When Fauchier and I started this company, we had such high hopes and dreams. And we achieved them to levels that exceeded all our expectations. Now...now someone is trying to destroy everything, and I don't know why."

"Mr. Derek..."

He looked at Elena. "Sure you still want a piece of the company, Elena? The way things are going, there may not be one to direct."

"What is this?" It was Martina's turn to be shocked. "What means Elena direct Terpsichore? Did you know this?" she demanded first of Broderick and then of Caroline, who was approaching with Detective Harris.

"Know what?" Caroline and Detective Harris said at the same time.

"Elena directs Terpsichore," Martina blurted.

"Martina, that is not exactly..." Elena said.

"Is that a fact?" interrupted Harris, his eyes boring into Elena's.

Elena could almost feel the detective's brain wheels turning.

Caroline looked flabbergasted.

"Partly true," Broderick answered.

"She owns half of the company and all of Fauchier's works. At least, according to his latest will," Derek clarified. "I was going to address this at the next staff meeting, but I may have to move that announcement up for after class tomorrow. Report on the steps we're taking to contest it. Oh, that reminds me. Harriet?"

Harriet extended a thick stretchable file to Elena.

"What is that?"

"The dancers' contracts for review," Harriet said. "Other miscellanea, like salaries, office costs, improvements, etc. Fauchier would review and confer with Derek on these."

"That responsibility falls on you now, according to this new will," Derek said. "We'd be derelict if we don't follow its terms for now, according to our lawyers. That is, until there is a final ruling on what's what."

"And since Mr. Derek doesn't want to be in breach of anything, just in case," Harriet added. "Derek asked me to give you all appropriate copies."

Elena placed her hands behind her back. She was not going to touch that with a ten-foot pole.

"Send them to my lawyers," she said. "I'm not supposed to do anything or make any decisions until they look things over and give the OK."

"But that will delay things," Harriet complained.

"I'm sorry. It's out of my hands."

Elena grabbed her things from where she'd left them on the floor and exited the theater with Jake not far behind.

BY THE TIME everyone gathered in Elena's brother's apartment that evening, it was close to nine o'clock. The silence was thick, not due to any tension, but because everyone was eating fast and furiously, the soft whirr of the washing machine and dryer creating background counterpoint to the utensil noises.

"Is there any more fried rice left?" Fred asked. "I'm still hungry."

"You are always starving," Elena said, and handed over the rice container.

"Hey, I'm a growing boy," he said, emptying the remaining rice onto his plate.

"What you are is an opportunist where free food is involved," Elena told him.

"Be careful you don't grow sideways," Francesca said, laughing.

"Well, since we're reasonably less hungry now," Jake said after a brief glance at Fred. "Let me be the first to address the elephant in the room." He grabbed a crab Rangoon and bit into it appreciatively.

"It's more like a giant turd that keeps on giving," Anne said.

"I want it to be so over," Francesca added. "It's just so awful."

"What I'm interested in is the accusations Caroline blurted out back there," Jake asked.

"Any veracity to them, Anne?" Francesca asked. "You know I don't follow company gossip. Well, not always."

"Wait, what did Caroline say?" Fred asked.

"That's right," Elena said. "You weren't there."

He looked around the table for a volunteer to dish out the goods. "So?" he prompted.

"She practically accused Martina of being the culprit of the vandalism and, probably the attacks," Francesca said.

"And a possible reason why the Royal released her from contract." Elena finished her ribs and pushed her plate forward. She couldn't indulge in takeout too often, but it was nice to binge once in a while, especially with the type of food that would add on the pounds just by breathing in the aroma.

"There's no backbone to that accusation," Anne said.

"And don't forget that ridiculous statement about passionate temperament and experiences from the ever-fawning Broderick," Jake said.

"What do you think that was about?" Francesca asked. She pushed away her plate, which looked as though someone had licked it clean. "I mean, I get her passionate temperament in her dancing, but experiences? Martina's *young*. Really young."

"Idle gossip or true, Anne?" Jake insisted.

Anne sighed. "I know French wine doesn't really complement Chinese food, but can you open a bottle?"

"Or two," Fred added.

Elena grabbed Jake's empty plate and hers. "Help me clear this up first and then we can hang out in the living room."

Within seconds, everyone helped putting away dirty dishes, stowing what little leftovers there were in the fridge, and cleaning the table. Once done, Elena shooed everyone to the living room, turned on the dishwasher, and chose two favorite Pinot Noirs from the small wine refrigerator in the kitchen. She handed Jake the bottles and the cork opener.

"Can you do the honors? I'll grab the wine glasses."

Once everyone was served, Anne swirled the wine, as if fascinated by its red kaleidoscope swirls. Elena knew she was considering what to divulge.

"You know Martina is eighteen, right?"

"That young?" Elena said.

Anne smiled. "You were only sixteen when you started in the corps at Terpsichore."

Good Lord. Had she been that young? She'd felt so adult back then.

"Well, when the Royal hired her, she was this wunderkind from St. Petersburg from the Vaganova school, and within the year, she'd been promoted to soloist. That's when the trouble began."

"What troubles are we talking about," Jake asked.

"Let me preface with the fact that what happened was nothing illegal, at least not in the UK," Anne said. "Still, the tabloids there are mercenary and ruthless. And Martina, young and away from home, reveling in her newfound stardom, didn't know better." Anne sipped her wine. "At least, I hope she didn't. You never know nowadays."

"Who was the older man?" Jake asked.

"Well, that's a hell of an assumption," Elena said.

Jake's megawatt smile appeared.

"But accurate," Anne said. "Thirty-three years her senior to be exact, and married. The man became obsessed with her."

"And I'm sure that after much wining and dining, gifts, and promises, he got what he wanted," Jake said.

"True. But I think the man was more in lust with her youth, energy, and passion rather than her. Francesca was right in saying Martina pours all her passion into her dancing. She may have seen this liaison as a meteoric step to higher prestige and stardom. A secure future."

Elena stopped sipping her wine. "So, what happened?"

"I bet the man's wife happened," Fred said. He'd retrieved his clothes from the dryer and was folding everything neatly.

Anne nodded. "To Martina's misfortune, a balletomane posted a picture of her and her lover dining in a restaurant on social media. Someone recognized the man, and, well, what can I say?"

"What a sleazeball," Francesca said.

"But a very juicy story, for the tabloids. Sordid details, some true, others not, were printed in all the smutty news rags, paparazzi began following Martina and the man everywhere, and the faculty, staff, and dancers of the Royal were hounded by journalists. The wife, needless to say, was not a happy camper. After all, her fifty-year-old husband seduces a seventeen-year-old Russian-born ballerina."

"Good lord," Elena said. If they'd been caught here in the States, the man would have been charged with perverting a minor at least, and possibly rape. Well, maybe. Money can erase a lot of impropriety and lawlessness.

"Still, why the brouhaha? It's not as if this doesn't go on most of the time lately," Jake said.

"Probably not enough circumspection and decorum from Martina and her lover's part to satisfy such a prestigious company as the Royal," Elena said.

"Not to mention the embarrassment of constant harassment and the reputation shredding," Francesca added. "Those so-called journalists over in Europe can be brutal. Ask my friend in Spain. She dated, for a while, a famous singer, and her life became hell, with cameras shoved in her face practically twenty-four seven, impertinent questions, pictures of them at the house, at the beach, in her dressing room, at the theater, the studio. Even dining quietly at a restaurant became a zoo. And let's not mention the paparazzi practically kissing bumpers with their cars. That, to her, was the last straw."

"Visions of what happened to Princess Diana in Paris, right?" said Anne.

"Yeah," Francesca said. "Even though she really liked him, she broke things off."

"And the cameras went to better pastures," Elena said.

"I'm sure Martina and her sugar daddy would have been replaced within the week by another more entertaining scandal," Jake said. "What happened to change the dynamics?"

"Sugar daddy." Elena made a face at Jake. "Very archaic of you."

He blew her a kiss.

"The board of trustees for the company the man owns is what happened," Anne said. "Choices were placed on the table. Either Martina was fired immediately, or a ton of foundation money allocated every year to the arts would be taken elsewhere. You see, the wife of Martina's lover is the co-chair on her husband's company board," Anne said. "Reputation and money on the line. A *lot* of money."

"I can guess what choice was taken," Jake said.

Anne nodded. "The artistic coordinator there, a friend of Derek's, called when it became inevitable that Martina had to go. Derek, at the time, was looking for a talented soloist, and he snapped her up immediately. But..."

"Her peccadilloes followed her," Jake finished for her.

"I remember when she first came to the company," Francesca said. "A lot of tongues were wagging about how she was a troublemaker. But I never saw that."

"That's because Broderick and Derek protected and guided her," Anne continued. "She was advised to keep her head down, do her work well, and stay out of trouble."

"Wow," Fred said, putting the last of his clean clothes inside his rolling suitcase. "This is better than a reality show." He glanced at Elena. "And you know how I love reality shows."

Elena agreed with Fred. Who would have thought all this nastiness was happening behind the scenes? Good grief. Their lives in Monaco were tame and naïve by comparison. Or was it because Fred was happily married, with a wife who shared his passion and career? Or that she'd been so focused on her dancing, making things work at a new company while advancing her choreographic goals, that she'd never noticed if similar things were happening in Ballet Etudes?

"But let's get real here." Jake served everyone a new round, emptying the bottle. "Whatever happened back in England, that doesn't explain what's been happening here. These attacks are up close and personal. Maybe not the initial vandalism, but definitely what happened to Justin and Tess. Those have nothing to do with Martina being sacked because of moral turpitude."

"But Justin was sniffing around her," Francesca said. "Maybe Caroline put the brakes on him."

Elena scoffed. "Justin is an opportunist. Always has been. He wouldn't let Caroline or anyone else stop him from taking advantage of anything that'll get him where he wants. And he's been sniffing around young potentials to advance his career since before he dragged me into his net."

"I don't know, Elena," Anne said. "I think Justin was really in love with you."

Elena blushed.

"But wouldn't it follow, logically, I mean, that Caroline, not Tess, would be the focus of the attack?" Francesca said.

"Let's not forget who was supposed to be on that table at that time," Jake said, his expression serious now. "And that wouldn't explain the attack on Justin either. No. This has an element of anger, whether caused by resentment, a need for revenge, or by pure rage at something, or someone. That is what has to be determined."

"Again, why?" Elena asked. "What could possibly be the motivation?"

"Maybe it's about secrets," Francesca said out of the blue.

"Secrets? What secret could anyone have to cause all this mess?"

"We all have secrets," Anne said. "You had one, Elena."

That shut everyone up for a few seconds. Elena gathered the empty wine glasses and took them to the kitchen. Jake was still nursing his.

"Maybe Martina has more skeletons in the closet than previously thought," Fred said.

"That's hard to prove unless someone fesses up," Francesca said.

"Well, I know Derek has more than his share hidden in the closet," Anne admitted. "And who knows the ones Broderick may have."

"But that could be said about all of us," Jake said.

"Hey, don't lump me in with everyone else here. I'm only visiting," Fred said, and zipped shut his suitcase.

Humor replaced tension for a second.

"Do you think Tess saw who attacked her?" Elena asked.

"It's possible," Jake said. "But lying on the table face down doesn't bode well for identification."

"Unless the attacker said something," Fred said.

"A possibility," Jake agreed. "But I'm sure Detective Harris will keep that information close to the vest, if it happened."

Fred yawned and caught himself before nodding off. "Sorry. I'm tired."

Anne checked her watch and gasped.

"Damn, it's late." She grabbed her purse and pulled Fred from his seat. "Come on, Fred, before you pass out on Elena's couch. We'll share a cab and drop you off at your hotel."

"Thanks for the meal and the company," Francesca said.

"Coming, Jake?" Anne asked.

"Not yet," Jake said, not moving from the sofa.

"Try not to keep her up too late," Anne said, raising her voice out in the hall. Francesca's muffled giggles echoed behind her.

"Some friends," Elena said.

"But good ones."

Elena waited with the door open. Jake still sat on the sofa, a faraway look in his eyes.

"In or out?"

That seemed to snap him out of his reverie.

"Like the burger joint in California?"

"Very funny."

He patted the sofa cushion next to him. Elena sighed, closed the door, and sat.

"There is nothing I'd rather do than to stay," Jake said as preamble. "But..."

"Who said I'd allow it?" she interrupted him.

His smile was disarming. He knew better. So did she.

He kissed her to prove it.

"I don't want to keep you," he said. "We've all had a stressful day, you especially. But I don't want to say certain things in front of the others."

She waited.

"About the letters on the medicine bottle," he said. "I'm still assuming it is a medicine bottle and Detective Harris let that slip out without realizing it."

"Think he was lying?"

He shrugged. "Anything goes in an investigation."

"Have you gotten anywhere with the search?"

"Do you know how many brand names of medicines there are? Not to mention the generic names for those, plus over-the-counter medications, and homeopathic?"

"Not a clue."

"It's an eye opener to say the least." He drank the wine that was left in his glass. "I also thought, at first, that those letters could be a patient's name."

The *c iz* flashed in her mind for a millisecond. "Hell, no. You don't mean..."

"Martina? It did cross my mind, and would have simplified the search for my very irate staff member. But the letters are out of order. They don't sync with her last name, or any other name from the roster at Terpsichore. So, no. That would be barking up the wrong tree and waste time. Another avenue of search would have been the pharmacies, but given that I'm not police, well, I can't get a warrant to overrule HIPAA privacy from pharmacies in all boroughs. Not that that search would be too fruitful either. Hell, nowadays, medications can be bought online from all over the world and delivered to your door. Better to find a corresponding name and its purpose. That could point us in the right direction."

"Do you have any news on Tess?"

"She's conscious, resting, and should be released tomorrow. But no other news. I'll try to see her first thing tomorrow before they release her from the hospital." He glanced at his watch. "I'd better leave."

"Must you?" She feigned distress.

"Minx." He pulled her up, held her hand walking to the door, and didn't let go even after she opened it.

"Night."

"Be careful tomorrow, Elena," he said, his expression devoid of humor. "It will be chaotic at the theater with dress rehearsal. Too many strangers and comings and goings for my comfort. And what Derek did to you back there today, making you out as the bad guy for not reviewing contracts and delaying things with lawyers, was way out of order. And, I don't trust Broderick either."

Elena nodded. She knew that by tomorrow's company class, everyone would know she had a stake in the company, that every single staff member would be at her mercy as far as contracts, budgets, and salaries went, and that nothing could be done until the lawyers hashed it out. Not only that, but Derek would lay out for all to see the open hostilities, affecting every single member of the company and school.

It wasn't fair, this playing dirty. Then again, she wasn't surprised.

Chapter Eleven

The applause signaled the end of class. As usual, Elena was soaked in sweat, but she didn't mind it too much today. She'd needed to sweat away all the excess calories she'd consumed last night.

But that food had been worth the slight bloating today.

On the other hand, class work had been more demanding, and the adagio during center work had been slow and brutal. Broderick had been true to irritable form.

"You think he's in a bad mood?" Francesca said, more as a statement of fact rather than a question. She toweled herself dry, as sweaty as Anne, Fred, and Elena.

"I'm sure he's punishing us for his own stress," Anne said, giving Broderick the evil eye. "Hate when that happens. God, I'm getting too old for this crap." She drank greedily from her water bottle

"Well, Derek didn't improve things with his announcement before class," Francesca added.

Elena wiped off more sweat and put on her ripstop warmer pants, followed by her warm-up booties. Mr. Derek and Broderick had arrived a few minutes before class and had announced there would be delays in contract renewals and salary reviews due to new unforeseen circumstances regarding Fauchier's latest will. He had then explained the hiccup, Elena's involvement in the process, and that things should be hashed out the week after the gala. Hopefully. In the meantime, no change in Justin's condition and Tess was recovering well from a very mild concussion. Unfortunately, she wouldn't be able to dance at the gala, as per doctor's orders, so Lauren would be replacing her as the Queen of the Wilis. He mentioned the dancers who would now be dancing Moyna and Zulma, the Queen's retinue, and how Anne had been gracious enough to step in to fill the void in the corps after this last-minute substitution. He finished by telling everyone he'd keep them informed about the negotiations and thanked them for their patience and continued loyalty to Terpsichore.

Well, to say that the disclosure of current affairs had not gone down well was the understatement of the year.

When that bombshell announcement was dropped, complaints, questions, protests, and simple disgruntlement had erupted. Amid all the grumblings, Elena had seen the rippled shock waves going through all the members of the company; had felt the curious, the speculative, the calculating, and the angry stares of all bearing down on her. Had heard the continuous whispers and the hushed, snide comments even after class had started. No one had to tell her that, later on, she'd be pursued and shadowed, every member vying for answers, together with attempts at jockeying for a favorable position or outcome to salaries and contract negotiations. Others would probably vent their frustrations and anger at the sudden changes and shifts in the power structure of the company.

No one ever liked sudden change, especially potential, unfavorable change.

Thank you, Derek Michaels, for making my life way difficult.

"The rumor mill is in full swing," Francesca said. "I'm getting texts right and left from people I never communicate with." She jammed her toe shoes in her bag. "As if I'd tell them anything."

"Join the club," Anne said, finally silencing her own cell phone, which had been pinging regularly since she'd switched it back on after class. "They wouldn't bother if they knew I don't have Derek's ear anymore."

"I'm still surprised Derek didn't give you Myrtha's role," Elena said, and didn't add he should have done, out of respect and courtesy to Anne.

"I offered, but he wanted to give Lauren the chance," Anne said. "Analisse can't say enough about her talent and Broderick has been chomping at the bit to bring her up the ranks. And you know how Derek..."

Whatever else Anne had wanted to say, Analisse interrupted it.

"Thank you, everyone. Dress rehearsal starts at two o'clock sharp. Curtain call one fifty. We'll go through everything in the order of performance day. No delays. You know the drill. Accessories and costumes will be delivered to your dressing rooms soon, if they haven't been dropped off already. Hairstyling has the schedule online and posted on the door, but the sooner you get it done, the better. If you're missing anything, let me or Maricela know. She and her crew will be doing the rounds to check things and help with costumes. And the stage trapdoor is still inoperable, so the theater crew has blocked the area by taping a plywood board over the open space. Lauren, you'll need to come out from stage left in your *bourrées*. Please don't trip over the plywood, ladies. We don't need any more injuries. Oh, and for the younger members of the group—get rid of those dark gel nail polishes you're sporting. You may think it's perfect and emo for vengeful ghost Wilis, but no." She clapped. "OK. Let's go, people."

Everyone scattered. Elena gathered her things and headed to the lower floor with her friends.

"Meet you in fifteen for hairdressing?" Francesca asked.

"The earlier the better," Anne said. "Want some extra time to eat something and relax."

Elena nodded. After a brief goodbye in the hallway, she headed toward her own dressing room. She avoided looking at those milling around on the off chance they'd want to stop or confront her, whichever the case may be. But everyone was busy getting ready for rehearsal and didn't seem to have the time, nor the inclination, for a serious tête-à-tête. Besides, the theater crew and orchestra members were added to their numbers, and instrument tuning and arpeggios from wind and string complemented those of voices, thuds, and hammerings that echoed throughout the area. Familiar. Homey. Part and parcel of every pre-performance.

She would have enjoyed it, if not for the present circumstances.

She turned into the hallway. Elena didn't believe in portents, but she'd felt uncomfortable ever since realizing the individual changing room they'd assigned her was exactly two doors down from where Tess had been attacked. Usually, she loved being alone while preparing for a ballet, enjoying the quiet and privacy an individual dressing room afforded, but she would have foregone that this time. She'd have preferred the boisterous changing room of the corps for the moment, or even sharing a room with disagreeable Martina. Thankfully, the police had taken down the 'do not cross' tape sometime last night.

Her Juliet gown, hanging from the door frame, greeted her arrival. She unhooked it, stepped inside and began the routine of placing makeup, brushes, lashes, shoes, tights, sewing kit, hairpins, perfume, wipes, and all her paraphernalia on the table and on the extra chair. Organized everything as she liked it. As promised, Francesca poked her head in fifteen minutes later.

"Ready?"

Elena picked up the Juliet hair accessories left with the costume, the hairnet and hairpins, her purse, bag, and they headed over to hairstyling.

Forty-five minutes later, hair done and accessories in place, they ambled back to Elena's dressing room.

Her phone pinged, and the ringtone from another of her brother's scores echoed within her handbag. She fished for it, knowing who texted her. She'd chosen that particular music for Jake.

"Morning, Sunshine. I'm in the office, but I'll stop by before dress rehearsal. Heard Derek ruffled some feathers this morning announcing your involvement in Terpsichore. Keep Fred, Anne, and Frannie close. BTW, do you need anything? Water, salad…me? Ask the others if they'd like something (not the me part). See you soon. Be careful."

"Oh, I know that smirk," said Anne.

Francesca twirled and cooed like a dove. "Someone's in lo-ove."

"Oh, be quiet." Elena swatted at Francesca, blushing. "If you must know, Jake asked if we needed anything before dress rehearsal."

"Ah-ha," smirked Anne, and Francesca repeated it, as skeptical as Anne.

"You're both incorrigible. Jake asked about food or water." She turned over her phone and waved it, showing the text. "There. See?" But she quickly hid it so they wouldn't read the 'me' part.

"That man is a godsend," Anne said. "I'd rope him in soon."

Elena agreed.

"Chocolate would be nice. Go ahead. Text him." Francesca waved at her to get on with it. "Dark chocolate with almonds for me."

"I'd kill for a smoothie," Anne said. "Pineapple with strawber... Didn't you leave your door closed?"

Elena stopped. First off, yes, she'd left her door shut. Now it had an open gap of an inch or so. A sudden, visceral feeling that all was not well overpowered her. *Be careful.* Jake's warning reverberated in her mind.

She never understood why she kicked the door in, not even later, when she'd had time to analyze her reaction. The thing slammed hard against the wall with enough force to crack the plaster behind it and crashed back shut again.

Anne and Francesca were shocked, for a moment. Seconds later, the shock gave way to a burgeoning hilarity.

The hilarity won. Francesca started chuckling, then laughing. Anne followed suit. Contagion ensued, this side of hysterical.

"Well, if there was anyone behind that door, they're toast," Anne said.

They dissolved into more laughter.

"What's funny?"

Martina's voice paused the laughter for a surprised second and then they cracked up again.

"Why is everyone laughing?" Caroline asked, poking her head out from her dressing room at the other end of the hallway. Others, among the crew and orchestra members filtering in, started to loiter in the vicinity, intrigued.

Martina shrugged. "They're not saying."

"You had to be here," Anne said, wiping her eyes.

The three of them were raging idiots, Elena thought, but she opened the door carefully. It swung in an easy arc, with no obstruction behind to block it.

Smiling at her prior ridiculous reaction, she turned on the light and froze.

The words YOU'RE NEXT, scrawled garishly across her mirror with red lipstick, *her* red lipstick, was the first act of vandalism within the room.

"Oh my God, Elena," whispered Francesca, horrified.

The second act was that someone had taken her toe shoes and, in a fit of rage, had broken all her pressed-powder eye shadows with them, staining the shoes in a manic kaleidoscope of color. All her lipsticks had been opened and broken, crushed against the table, making it seem as if the thing had open cuts or red pustules. Her cake foundation had been thrown on the floor and crushed, tights cut and ripped with her scissors, which now lay abandoned on the floor. Her ballet bag had been upended and spread on the floor, stained beyond repair.

The only thing untouched was her Juliet costume.

Elena stared at the flowing dress in inane wonder as it hung, unscathed, amid all the destruction. *Well, that was a relief.* The costume would have been very expensive to replace and her current budget couldn't afford such a monetary hit.

"I'm texting Derek," Anne said. "And Jake. Frannie, take photos."

Elena remained frozen. Who on earth would do such a thing? Really. Why embroil her in what had been happening in Terpsichore way before she arrived for the gala? She didn't belong to Terpsichore anymore.

You, dunce. Now you do. And Mr. Derek announced it to the world this morning.

"What a mess."

Martina's voice, out of the blue, snapped Elena out of her immobility.

"Was this you?" Elena stabbed an accusatory finger at her.

"You joking, right?"

"Did you do this?" she repeated, having difficulty controlling her voice.

Martina was beyond offended. "Do not put blame on me for this, this..."

"What on earth is going on?" Caroline asked, poking her head around the doorframe. It took a second to absorb the vandalism. "Oh."

That did it. Caroline now became the target of Elena's wrath.

"Was this your work?" She pointed to the ransacked room and her voice got exponentially louder. "I know you hate my guts, so I wouldn't put it past you."

"What?"

"Well, did you?"

Caroline's fury ignited. "Hell, who do you think you are, accusing me of something like this?"

Elena wanted to scream like a banshee, or hit someone. Anne, who recognized the warning signs, stepped closer.

"Elena, don't."

By now, sensing a drama brewing, people crowded the hallway and doorway. Some phones were high in the air, in the process of snapping candid photos or recording everything to post later in dance vlogs. Others were texting furiously.

But Elena wasn't listening. She was looking at the surroundings, searching for anything that might give her a clue as to who had vandalized her space. On the ground, by the chair, there was a smudge, as if someone had slipped on the foundation spread there. The doorframe sported a few smudges of color too, pink being the most obvious. Unfortunately, it didn't mean anything. Those were more likely eye shadow castoffs from the toe shoes while used in their destructive agenda.

But she was on the hunt now. And she couldn't delay. Already those crowding the hallway were obliterating all evidence.

Elena pushed people out of her way, looking everywhere for signs of smudged color. Whoever had done this had to have done it quickly, leaving on them evidence of the destruction. But where on earth was that evidence? Frustration gnawed. By God, she wanted to chase down this Lady Macbeth so badly. And, once caught, well, her sorry ass would be toast.

"What are you doing?" Francesca asked, worried.

She kept pushing and looking on the ground, the walls, people's clothing. Frustratingly, the floor was so riddled with smudges, scuff marks, and dirt that she couldn't really tell if there were any traces that could show where the vandal had run to. Wait. Was that a hint of her cerulean blue by the floorboards near the exit?

She turned on Martina next and grabbed her hands, turning them over. Turned the woman in a three hundred and sixty, inspecting her clothing, her booties, her arms, and hair.

They were clean.

Next, she got hold of Caroline's hands.

"What the hell?" She swatted away Elena's impertinence. "Are you insane?"

Elena let that slide. Caroline and Martina could have washed their hands, changed, even taken a shower.

She pushed more people aside and rushed over to Martina's cubicle at the other end of the corridor. She lifted and pushed aside clothing, shoes, searching.

By now, a small cortege of the curious followed her every move.

"What are you doing?" Martina practically screamed it.

Elena ignored her, heading for Caroline's dressing room. But the other woman was faster.

"Oh, no, you don't." Caroline splayed out her arms, ready to defend her territory with her body.

"Get out of the way."

"Not on your life."

"What the hell is going on here?"

The exasperated voice came from none other than Broderick, which irritated Elena even further.

"My room was vandalized, that's what. Everything is ruined."

"You've got to be kidding me."

Francesca grabbed his hand and dragged him back to Elena's dressing room. "Look."

"And this woman," Elena said, following him with reluctance, pointing back at Caroline. "She won't let me check her room."

"Now, Elena," Broderick said, but he stopped short when he saw the evident destruction and the YOU'RE NEXT splayed out in all splendor across the mirror.

"You're sick," Caroline said. "She's sick, Broderick."

"Whoever made the mess had to leave evidence on themselves, their room, even their clothes. That is if I'm not too late," Elena said with disgust. "This could only have happened when Anne, Frannie, and I were at hairdressing." She crossed her arms and stared at Caroline. "Are you hiding something? Is that why you won't let me into your room?"

"Ok, that's enough," Broderick said, exasperated. "Everyone is a bit stressed and..."

Stressed? Elena was about to let Broderick have it when Caroline played diva.

"You've got some nerve, Broderick Newsom." Caroline's anger vibrated her body. "Stressed? We've been terrorized for months and nothing's been fixed. To boot, you've done diddly about security here. And you promised, *promised,* you'd resolve this. Promised Jake would get to the bottom of this. Now, look what's happened. Justin at death's door, Tess concussed. Who's going to be targeted next?" She pointed her finger at Elena as if a ballistic missile could fire from its tip. "And now, *this person* is accusing me, and Martina, for the vandalism inside her room." She turned on Elena. "You should be pointing a finger at yourself, lady. Ever since you arrived *everything's* been messed up." Her expression turned nasty. "I wouldn't put it past her, Broderick, to have created this mess herself in order to divert blame to one of us."

Elena almost launched herself at Caroline. Almost, because Jake materialized out of nowhere and dragged her out of the way.

She began to wriggle in earnest.

"Whoa there, my prodigious termagant," Jake whispered in her ear. "Let the lesser mortals battle this thing out." He nodded to Francesca and Anne.

"We're wasting valuable time," she said, complaining at the brakes put on her. "Time is critical here, Jake."

"Let me do the snooping," Jake whispered, and before she could respond, he faced the crowd in the hallway.

"Okay, show's over. Everyone, back to work."

Despite the mumbles and grumbles, everyone scattered, except for Broderick.

"Listen, Elena, I'm really sorry about this." He scanned the destruction in the room once more. "This is beyond terrible."

Elena simply nodded.

"Listen," Jake said. "Why don't you hunt down another room for Elena? She needs to replace her things, so I'll get her started on a list. Get Analisse to help with that. Let me know when Detective Harris arrives."

"This should have remained an *internal* issue."

"But it hasn't, so we'll have to deal," Jake said. "Go, Broderick. You have a dress rehearsal to oversee. Derek's on his way. We'll handle things from here."

They stood waiting until the hallway cleared, with Anne and Francesca flanking her like bodyguards. Martina and Caroline were nowhere to be seen, probably steaming in their rooms about the injustices done to them.

Elena, at this point, didn't care. A sudden lethargy settled on her.

Jake, suspecting she was at the end of her tether, pulled her into the messy dressing room.

"You need to get ready for your rehearsal," he told them. "Salvage what you can. I'll have one of my men stand guard over your things."

"But..."

"Jake's right, Elena," Anne said, always level-headed. "Dress rehearsal waits for no one. You can use my makeup or Frannie's. We barely have a half hour before curtain call. After we're done, there's a Sephora near here. We'll make it a girlfriends' day out. And, don't worry. Derek will reimburse you. I'll make damn sure he does," Anne whispered the last.

"For now, take stock of what was ruined," Jake continued. "Type a list on your phone notes app. That way you can message it to me, Derek, Broderick, and Analisse. Did you take any photos?"

"Frannie did."

"Good. Send them to my phone. I'll be cataloguing everything too. Detective Harris should be here soon."

"I bet he was thrilled," Elena said.

"Not quite," was all Jake answered.

Elena looked around the damage. She picked up a pair of toe shoes by the ribbons and raised them eye level for all to see. The satin was stained beyond hope, a mess of clashing colors. The other two pairs were in similar condition.

"Look at them. They're ruined."

"We can go get you new ones tomorrow," Francesca said. But her attempt at optimism fell short.

"Michel handmade them special for this performance. I hadn't used them yet."

And saying that, Elena deflated like a burst balloon. She dropped into the chair and burst out crying.

"Oh dear," Anne said.

"Oh, honey, come here." Jake lifted and cradled her. "It's okay." He rubbed her back. "Let it all out."

Francesca came and hugged her as well. Anne simply patted her arm.

A discreet tap on the door announced the arrival of Derek, followed by a very serious Detective Harris.

Chapter Twelve

"ARE YOU OKAY?" FRED ASKED.

They were on stage, behind the closed main curtain. So were the others who danced in the first part of the show. Everyone was spread out on stage, and each kept clear of the others' space, practicing moves, jumps, perfecting balances, turns, and executing whatever part of their variation required attention for flawless delivery at the performance. The *Giselle*, act 2 group, which took over the stage after intermission, were backstage or in the wings, warming up.

Fred and she had been going over her pirouette variation and she'd been off balance, or, because of her lack of concentration, hadn't gotten near enough for him to grab her comfortably.

"I'll be fine," she insisted.

"Are you sure?" His voice couldn't mask his concern. Like everyone else in the company, and in the whole freaking world, Elena thought disgusted, word of the debacle in her dressing room, its aftermath, and her loss of control, had been all over the theater. Even the stagehands and orchestra members had asked how she fared, giving her commiserating looks as they passed by.

Afterward Jake had crammed her in the dressing room with Francesca and Anne, introduced them to the man who would be taking up guard duties, and informed them the man would stay inside the room, keeping watch, as soon as they left for rehearsal. In the meantime, that same man would be standing guard in the hallway, by the door.

"Want to go over it again?" Fred asked.

She nodded, trying to get back to some semblance of normal. Elena pressed her toe shoe platform on the floor, forcing her arch forward and did the same with the other foot, giving herself time to refocus. Unfortunately, glancing at those shoes, beaming back at her in all their psychedelic-colored damaged splendor, reminded her of how ridiculous she looked. They didn't match her costume, were garishly obvious, and Elena was sure all eyes would be focused on them rather than her dancing. Well, screw everyone. She'd refused to waste her time going to her brother's apartment (or have Jake go, when he'd suggested it) to dip into her emergency cache of toe shoes, three or four pairs usually, for occasions such as these. Usually, Terpsichore supplied their dancers with custom toe shoes if a debacle occurred, which sometimes happened. Analisse had offered replacements. But she'd simply thanked her and had refused to back down or out from wearing these for dress rehearsal.

An in-your-face kind of moment. Let them try to criticize.

Besides, getting into a toe shoe brand she'd never used before could mess up her feet. And she didn't need blisters in places she'd never get with her own.

"Let's go over it again," she said.

Elena concentrated on the muffled background instrument tuning of the orchestra, which kick-started Prokofiev's music in her mind, and focused. This time around, everything went flawlessly.

"Want to go over anything else?" Fred asked.

Before Elena could answer, Analisse strode center stage to impart last-minute instructions.

"Listen up. Program lineup: Overture, curtain up, Martina center stage, full lights. Variation. Bow, bow, bow, exit, lights down. Francesca and Randy, you should be ready by then on opposite wings. Lights on, back screen projection on, music cues your entrance. Variation. Bow. Exit. Lights down. Caroline and Mario, you silently walk center stage, pose. Screen background projection appears. Intro music. Variation.

Bow. Curtain down for scenery change. Overture R&J, curtain up, and you enter Elena from stage left. Russell? Wave at Elena, please."

Elena turned around, saw the young stagehand waving his hand, and waved back.

"Okay. He's the one who'll guide you up onto the balcony balustrade. Fred, ready at wing, stage right. Variation. Bow, bow. Curtain down. Intermission. Any tweaks will be done after each variation is finished. Broderick and I will be making notes and sharing them with the maestro, as well as the house and stage crew. Then on to the *Giselle* group's turn. Leave your costumes in your dressing rooms, please. Wardrobe will pass by later to collect for cleaning. They'll redeliver for the gala. You, however, can go home and relax. Tomorrow, nine thirty, here, sharp." She clapped. "Two minutes. Break a leg everyone."

Elena felt a slight bump on her rear and a soft whisper of 'break a leg' from Francesca. She smiled, turned and did the same to her friend. Then it was Fred's and Anne's turns to give and reciprocate.

"You look positively unique with those shoes," Francesca said.

"She may start a trend," Fred said. "Like a good luck charm for dress rehearsals."

Elena laughed. Fred always had that effect. The male version of Francesca, always looking at the bright side of things.

"And you look positively radiant in that tutu," Elena said, studying Francesca, who looked statuesque and elegant in the red and black creation.

"I do, don't I?" She turned one way, then the other, admiring the beautifully crafted costume.

Lights flickered. It was time for rehearsal.

Everyone moved to their respective entrance positions near the wings, while Martina ambled center stage and got into place.

Elena took off her leg warmers, scouting around to see who was where. From experience, she knew she had between ten to fifteen minutes tops before Martina was released from the stage. The others would be focused on her performance. Two seconds ago, an idea had popped into her head and she wanted to implement it before anyone saw she was nowhere near the stage. And she didn't want to get caught while she snooped around.

Anyway, no time like the present.

"I'm going to drop these off at the dressing room," she told Francesca and Fred, who half heard and nodded automatically. She elbowed Anne. "Let me know if something changes and they need me." She gestured her intent with the warmers. "I'll be right back."

Strolling, as if with no purpose in mind, Elena headed downstairs. Once there, she trotted to the dressing room she now shared with Anne and Francesca.

"Hi," she greeted the guard Jake had staking out their room. She lifted her warmers. "Dropping these off. Any news?"

"All quiet, really."

"Well, that's a relief. Is Jake around?"

The man shook his head.

"Well, thanks for keeping an eye on things," she said.

He went back to reading or watching whatever was on his phone.

Elena, instead of turning right to return to the stage, turned left. Caroline's dressing room was two doors down.

Don't tell a ballet dancer she can't do something. You will find they will OCD until they can.

She was on a mission.

Reaching the door, she turned the doorknob carefully, expecting it to be locked. But the door opened as smoothly as any and she scooted inside before anyone could catch her at it.

"Goodness, what a mess."

The room was a hive of littered personal items, placed in disarray all over the room. She couldn't understand how Justin and Caroline lived together, if she was this untidy at home. Justin, unlike some men she knew, was extremely neat and organized, and hated things out of place.

Well, guess it was true about opposites attracting.

Elena shrugged.

She ignored the makeup table and reached underneath, where Caroline's ballet satchel was stored. As furtively as she could, she emptied its contents on the floor, rummaging through clothes, underwear, shoes, ballet slippers, and the entire cornucopia inside a ballet bag.

Nothing.

Nothing stained. No telltale signs of Caroline being the perpetrator of the vandalism.

She shoved everything back inside, not bothering with order, while keeping watch for anyone passing by or listening for any noise that might indicate someone's approach. She shoved the bag back where she found it, doubting if Caroline could ever tell the difference if someone had rummaged inside her bag today. The contents had been in no apparent order to begin with.

She grabbed the sneakers next, scrutinized soles, interiors, edges, ribbons.

Nothing there to see either.

She paused, hearing muffled conversation somewhere at the other end of the hallway. A minute passed and nothing happened. She relaxed.

Her next target was Caroline's purse, abandoned carelessly on top of the easy chair. Here Elena was more careful. Although the bag itself was an enormous cave of space, it was personal, and any woman would know if someone had rummaged inside. It was filled with the usual: wallet, keys, makeup bag, brush, hair bungees, and what looked like vitamin bottles. She was about to check those when she spotted the phone.

It probably was locked, requiring a code or fingerprint. But one never knew. It wouldn't hurt to try.

She lifted it slowly.

"What the *hell* are you *doing?*"

Elena almost dropped the phone on the floor when she heard the whisper. She jumped around to face Anne, who was looking at her with such an incredulous expression, Elena wanted to laugh.

"How on earth did you find me?"

"I followed you. I knew you were up to something when you said you were dropping your leg warmers in the dressing room. You've *never* left stage during dress rehearsal, always watching and keeping warm in the wings."

It didn't pay to have someone know your habits so well.

"Well, if you must know, I'm checking Caroline's things for evidence. She didn't let me before."

"Are you *insane?*" Anne still spoke in a hoarse whisper. She looked around as if Detective Harris were on the prowl to catch evil-doers like her. "Drop that."

Elena shrugged. "It's probably locked anyway." She placed it back where she'd found it.

"You need to get back upstairs," Anne said. "Martina's almost done with rehearsal, and she's pissed."

Elena closed the dressing room door carefully and rushed after Anne.

"What happened?"

"The orchestra seems to be on a caffeine high," Anne said. "The tempo was disastrous. Twice as fast in most sections."

Normally, the orchestra followed the conductor's baton, so it was more likely that he was directing things too fast due to normal enthusiasm, or, maybe, he'd enjoyed a very nice lunch with a few alcoholic beverages to complement his meal.

It had happened before.

They reached the backstage area as Broderick suggested the final corrections for the conductor to annotate in his rehearsal score. The latter signaled, and the orchestra began a few measures before the problematic section, while Martina marked the variation until she picked up her cue.

"But isn't Kess conducting the gala?" Elena asked, craning her neck to see into the orchestra pit. Eric Kessler was music director for the company.

"Yes, but one of the guest conductors took on dress rehearsal," Anne said. "Kess couldn't make it today."

"Where'd you disappear to," Francesca whispered.

"Never mind," she answered.

Martina finished her variation and stood looking into the auditorium.

"That was much better," Broderick said from the orchestra seats. "Feel comfortable with that tempo now?"

"Yes," Martina said.

"Perfect. Thanks, Pino. Make sure Kess is aware of the tempo change," Broderick said. "Go relax, Martina. Good rehearsal. Next," he shouted.

"That's me." Francesca exhaled forcefully and pressed the platform of each toe shoe on the floor, getting any kinks out of her arches and ankles, and as a sign of readiness to tackle anything.

They all did that.

Thankfully, the tempo for Francesca and Randy's variation was perfect. Not so much for Caroline and Mario. It seemed Luca Pino, guest conductor, not too par excellence today, wanted to rush through rehearsal and had forgotten, somehow, that Fauchier's work was an adagio, not an allegretto. Broderick had to stop the rehearsal several times in order to instruct the conductor, and Caroline got progressively more upset, so much so, that her mood affected her balances and Mario's timing for lifts was off.

Five minutes later, with a lot of back and forth, Broderick released the duo.

A tap on her shoulder and a whispered, "Ma'am, you're next," from the stagehand, signaled Elena's turn was up.

By the time Fred and she were in the fish lift toward the end of the variation, Broderick had stopped the conductor three times to tweak the tempo. That meant running the variation several times from different places and extending rehearsal of parts that were difficult and exhausting.

By their fourth repetition, Fred and she were not amused. It felt as if Maestro Pino was playing jokes on all of them just for the heck of it.

"If he keeps messing up," Fred whispered to her as he brought her down. "He's going to kill us." He groaned as he lifted her for the last time.

"More you than me," she whispered back, smiling and pretending they were having the time of their lives. Poor Fred. Their Romeo and Juliet variation was hard enough without a schizoid conductor leading the orchestra. Fred's thigh muscles must be having screaming spasms by now.

Somehow, they muddled through the rest of the variation. Now, in stage center, they listened to Broderick's last suggestions with a stony face.

"In your *piqués* Elena, tighten the circle a bit more around Fred, that way, you'll time your *penché* perfectly with the music. That's about it from me." Broderick said. "Anything else you need to go over?"

Elena's answer couldn't come fast enough. "No. We're good. Right, Fred?"

Fred simply nodded. He couldn't have answered if he'd wanted to.

"Good," said Broderick.

Analisse stepped on stage and herded the *Giselle* group together.

"I'm heading out to the hotel," Fred said and gave Elena a cheek peck. "I'll see you tomorrow. I need to rest."

Good advice, she thought, but not doable for her at the moment. She needed to replace all her broken and vandalized goods first, then she could go to the apartment and rest.

Heading for the dressing room, she wondered if she'd see Jake anytime soon.

"So, they couldn't find anything?"

Although her tone held a good dose of skepticism, Elena was mellow. Jake had appeared at the apartment two hours ago with her favorite Italian restaurant takeout and a bottle of a very expensive Brunello di Montalcino. Someone had been snitching on her likes and dislikes to Jake, and she'd wager on Anne or Francesca being equal culprits. Knowing both women well, Elena bet Francesca had been the easier target to get the goods on Elena.

Elena suspected Mr. Scherzo wanted to keep his assault—on steroids—to impress her. And, she had to admit, he was doing a great job at it.

Not only that. She was profiting from his need to dazzle very nicely too.

"Nothing," Jake admitted. "And we looked everywhere, including the trash cans in the theater. Detective Harris may extend his search outside the area. Maybe."

"Maybe?"

Jake sipped at the wine. They were sitting on the sofa, his arm cuddling Elena to his side.

A very satisfactory position.

"He doesn't have the manpower or the budget to pay his people overtime, especially when he deems the incident, and I quote, 'A petty, internal, jealousy squabble.'" He downed the rest of the wine and placed the empty glass on the center table, snuggled her closer to him, and sighed the contented sigh of a man well pleased. "Doesn't see the correlation between Justin's and Tess's attacks to the vandalism. And Derek agreed. Convinced him to focus the city's resources on Justin's attack, and leave the internal crap to him." He planted a kiss on the top of her head. "Harris mentioned you are a very unlucky lady."

"You mean, unlucky I'm still a suspect, or that I'm jinxed?"

His laughter reverberated all along her body.

"I think both."

"This is so insane."

"Yeah, I know," he said. "One thing though, Harris has something up his sleeve. Wants to address the company right after class tomorrow. Derek gave the okay."

That piece of news intrigued her.

"Any inkling?" She looked at him.

"No. And I'm not going to obsess about it." He caressed her cheek. "We'll find out tomorrow. Right now, I have more interesting things to do."

And with that, he kissed her, proving his point.

Minutes later, back to the previous cuddling position, Elena asked, "Any news on Justin?"

"It doesn't look good, Elena. His parents arrived yesterday from Toronto and want to take him back home. That means taking him off the respirator."

Elena closed her eyes at that. What a horrible decision for a parent to have to make, she thought.

"I feel so sorry for them," she said.

"Me too," he said, with heartfelt pity.

"Poor Justin," Elena said. "We all deal with injuries, and it's a constant worry for every one of us as a possible career ender. But we never consider life-snuffing injuries. Caroline has to be devastated."

"I don't know how she copes, in all honesty," Jake said.

"She has no other choice. Besides, it's what she lives for. What she has always lived for." Elena yawned. Between the stress, the rehearsal, and the good food, she was fading fast. "You know, years ago, just before I left Terpsichore, she told Mr. Derek that she would die rather than stop dancing." She yawned again. "I would never want to be placed in that position, but I can't think death is somehow preferable to not dancing."

"That's because you have your family, your alternate career path to support you." He squeezed her shoulder. "You have me, now. Caroline only has the company and Justin."

"And that, according to Anne, was on the rocks."

"Drone attracted to a different, younger flower?" Jake asked.

"You, sir, are on the ball, as always." She yawned.

"Okay, if that last yawn was not a signal for me to vamoose, I don't know what is. That..." He stood. "Or I'm boring."

"I'm sorry," she stood as well. "I'm just tired."

He caressed her cheek. "I know. If not, I'd be insulted."

He led her to the front door but stopped short from opening it.

"Listen." He faced her. "Be careful. Derek is in denial about the vandalism..."

"What?"

"Not in the way you're thinking. He can't accept someone in the company is so hell-bent on damaging its reputation. Can't even fathom someone has a vendetta with the company, him, or any of its director-ship. Hell, even another dancer, for all I know. So, he's turning a blind eye on that. Nevertheless, he *is* focusing all his energies in battling things out with you. He's arranging to interview each of the principals that are up for renewal tomorrow, with you present."

"I'm not sure..."

"That you should be there? I agree. But he wants to force your hand. And that will create a lot of animus toward you, not only with the members of the company, but also label you as a possible troublemaker and opportunist. Won't look good for you in the ballet world."

Good grief, she thought. That was all she needed.

"And, I don't know," he continued. "I have this odd feeling things are coming to a head. Anyways." He put his hands on her waist and, as he'd seen in their many rehearsals, he lifted her on her tippy toes until she was barely inches from his lips.

"Good night, good night," he whispered, deviltry and something deeper reflected in his eyes. "Parting is such sweet sorrow, that I shall say good night till it be morrow."

At her startled look, his megawatt smile appeared. "Hey, I do know a little Shakespeare."

And with that, he kissed her to end all kisses. Soft and exploratory, at first. With a degree of care and wonder that Elena felt she was adored, cherished. Then deepening it. Demanding response. Reveling at her reciprocation. No man, ever, had ignited such heat and passion as this man had in her.

And he knew it.

And with that simple move, her Scherzo man transformed into her Romeo.

Chapter Thirteen

THERE ARE DAYS THAT SHOULD BE ERASED FROM THE calendar...

Skipped over...

Bypassed...

Deleted.

Today was such a day.

Everything that could go wrong, did, starting with the announcement that Justin's parents had taken him off life support and his condition was going downhill fast.

Caroline was beside herself. She barely made it through barre work before Broderick told her she was excused. She rushed out, crying quietly.

Detective Harris had arrived at the theater promptly after their nine-thirty class, and had announced that his officers would be searching through all lockers at Terpsichore central, and he was also asking to reinterview everyone, specifically with regard to their medical history.

The outbursts from the last was worthy of a volcano erupting. But Harris stood immutable, reminded everyone that he was investigating Justin's attack, which could potentially turn into a murder investigation if the latter died. That shut everyone up. He further stated that, apart from those rehearsing at the moment, everyone else was expected to report to Terpsichore headquarters immediately.

"Ah. There you are," said Harriet, as soon as Elena stepped into Terpsichore. She seemed to have been keeping an eye out for her from reception.

"Sorry about the delay. Subway issues. You texted that you had to see me?"

Harriet nodded, stepped outside the small office, and proceeded to foist two file boxes at her.

"What on earth are these?"

"Performance reviews of staff, dancers, and teachers alike. Miscellanea of expenses, salaries, etc., for you to review."

"Woah. Wait a minute. Is this what you tried to give me the other day?"

"Sure is."

"Harriet. I don't have the expertise, let alone the background to approve or disapprove of any of this. Besides, I'm not to do anything without the lawyers seeing it first. Take it back." She tried to shove the boxes at Harriet, but the woman refused the bait.

"My orders were to give them to you. Done. Now, you have an interview with Detective Harris in..." She scanned the ballerina wall clock behind the desk. "In five."

"Oh, good grief. Where?"

"Women's lockers. I'm off." And without further comment, she left via the connecting door to her office, closing the door with a snap.

Elena wanted to scream. Instead, she dumped the file boxes on top of the receptionist's desk and called her lawyers. After a brief discussion, they advised her to a) not peruse such documentation without them seeing it first, b) that they'd review all documentation later in the week, and c) they'd send a courier in the afternoon to pick up the box files at Terpsichore. With that said, Elena hung up, peeled off a Post-it note next to the computer on the desk, slapped it on the boxes, and left written instructions about the pick-up.

Five minutes later, she walked into the lockers. Detective Harris and his partner were looking through Francesca's things. Her friend, for once, looked annoyed.

"What are these?" Detective Murdock, decked out with latex gloves, retrieved several medium-sized bottles from the top shelf of the locker.

Elena stared. They resembled the ones she had seen in Caroline's purse.

"They're my multivitamins."

He nodded and promptly took one pill from each bottle, dropping each capsule in its own separate bag. After sealing each, he carefully labeled them.

Francesca glanced at Elena and grimaced in frustration.

"And this?" Detective Harris lifted a small jar. He was riffling through Francesca's ballet bag.

"My moisturizer. You can read the label."

Harris merely smiled. "And this?" Another tube went up.

"My Tiger Balm. For sprains and muscle pain."

He nodded and kept rummaging. A few minutes later, satisfied with the answers, he handed the bag back to Francesca.

"Thank you, Ms. Mori."

Francesca huffed and snatched her bag. Then closed her locker with a bang and snapped the combination lock shut.

While the detectives conferred on the side, Francesca joined Elena.

"The nerve," she whispered. "Asked all sorts of medical questions, including contact numbers for all my doctors, including my gynecologist for God's sake."

"Why on earth?" Elena whispered back.

"No clue. Not a peep from them. They're as tight lipped as a cramped muscle."

Elena almost let out a nervous giggle.

Almost.

"Martina is up in arms. They took samples of her vitamins too. She accused them of being worse than Gulag guards."

Elena understood. Anyone coming from the ex-Soviet Union knew about police abuses.

"Allowed them to riffle through her things in the locker, but didn't answer a single question about health and doctors. Told them basically to go to hell and get a permission." Francesca chuckled. "Harris corrected her, telling her they would issue a warrant, not a permission. She was nervous, you could tell."

"Well, aren't you?"

"No," Frannie said. "I'm pissed, not nervous."

That was a first. It took a lot to get Francesca angry. And, let's face it, Elena thought, the questions posed by the detectives would get anyone riled up. The nerve.

"Wait till they get Anne in here," Elena said. "They don't know what recalcitrance is."

"Ms. del Carral?"

Francesca leaned into her. "Be careful," she whispered close to her ear. "He's shifty and devious."

Elena nodded.

"See you at the theater." She waved her goodbye.

"Ms. del Carral, please?" Detective Harris pointed to the bench in front of the lockers.

She sat.

"Did they assign one of these to you?"

She pointed to his left, toward the end of the row. "That one. The one with no lock." At his raised eyebrow, she clarified. "I'm not a company member. I only used it a couple of times to store my ballet gear when in class or rehearsal here. That's all. The rest I always took with me." She hefted her bag and opened it.

Detective Harris motioned to Murdock to check the locker out with a nod of the head and began rummaging inside her tote.

"It seems ballet dancers are all creatures of habit," Harris said after a few seconds.

Elena smiled. "Yes. Our bags are clones of each other. The only differences are the brands, labels, and makers of our ballet gear. Also, personal preference as to style."

She heard the metallic sound of the locker opening. She reached inside her duffel and lifted her rehearsal leotard. "Take this, for example. I prefer the low cut, long sleeve for rehearsals and..." She picked another. "This V-neck camisole one is for class. Frannie prefers the short sleeves." She picked up an object from the bottom. "I swear by this foot roller. Frannie prefers the ball." She dropped everything back in again and shrugged. "Elastic bands differ in strength too. It's a matter of personal preference and what works with your body."

Without looking up from his rummaging, he asked, "Do you have any serious medical conditions?"

That braked her thought processes. With what Frannie had told her previously, and what she'd heard the detective reveal a while back about the bottle she'd found holding medicine, Elena played dumb.

"You mean like asthma? Or surgery done?"

His glance was penetrating.

"Well, my appendix was taken out when I was eleven, if you really want to know."

He seemed annoyed with her answer.

Good.

"And, let's see, I had an issue with my Achilles heel a while back. Had to get steroid shots for that. Let me tell you, that was painful. And worse," she leaned into him as if confiding to a friend. "I was put on rest for two weeks. Literally climbing the walls with the inactivity."

"Ms. del Carral..."

"I've also had several painful corns removed."

"Is this a joke to you?" Harris asked, annoyed.

She sighed. "Sorry."

"Apart from your appendix, anything else of concern?"

Elena shook her head.

"Dan?" Murdock said.

"What?" asked Harris.

"Come take a look."

Elena didn't like the tone of voice from Detective Murdock. Something was up. She followed Detective Harris and peered over his shoulder.

Detective Murdock had opened a similar bottle of what looked like Frannie's vitamins, and was cradling several vanilla-colored, oval pills in the palm of his gloved hand.

"What are those?" she asked.

Detective Harris faced her. His demeanor had changed from tolerant to aggressive and suspicious.

"Why don't you tell us what those are?" He pointed to the pills. His tone was harsh.

"Don't ask me," Elena said. "Those are not mine."

"They were in your locker."

"Like I said to you before, Detective, I only used that locker to store stuff while I was in class. I didn't put that there."

"Enough." His chin jerked toward Murdock's hand. "Check them out now, Steve. Then take them to Forensics. We need to know if they're the same. In the meantime..." He took her arm. "You are coming with me to the precinct. This has gone on long enough for my taste."

She snatched her arm back.

"Whoa, there. I'm not going anywhere with you." She started backing away, only to bump against Murdock, who had blocked her retreat.

"Ms. del Carral, either you do this voluntarily, or I'll arrest you, right here and now, for assault and attempted murder." Harris lifted his cuffs.

"Are you serious?"

"Deadly."

In the middle of this confrontation, stepped Anne, at first oblivious, then curious, then concerned.

"Detective Harris, Harriet said..."

"Anne," Elena interrupted in desperation. "They want to arrest me."

Anne was about to dismiss Elena's statement, but reconsidered after seeing their expressions.

"Ridiculous."

"We found a suspicious substance in Ms. del Carral's locker," Harris said. "So, we're taking her down for a little chat at the precinct."

"You can't do that." Anne was beyond blustering.

"Again, Ms. del Carral," Harris said, ignoring Anne. "We can do this without fuss, or you can do a perp walk for all to see. Your choice."

"Anne, call Jake. Tell him what's happening."

"Steve, grab her purse and ballet duffel." He grabbed Elena's forearm. "Let's go."

TWO HOURS LATER, a furious Jake sat next to Elena inside what she assumed was an interrogation room. He'd arrived half an hour after Detective Harris had dumped her in this closet of a room, with gray walls meant to depress anyone who sat there, and which smelled of humidity, old sweat, and stale cigarette smoke. She kept her arms on her lap, not daring to place them on the small table facing her. God knows what had happened on it. The room felt dirty.

"This is ridiculous," she said for the third time.

Jake stayed mute.

"I'm going to miss rehearsals," she added, frustrated no end.

"He's doing it on purpose," Jake said, his voice low and dangerous.

"I'm surprised they let you in here with me," she said. "Thanks."

Hearing her wobbly voice, Jake turned to face her. He lifted first one hand, kissed it, and then did the exact same thing with the other. "I'm here as your advocate. They had no choice."

But Elena knew he was here for a much more important reason. Could someone fall more in love yet?

She sighed, contentment filling her soul, despite the circumstances.

"Okay, let's go over this again."

"But I don't have anything to add," she said.

"You said Murdock found the bottle with those pills inside the locker you've been using."

She nodded.

"Any idea who may have left them there? Were they there when you started using the locker?"

"No and no."

"And Harris kept asking questions about medical issues? Serious medical issues?"

Another nod.

"And the pills were small?"

"Yes. Vanilla colored and oval shaped. They reminded me of the medication Roberto uses for his allergies."

"Harris wouldn't bother to drag you in here if those had been over-the-counter medications," Jake said. He seemed to be considering something. "It's more serious than that."

"Well, he's not saying what."

Jake smiled with the first hint of humor stamped on his face.

"No, he's not one to share important information."

Elena leaned forward. "He even asked Frannie about her gynecologist."

"Really?" He considered something, then out of left field he asked, "Why are you whispering?"

"I don't want them to know I know."

Jake chuckled. "Elena, Harris has been watching and listening to us for the past hour." He lifted his face and said to the air in general. "Isn't that right, Detective? Shall we stop this farce?"

Two minutes later, Detective Harris entered the room. He dropped Elena's ballet satchel on top of the table, with several evidence bags next to it. Her purse had been added to its contents.

Elena made a face. She'd have to disinfect that thing once she got to her brother's apartment. Maybe even chuck it altogether, buy a new one, then stick the cost for them up Derek's behind.

Then she stared. Inside the clear plastic evidence bags were some of her things from inside her tote and purse. Black smudges were smeared on some of the items. She practically exploded.

"I didn't give you permission to search through my things."

"Bad move, Detective," Jake tut-tutted. "Now Ms. del Carral will have ample cause to sue for harassment and illegal search. And she didn't give her consent to have fingerprints lifted from her personal items either," Jake added.

"My fingerprints?"

"That's why he wanted you down here." He sounded certain.

"What?"

"I have probable cause to search without a warrant," Harris said, immutable.

"Ah, Harris. But not to lift her fingerprints if you're not charging her. You know better."

"Charging me for what?" Elena wanted to hit something. "I have done nothing. Absolutely nothing."

"We only wanted to have a friendly chat with Ms. del Carral, that's all," Harris said.

Jake laughed. He didn't sound amused, though.

"A friendly chat could easily have been easily done in one of Terpsi-chore's offices," Jake said. "Not down here at the precinct, like a petty criminal."

Harris pushed the three bags toward her. "What are these, Ms. del Carral?"

"Didn't you read the labels?"

"I'm afraid I can't understand them."

Of course. They're in French, you moron.

"Get them translated. And your department owes me mega bucks for those. You've ruined them. I'll have to throw them away."

Wow. She was turning into a snippy little termagant indeed.

"Are we done here?" Jake asked. "You have what you wanted and the fingerprints didn't match the bottle you retrieved from that locker, if not you'd have charged Ms. del Carral already."

Elena stood. She snatched the bags and dumped them inside her tote. She wasn't about to leave any of her things with this man.

Harris didn't stop her. He walked to the door and opened it, as an invitation for them to scatter.

"You know we had ample cause to search," Harris said matter-of-factly. "All roads lead to Rome, people say. And I'm afraid all roads in Mr. Bakare's incident, plus all that has followed, have led to you, Ms. del Carral."

"That may be so," Jake admitted. "But you should look closer to home. Ms. del Carral lives in Monaco and only arrived a week ago. She hasn't worked for the ballet company for more than five years. This mess began months before she arrived and has a very personal flavor to it. It is linked exclusively to Terpsichore. Search for your motives there, Detective."

"We are," Harris said. "Things have been done for elimination purposes."

"Really," Elena burst out.

"What is curious, though," Jake interrupted, "is your insistent questioning about medical issues. Care to elucidate on that?"

Harris merely watched them.

"You could have asked nicely," Elena told him, at the door. "I would have cooperated. But the way you've treated me today, well, I'm not amused at all, and I'll be speaking to my lawyers about this."

"And the harassment stops now, Detective," Jake said in farewell. "If not, I'll have my own lawyer contact your Chief. They're very good friends, you know."

Harris smirked. Murdock met them and escorted them out of the precinct.

Good riddance to annoying detectives.

BY THE TIME they arrived at her brother's apartment, it was close to five o'clock. Rehearsal with Fred on both R&J and *Concerto* was a dud. Text messages from Frannie, Fred, and Anne on her phone had also exploded. Eighty-five messages, desperate to find out what was going on, the anxiety for her evident in the frantic face and prayer emojis cluttering text space.

She threw her tote in the corner in her bedroom.

"By the time I go home, I'll be bankrupt from having to replace everything."

"What are your plans for today?" Jake asked from the living room.

Today is almost gone.

She looked around the bedroom, not really seeing anything. She wanted to kick, and scream, and tear someone's hair out. She needed action.

"I don't know." She walked to the mini fridge and grabbed a bottle of water. She gulped half of it down. "I think I'll take a shower and go to class at Rick and Nat's. There's a Target near their studio where I can buy a new tote. Then I need to replace my ruined makeup and moisturizers. Find out what else Harris and his crony put their paws on and replace that, let alone wash everything in there." She shivered and drank some more. Gestured. "Want some?"

"Nah. I have to get back to the office. I have an idea." At her evident curiosity, Jake shook his head. "Let me find out first if it pans out."

She nodded.

"Text your friends," he said, walking to the door. "Let them know you're okay. Have some dinner with them." He took out his wallet and gave her five twenties. "Here. Take cabs. Try not to be alone."

"I can't take your money."

"If that amount falls short, get receipts. I'll get it back after I do my expense report for Terpsichore."

He gave her a quick, but deep, kiss, and left as quickly, already on the phone as he walked to the elevators.

"WELL DONE, EVERYONE," Gustav said, as the entire group clapped in acknowledgment of a great class. Elena had never taken classes with this teacher, but Francesca had persuaded her to. She even got enthused enough to join Elena. So had Fred. Their fourth musketeer, Anne, had balked about joining, saying she was going to spend an evening with her significant other. She needed it after the scare Elena had given her. Her activities tonight would consist of good food, wine, company, followed by a great romp in the hay.

"Isn't he wonderful?" Francesca said, wiping sweat with a hand towel. "I told you Gustav was good."

"Thanks for motivating me," Elena said, grabbing her new tote with all her new purchases stuffed inside. She pulled on her jeans. "When I heard Rick wouldn't be giving class tonight because Nat had an activity she couldn't miss, I almost didn't come."

Fred glanced at her new bag. "Nice. Got everything else you needed replaced?"

"And then some," Elena said, smirking. "Derek will be shocked when he gets my receipts. Properly vetted and approved by me. He wants me to vet and approve everything else."

"Well, there you go," Francesca said.

"Have you eaten anything yet?" Fred asked. "I'm starving."

"When aren't you?" quipped Elena.

"Let's go to Giovanni's," Francesca said. "It's close to your hotel, Fred. And the food is to die for."

"It's a bit of a splurge, Frannie," Elena said. Dancers could rarely do it. Their salaries weren't high to begin with, and most of it went for ballet gear, food, and rent. Everything else was an extravagance. And she knew that restaurant in particular because her mother and Fauchier used to go there often. A bit pricey back then. She was sure it was more so now.

"I don't care," Francesca said, zipping her tote with finality and hefting it on her shoulder. "All this has left a bad taste in my mouth. Not only that, but we have to enjoy ourselves more. We're always focused on work, work, work."

Yes. There was that too, Elena thought.

"That's because it's rare we have time off, like now," Fred said.

Francesca walked down the long flight of stairs leading out of the dance studio and onto the sidewalk.

"Well, I need a shower and some decent clothes." Elena clicked her phone on and checked the time. "Meet there at nine thirty?"

Everyone scattered to their respective abodes.

At exactly the appointed time, they were seated at Giovanni's, sipping a very good chianti and gorging on zucchini sticks and calamari *fritti*.

"God, these are really good," Fred said, grabbing another handful and dropping it on his plate.

Elena dunked calamari in the restaurant's spectacular marinara sauce and savored each munch. She'd forgotten how tasty the food here was. The last time she'd been here, her two siblings and she had been celebrating her mother's wedding to Fauchier.

Seemed like a lifetime ago.

Elena shook her head. Uh-uh. She was not about to bring back bittersweet memories at this moment. She wanted to enjoy her evening with her friends.

And it was a shame Jake couldn't be here. It would have made the night perfect.

Their entrées arrived, and the second gorging began. Once done, all three leaned back on their chairs, savoring the last of the wine.

"I can't eat a single morsel more," Fred said. "I'm not sure I'll be able to sleep well, I'm so full."

"That's a new one," Elena said.

"Want to be more decadent?" Francesca asked, after the waiter had handed them the dessert menu.

"No, not for me." Elena patted her takeout container. "I couldn't even finish my pasta."

"Bummer," Francesca said and handed the menu back to the waiter. "I really have a sweet craving."

"After what happened to you this afternoon, Elena," Fred said. "I don't know how you could have eaten. My appetite would have been destroyed."

"Class took care of that," Elena said. "Got all my stress and frustrations out in there."

"Everyone is talking about what happened," Francesca said.

Fred's laugh lacked any humor. "It's the only thing they're talking about. Analisse and Broderick had to reprimand everyone at the theater."

"Including the stagehands." Francesca placed her empty wine glass carefully on the table. "Everyone is jittery. The corps were distracted today. Randy almost collided with me."

"Really?" Elena said.

Fred nodded. "He later told me the only thing he could think of was whether the detectives would arrest anyone else."

"Anne kept crying too," Francesca said. "And Martina continued her complaints to anyone who was within earshot before and after her rehearsal."

Elena finished her wine. Rehearsal, it seemed, had been a mess. Not that she was glad she'd missed it, but she was sure it would have been challenging, especially after what had happened to her.

She was still rattled.

"Interesting enough, Caroline was the most calm," Fred said.

"Well, she didn't have to suffer Elena's ordeal," Francesca said. Irritation colored the edge of her tone.

"I've never been one to sympathize with Caroline," Elena said. "But what she's going through with Justin is worse, I think. She's probably so emotionally drained with all that is going on that what happened to me is unimportant to her. Besides, her refuge is dancing. Has always been. I'm sure she welcomed the distraction of rehearsal."

"Oh, you're right, I'm sure," Francesca admitted.

"Oh-oh."

The warning came from Fred, who faced the entrance to the restaurant.

"Don't look now, but I think our dinner is about to sour."

"What on earth are you talking about?" Elena asked.

He pointed his chin toward the entrance to the restaurant. Francesca and Elena turned and saw Derek and Broderick greeting the maître d'.

Just what she needed to complete her day.

"Quick." She turned and kicked Francesca under the table. "Turn around. Fred, ask for the bill. Wait." She grabbed his hand before he could lift it from the table. "That will attract attention. Let's wait until they're seated."

"Too late." Fred's face showed his regret.

A few seconds later, both men were beside her.

"Elena, dear."

She almost shrugged her shoulders in resignation, but she put on a smile and got up, gave Derek Michaels a greeting kiss. Fred and Francesca did the same.

She nodded to Newsom in acknowledgment. "Broderick."

"I see you've eaten already," Derek said, after glancing at their dishes and nodding to Francesca and Fred.

"Just finished."

Derek turned to the maître d', who was hovering politely behind both men, waiting to seat them. With a wave he motioned to their table.

"Tony. Put this on my tab, will you please?"

"Yes, Mr. Michaels." And the man waved their waiter over to whisper his order to him.

"You don't have to do this, you know," Elena said.

Francesca pinched her back.

Derek's face turned apologetic. He took Elena's hands in his own and squeezed.

"I can't begin to tell you how sorry I am about what Detective Harris did to you," Derek began. "It was unfounded and inexcusable. I know we've had our differences lately, but this... I'm sorry I wasn't there for you."

"Jake was," Elena said with a soft smile.

"Yes, Jake." Derek's lips thinned. In disapproval? Elena wasn't sure.

"He's become quite the staunch defender of you, hasn't he?"

Well, no one else has.

She said nothing.

"Listen, it's late and I don't want to keep you. Try to rest. But stop by my office early tomorrow. I need to consult you on a few issues."

"Mr. Derek," she protested, but he cut her off.

"Please, Elena. Eight thirty? Before class?"

After a few seconds, she nodded.

"Thank you, dear."

Without saying anything else, both men turned and followed the maître d' to their assigned table.

Elena watched, half in pity. The man she had always admired and loved like an uncle, tonight walked with shoulders bent, his gait slow and shuffling, so unlike his usual erect posture and purposeful strides.

The recent events had definitely weighed him down.

Derek Michaels, for once, was showing his age.

Chapter Fourteen

WHEN ELENA ARRIVED FOR HER MEETING WITH MR. DEREK, Harriet herded her into her office to give Derek Michaels a chance to finish conferring with one of the company's dancers in his. With that said, same Harriet had promptly left Elena to her own devices, claiming she had a million things to do before the gala.

Elena, who had not woken up in a very good mood, sat down in a huff. Then stood up. She couldn't stand still and roamed the office, not paying attention to the murmur of voices filtering through between too-thin walls.

"You can't do this."

The loud voice stopped Elena in her tracks. It sounded like Caroline. She tiptoed closer to the connecting door.

"This can't come to you as a shock, Caroline," Derek said. "Your technique has been slipping for a while now, and you've gained some weight. That affects your extensions. One of your partners complained, saying lifting you was becoming increasingly awkward and strenuous. Broderick and Analisse both agree your performances have been subpar lately, both in class and on stage. You're beginning to injure more easily. Must I go on?"

"You can't blame me. You know what's been happening, especially now."

"That's why we're not terminating you immediately and are giving you the remainder of your contract to get back up to speed."

Broderick's voice.

"Martina, on the other hand, is getting better, sharper, more dominant with each performance," Derek continued. "We're promoting her to principal, and that is final."

"You're still first soloist," Broderick said.

As if that made up for not being principal dancer anymore.

"But that is not the same thing." Caroline was beside herself. "I won't be dancing my favorite ballets. And, pretty soon, knowing you both, you'll demote me further until I'm like Anne, dancing whatever she can get. That is not fair."

"May be not fair, but it is the reality of our profession," Derek said. "Surely you've been making plans for your future, right?"

"Justin and I talked about it, but we never came to a decision."

Oh boy.

"Well, I'm sorry to say Justin was on his way out," Derek said. "We told him, just before we hired Martina, about our plans not to renew his contract at the end of the season."

So that was why Justin had been honeying it up to Martina, like Anne and Francesca had said.

"You were getting rid of Justin?" The incredulity in Caroline's voice was palpable.

"He's been on the way out for years, Caro," Broderick said. "I'm sure he was trying too hard, when he had his accident. The reality is he can't keep up with the dancers rising through the ranks."

"Unfortunate, this accident," Derek continued.

Elena jumped when she heard a bang. Sounded like a chair being thrown on the floor. Or at a wall. Or at someone.

"I won't put up with this, Derek." Caroline's voice trembled in her anger. "I'll sue you and Terpsichore for, for, age discrimination."

"Get real, my dear," Derek said. "That will never wash in a ballet company, and definitely not in court. Besides, your contract stipulates I can terminate employment for any reason, particularly if you become a detriment to the company."

"Caroline, we're giving you more than six months to get back to form." Broderick practically whined it. He never did like confrontations, Elena thought.

"You're an evil bastard, Derek Michaels, waiting until Justin's at death's door to tell me this."

"It's stark reality, my dear. And an economic one, as well," Derek told her. "Martina is attracting more fans to the theater. Sadly, you aren't. She's also getting more popular with her dance vlog. I have to consider the good of the company. So, this is final."

"Caroline..."

But the outer door to Derek's office slammed shut. Caroline had made her exit. And Elena was sure, knowing the woman, that Derek would have a fight on his hands. Caroline had given the company all her youth, talent, and energy. Had her mother experienced this dark side of Derek Michaels? Had Fauchier been as ruthless as Mr. Derek? Somehow, Elena doubted it. Her mother would not have married someone who could discard a loyal dancer like an old toe shoe. Or was she so stupidly naïve to believe ballet companies could not possibly function the way she'd witnessed right now? She knew she'd been extremely fortunate in her own career. Then again, she'd worked her tail off to stand out from the regulars. Her advancement in the world she loved had been fluid and with no drama, and further helped by the sponsorship of a few godfathers of her own. In Monaco, at Ballet Etudes, she'd been gifted with a future when allowed to choreograph her *Concerto in D*. Her *Black Rhapsody* had been backed by a selfless, tour de force choreographer, who'd not only praised her work to the potential jury members Elena had planned to send her work to, but who had encouraged her talent and drive until his untimely death. All roads led to Rome, Detective Harris had said. Well, all roads had converged to give Elena a solid future when faced with a too-early retirement as a dancer, an option Caroline and Justin didn't have. Or Francesca. Or Anne. Or any other dancer, including Fred and his wife.

Maybe that had been the reason Anne had been so blunt to her all those years back. She had to have known the ruthlessness of Derek, and had guided Elena well.

Did Jake know too? Was that why he was defending her so vigorously against Mr. Derek?

Elena glanced at the wall clock. Five minutes to her meeting. What to do? What to do? If she tapped on the connecting door now, they would suspect she'd heard the conversation. But, wasn't that the reason Mr. Derek had called the meeting this morning? As a shareholder of Terpsichore now, so to speak, she would have to take part in these decisions.

Could she be as ruthless as Mr. Derek proved to be? Would she be as harsh? And did she really want to become that type of person? Oh, phooey. To hell with everything. She needed to find out what Derek had in mind. She gathered her stuff, walked out of Harriet's office, and knocked on Derek's. Elena stepped inside as soon as permission was given.

"Morning," she greeted both men.

"Thank you, Broderick," Derek said, dismissing the man with a nod. "I'll see you later at the theater. And this won't take long," he continued. "Elena should be on time for class."

As soon as Broderick closed the door, Derek pointed to the chair facing him.

"Elena, please."

She sat, but not in comfort. Her spine was straight, almost in battle prep.

"Like I told Broderick, this won't take long." He stared at her for a few silent moments. "How long have I known you and your family, Elena?"

So, he's going for the beloved-friend-of-the-family routine. Your best interests at heart, blah, blah.

"Close to twenty years."

"Understand that I've come to this decision as if Fauchier himself were proposing it."

"Mr. Derek, you know I won't agree to anything until I consult with my lawyers."

"I am well aware of that. No," he shook his head. "What I want to discuss is for your consideration, but I highly recommend you accept it. It's a one-time-only offer. I won't present it again."

Her spine straightened even further.

"I've talked it over with my wife and Terpsichore's lawyers, and I think what I'm proposing will be the best for all."

Her noncommittal ah-ha said it all.

"I want to buy you out."

"Buy me out."

"When Fauchier died, he held fifty-percent shares of the company. That reverted to me upon his death."

"As well as all his percentage of profits from the proceeds of ticket sales, the school, and the staging of his works at other companies," Elena added.

Derek stared. It seemed he'd never considered Elena would be so well informed.

She almost smirked.

"Well," he said a few moments later. "My lawyers are writing up the proposal, but I wanted to give you a heads-up. I'm willing to give you full price on the shares Fauchier held at the time of his death. I am also willing to give you a reasonable percentage of everything, but that won't be a cumulative sum inclusive of everything up to today."

"In other words, you're suggesting I should accept only a pittance in comparison to what Fauchier would have collected were he still alive today."

Elena wasn't surprised at the terms of this buyout. What it boiled down to was false advertising, bragging about his and Terpsichore's generosity in this suggestion, claiming the lump sum to be agreed upon was the best offer available. And that she should be grateful and accept it. Her lawyers were studying the figures involved and had given her an estimate of the earnings Fauchier would have claimed. And the expected figures were astronomical. A nice retirement nest egg if things came through.

"All this as a lump sum?"

"Now, Elena." Derek put on his best condescending smile. "You know better than that. Terpsichore's profits are minimal once expenditures and taxes are deducted. It would have to be a long-term, specific stipend."

"Like an annuity."

"Precisely."

"And for the staging of Fauchier's works?"

"Ah." He leaned back and steepled his fingers. "I'm willing to share on that, but for a limited time. After all, we've functioned on the basis that Fauchier left all his works to aid in Terpsichore's financial support. I don't think the new will changes those terms. Now, getting back to this proposal. It will stipulate you should earn from those for a period of one year, but afterward, all rights and profits would revert exclusively to the company."

"With *Black Rhapsody* to be excluded completely," she said.

"Yes." His tone said he was not happy about that.

Elena didn't comment. He was offering her now a buy one, get one at fifty-percent deal, the only caveat was the discount applied exclusively to the cheaper item and only for a limited time. He could easily delay the staging of any of Fauchier's works until after the stipulated date was done and gone. He would get all the earnings later. She...nothing.

How generous.

"Well, Mr. Derek. Thank you for giving me a heads-up." She stood and grabbed her things. "Can't be late for class."

"Please, Elena. Consider it." He stood as well. "It is a very generous offer."

"I'm sure you think so."

"Elena, you assume I'm spiteful and, hell, even cruel," he said with a tinge of sadness. "But Fauchier did a number on us. On me, actually."

"Not intentionally."

"True, but nonetheless did. I've been left scrambling after the shock of learning about his marriage to your mother. About how *Black Rhapsody* was never his to stage. The company is a voracious animal. It forever needs money—loads of money. The funds we do have are tied up in trusts. The rest rely on donations, and those are slim now. The gala is crucial to get us back on track in this flat economy. And, we're not subsidized like Ballet Etudes and other ballet companies in Europe and throughout the world. I'm responsible for all my staff. Livelihoods are at stake. If we can't come to an equitable solution, this is the end of Terpsichore." His sigh was deep. "Think about it. Consider it, please. Seriously."

Playing to my loyalties, again.

Derek must have read the meaning of her thoughts on her face.

"We all have to make sacrifices."

Elena opened the door, but paused. "I'll read your proposal, consider it, and talk to my lawyers as far as how best to proceed. But I can't guarantee that my decision will be what you want. Not right at the moment."

"I understand."

"I may have a counterproposal."

"Expected it."

She nodded and left.

"It's disgusting."

This distaste, coming from Francesca, no less, was a snapshot of the malaise running through the company.

"It'll pass," Anne said, rising slowly from her stretches. She seemed lethargic this morning, her muscles tighter. Francesca had been all over the place with her balances. Caroline too. Elena had expended all her frustrations on her *grands battements* and had almost hit Fred full in the face with one of them. The men were affected, as well. Jumps and *tours* were sloppy, timing off, and, well, Analisse and Broderick were not happy.

The only one who seemed not affected by anything was Martina. Control was perfect. Balances divine. Pirouettes flawless. Execution at center adagio impeccable. Elena smirked. The woman, who normally didn't need much encouragement to show off, was reigning over all.

Unfortunately, Martina couldn't seem to help herself, and if Elena were honest, she would be behaving exactly the same after the news of the promotion. Let's face it, Martina *had* something to brag about, and her endorphins were probably through the roof. In all honesty, however, the woman's Cheshire Cat smile throughout class grated, especially accompanied with repeated crowing about her new position to everyone within range. And witnessing the groups of little sycophants gathering and buzzing around her after the announcement, jockeying for a favorable position and for future partnerships, was worse.

In time, that same group would totally ignore and sideline Martina the moment she couldn't offer advancement and profit.

It had happened to Anne. It was starting to happen to Caroline.

What a career they had.

"What did Derek want?" Francesca asked, grabbing her stuff so the stage crew could move the portable barres by the wings to backstage. Elena, Anne, and Fred, followed suit.

"What's this about a meeting?" Anne asked.

Francesca explained what had happened after dinner the previous evening, since Anne had not been present.

"Well?" Fred asked. They dropped all their bags by stage right. Elena rummaged for her flowing skirt to rehearse with, while Francesca and Anne donned their leg warmers.

"He's proposing to buy me out," Elena said.

Anne looked surprised. "With what money?" she asked, a heavy hint of disdain in her voice. "He's miserly to the max and is always complaining about lack of funds to keep things going. That we all must sacrifice for the good of the company."

"Oh, trust me," Elena said, with equal scorn. "He went into the whys and wherefores of that. Said monies will be given in small amounts."

"Have you seen the proposal?" Francesca asked.

"No. He simply wanted to give me a heads-up about what he was planning."

"Well, let's hope it's a generous offer," Fred said. "You could use the money."

"Anyone could use the money," Anne said.

Elena gestured for them to gather closer. "Derek was in a meeting with Caroline when I got there. He's demoting her to first soloist."

The shock on their faces said it all.

"He can't do that," Francesca protested a bit louder than usual.

Elena shushed her.

"It's not fair," Francesca added a bit softer.

"Derek won't care," Anne said.

Elena looked at her friend. There was a look in Anne's face that disturbed her a bit. Anger tinged with what? Disappointment? She couldn't put a finger on it.

"He's done this before, hasn't he?" Elena asked, suddenly enlightened about circumstances years back.

"Yes," Anne said. "To you, as you guessed. It was a choice between keeping a fledgling, like you, with tons of promise, or keep a box office hit, like Justin, at the peak of his career." Anne glanced at Derek, who'd entered the auditorium and was discussing something with Analisse. "I'm sure he's regretting that decision, especially after the *Black Rhapsody* fiasco and your talents as a choreographer. The prized gift that got away."

"Wow."

"Exactly."

"What exactly?" Fred asked, puzzled.

"The reason why Anne gave me a talk, five years ago, about the pros and cons of staying at Terpsichore."

"More cons than pros," Anne added.

Elena nodded. "She also urged me to consider my future, not in yearly contracts with Terpsichore, and hope for the best, but as an asset to another company, where I would be appreciated more..."

"And most," Anne interrupted.

"And where I could have a long-lasting dancing future," Elena continued. "Which is exactly what I did. Thanks to her, my ballet career, both as dancer and choreographer, are as secure as I can make it, with me in control of my future."

Elena took Anne's hand and squeezed. "I am so grateful to you, Anne. And I'm so sorry it's happened to you too."

"But I saw it coming."

"Still, it must have been awful. Thank goodness you're prepared," Elena said, a soft smile on her face, remembering Anne had a new beau and a happy future. "Not so with Caroline and Justin. As a matter of fact, Broderick said Justin's contract wasn't going to be renewed later this year. He was out of the company."

"Don't look so shocked, dear," Anne told Francesca. "Derek was planning this for a while. Since he hired Martina, actually. And both he and Broderick have had their eyes on Randy and Mario as replacement for a while. Who will it be? It's musical chairs now, with Martina as prize."

"But that is so disheartening," Francesca said, zipping her bag shut with force.

"Name of the game," Anne answered.

"Is it always like this?" Fred asked. "I mean, such drama in a company and so much back stabbing? I can't relate."

No, he wouldn't, Elena thought. Fred's career had been running at a smooth parallel to hers. They also worked for a smaller company where, thankfully, most of the members worked well together and didn't seem to have those issues. But, behind the scenes, at directorship level, was it as innocuous as Fred thought? Maybe they did the same, but not overtly. Then again, Derek was not doing it overtly either. It was only the privileged position Elena held because of the debacle with *Black Rhapsody* that had opened the backstage door for her to see all the crap stored there.

Depressing.

"Ah, the king is ready for his subjects," Anne said, pointing her chin in the direction of the auditorium, where Derek was seating himself near the orchestra pit.

"Okay, people," Broderick clapped to get everyone's attention. "Let's get on with things." He pointed to Francesca and Randy. "You're up first. Derek's been dying to see how you're working together, now that you've had more time to rehearse together. Then we'll continue with Elena and Fred, followed by Caroline and Mario. Martina, you'll be last. After a ten-minute break, we'll do *Giselle.*"

Martina waved her hand to get Broderick's attention.

"Since I don't go now, I need to pick up a few things at store," she said.

"Don't be late," Broderick warned. "Don't think I won't fine you."

Martina dismissed his comment with a wave, gathered her things and was about to go into the auditorium when Anne interrupted.

"Martina, wait," Anne said. "Will you be anywhere near the Duane Reade over on Fifty-Ninth?"

Martina nodded.

"Oh, be a dear and get something that I ran out of for me there."

Martina wasn't too thrilled, Elena saw.

"Well, hurry up. What you need?"

Anne scooted after her, and they both went into the auditorium, heads close, as if plotting.

Francesca chuckled. "Anne is the only person Martina can't say no to."

"Probably believes it's profitable to keep Anne on her side," Elena said, looking after the pair as they exited through the swinging doors of the theater auditorium. "Until she realizes Anne no longer has influence or Derek's ear to whisper her recommendations."

Broderick and Analisse gave the ready cue. Elena pushed Francesca in Randy's direction, where he was waiting.

"The *Giselle* group should be glad to hear the trapdoor to the lift is finally fixed," Analisse said from where she sat next to Derek, while Broderick left the stage to join them. "Lauren, you'll be using it in rehearsal, so be ready downstairs. Stage crew will cue you. Oh, and Elena, make believe you're coming out on a balcony. No stage props today."

Elena grabbed hold of a rigging cable by the wall and began her stretches to keep warm. Fred marked his variation near her, mimicking steps with his hands and practicing poses. All the while, Elena watched her friend and Randy rehearse.

Not for the first time, Elena thought Francesca's presence on stage was magical. By contrast, Martina was technically perfect, flamboyant. Caroline more dramatic. But Francesca was lyrical, her movements like beautiful ripples in water. And Randy was excellent as well. They made a good pair.

"She's gorgeous, isn't she?"

The whisper came from behind her, but she didn't need to turn around to know who'd spoken.

"Wish my brother would surface from his musical world and notice."

Anne chuckled. "My dear, he's not in New York enough days for that. And if Francesca doesn't cooperate...well..."

"I know. I'll have to come up with some sort of Machiavellian plan to get those two together."

"What you have to concentrate on now is how you're going to keep the treasure you've found." Anne nudged her. Jake was walking down the aisle in their direction. "And vice versa."

"I know," Elena said on a sigh. Watched as Jake took a seat a few rows behind Derek. The smile was on. He waved at her.

She waved back.

"But it'll be a hell of a ride. I'm quite looking forward to it."

Anne's chuckle followed her as she ambled backstage.

Five minutes later, it was their turn to get on stage. As she passed Francesca on her way to get her things, she hugged her.

"You were awesome," Elena said.

"I know," she said and grinned.

Elena laughed.

"Go impress," Francesca whispered, nodding in the direction of Jake.

"I've already done *that*," she said, and ran over to the corner, where Juliet's balcony supposedly stood, the tips of her toe shoes tapping and echoing around stage as she went.

Fifteen minutes later, after fits and starts because Broderick's interruptions and suggestions were constant, Elena joined Francesca, who sat, legs stretched, eating a yogurt.

"I swear, he made us repeat things unnecessarily," Fred said, huffing.

"Getting even, I'm sure," Elena said. She took off her skirt and mopped her sweat with it.

"I agree," Francesca said, licking her spoon.

"No need to take it out on me, if they're angry at you," Fred complained.

"We come in a package deal, I'm afraid," Elena said. She bent to take her toe shoes off.

"Again? Same pose? Must be my luck."

Elena glanced between her legs. The inverted image of Jake, as wonderful as she had glimpsed at their first meeting, stood behind her.

"Or perfect timing," Elena said.

Jake maneuvered around Frannie's extended legs to reach Elena.

"Hi."

"Hi, back, gorgeous." And, without worrying about an audience, he held her face and kissed her in slow exploration, making a slow burn proliferate into a conflagration.

Darn, but this man knew how to stoke her fire.

Chuckles, sighs, and whistles exploded around them.

"Yum." Jake grinned. "Sweet and salty. My favorite combination."

"Idiot." Elena made as if to swat him, but bent once more to finish unlacing her toe shoes.

"Up for lunch?" Jake asked and made way for Martina, who rushed between them, dropping all her bags on the floor.

No apologies.

The woman had no manners whatsoever.

"Am I late?" she asked, breathless. "Don't want to get them mad."

Referring to Derek, Broderick, et al, no doubt.

"Nah," Francesca answered. "Caroline and Mario are up next."

"Good," Martina said. "Had to wait more time in line at Duane Reade than wanted to. Where's Anne?"

Elena slipped into her jeans and looked around. Anne was nowhere to be found.

"No clue," Elena said. "Try the bathroom or the *Giselle* group downstairs."

Jake leaned toward her. "Lunch?"

"Definitely," she said and stepped into her clogs.

But Jake's cell phone went off. He glanced at the incoming text and swore under his breath.

"This can't be good. Office," was his answer at her questioning look.

"No lunch?"

"Let me get rid of this." He stepped away for some privacy. "Yes, Monica. What's up."

Elena watched, curious, as Jake's face changed from casually attentive to disturbed.

"Are you sure?" Jake asked.

That sounded a bit ominous.

He hung up, grabbed Elena's hand, and pulled her further back into the wing, away from prying ears.

"Something wrong?" she asked, his anxiousness transferring to her.

"Elena," Jake's unease was evident. "The bottle you found next to Justin, and Harris had let slip wasn't vitamins."

"Yes?"

"It's definitely medicine."

"Okay..."

"My assistant hit on the combinations of letters. It's generic medicine, given to people who have symptoms of dizziness or vertigo."

"What?"

"Have you seen anyone who's had an issue with balances, or dizziness?"

"Jake, that could be any one of us on a daily basis," Elena said, but couldn't help thinking about how Caroline had been off lately. About Derek and Broderick's complaints in the office. "We have off days. Today is case in point. We were all over the place. Undue stress can do a number on our concentration."

But something else nagged at her, just there, at the edge of her mind. What on earth was it?

"But that wasn't all. According to my assistant, this drug has what they call a secondary indication, a use other than what the drug was originally approved for," Jake said. "It helps treat other illnesses."

"Like what?"

"I don't know. My assistant is digging into it."

Elena was horrified. If it were true, and someone was ill and being treated with this medicine, pirouettes, balances, even something as simple as running across stage would be a nightmare. Undoable. Life altering and career ending.

Oh God.

"Everyone. Stop."

Elena jumped. The shouted interruption, reverberating around the theater, was shocking.

What on earth...

"I want everyone's attention, please."

Elena turned just in time to see none other than Detective Harris and his shadow, Detective Murdock, walking toward them down the auditorium's aisle. This time around, there were four uniformed officers at their tail. At a nod from Harris, they separated, two policemen heading with Murdock toward the steps leading onto stage left. The other two stayed put next to Harris.

"Stop what you're doing right now," Detective Harris ordered, still at the top of his voice. "I want everyone on stage," he finished, and directed his next remark to Derek, "please," as an afterthought.

"What is the meaning of this?" Derek stood, obviously offended by the temerity of the detective interrupting sacred time. His demand was as loud as Detective Harris's had been.

"Who the hell do you think you are, Detectives?" from Broderick. Almost screeched. Always known to chime in with his two cents, whether people wanted to hear him or not.

"We're in the middle of a rehearsal, for God's sake," Analisse sputtered.

"I meant exactly what I ordered, Ms. Menia." There was no apology in the detective's voice as he strolled toward the stage. "If you would, the three of you, please join your dancers on stage." He raised his voice once more. "No one is to leave until I say so, especially those there." His fingers pointed to all the soloists from the first act of the gala. "I need a few words with you all. Move center stage, please, now."

"Come on." Jake steered Elena to where everyone was gathering.

Francesca rushed to meet them. "What is going on?"

"Do you think he's going to arrest someone?" Fred asked. He sounded more bewildered than scared. Then again, why should he be fearful when the mess didn't really involve him?

"We've got to warn Anne," Frannie whispered to Elena.

"We don't have time."

Elena studied Harris's expression as he approached them. It was almost as if it were saying "Gotcha" this time around. And his eyes kept shifting from one person to the next, piercing them all, as if he could coerce a confession right then and there from the guilty party. Because they were all suspects, Elena was certain.

"Ladies and gentlemen, please make yourselves comfortable." He opened his arms as if herding them all in a roundup on center stage.

Caroline, Mario, Martina, and Randy opted to sit on the floor. Elena, together with Jake, Fred, and Francesca, stood. So did Derek, Broderick, and Analisse. The rest of the stage crew, and those few from the ballet corps, hovered toward backstage, the dancers shifting nervously from foot to foot.

Detective Harris reached the stage apron and faced them. Elena felt as if she were in a courtroom, facing a judge about to render his sentence.

"Ladies and gentlemen. As you know, I was first brought in to investigate the assault on Mr. Justin Bakare. But, since then, the case has snowballed into the attack on Ms. Tess Baukman, another one of your members, as well as an incident of vandalism with intent to harm in this very theater." He pointed to Derek. "Your director finally informed me that the case of personal property destruction was not isolated to the incident here, but had been happening at your studios as well."

"Nice summary, Detective," Jake said. "But could you get to the point here?"

"All in good time, Mr. Forrester," Harris said and nodded to Detective Murdock, who in turn nodded to the policemen.

"Okay, guys," Murdock said. "You know what to do. Everything."

One policeman started searching their personal things, while another kept a blocking stance.

"What do you think you're doing?" the outcry was from Caroline, and echoed by everyone on stage.

"Get away from my things," Francesca practically jumped the policeman. Martina had to be held back by Murdock.

"You have no right to search anything," Elena said, incensed.

"I have every right, Ms. del Carral," Detective Harris said, lifting and unfolding a piece of paper. "This warrant gives it to me." And he handed it to Derek.

"This is an outrage," Derek said. "Broderick, call my lawyers."

"What's an outrage here, sir, is your lack of cooperation," Harris said. "There is someone sick in this company and you're closing ranks, keeping information about a medical condition from me."

Elena and Jake stared at each other the moment Harris said *sick*.

"What do you mean *sick?*" Analisse asked.

"Yes," Caroline added, but there was an edge of nervous agitation to it. She kept staring at the zips and plops of the policemen searching their personal items and purses.

"Detective," Derek interrupted. "Give me a break. All dancers, at one stage or another, are sick or injured. This is nothing new and you, sir, are wasting our time."

"I'm not talking about painkillers or Tiger Balm, *sir*," Harris said, with heavy scorn. "I'm speaking of a real illness, a career-changing one, one that could break the strongest into possible mental illness and retaliation."

Broderick laughed, albeit a bit nervously. "And I thought we had drama queens in this company. Detective, you take the cake." He turned to Derek. "You should hire him. He would make an awesome Baron Von Rothbart in *Swan Lake*."

"Laugh all you want, Mr. Newsom, but you have a problem here." Harris took out a folded evidence plastic bag from his pocket and unrolled it, keeping it at arm's length for all to see.

Elena recognized its content immediately.

It was the plastic bottle she'd found when she discovered Justin.

And something popped into her mind that she, at first, disregarded because it would be so awful, if true.

Jake pressed her hand. "What's the matter?" he asked.

"Cover me?" She began to back away inch by inch toward where Martina had dropped her purchases.

"Isn't that the plastic bottle you found, Elena?" Francesca interrupted her thoughts.

She froze. Leave it to Francesca to blurt unnecessary things out in her naïveté.

"And how do you know this?" Detective Harris asked her.

"Well, Elena told..." Francesca stopped. "Oh."

"Indeed, Ms. Mori. Everything points to Ms. del Carral there."

Here we go again with all roads lead to moi.

"Ah, come on, Detective," Elena blurted. "Give up. This goes beyond harassment."

Jake glanced her way, as she continued inching closer and closer to the wing.

"Quit stalling, Detective," Jake said, moving away from her, keeping Detective Harris focused on him. "Out with it."

"Our forensic department has analyzed the contents of this." He shook the evidence bag for effect. "And they identified the residue as meclizine."

She froze again as Harris's eyes bored into everyone there.

"What the hell is that," Randy Dimmig asked. "Is it a steroid?"

"No," Harris answered, a bit of disappointment in his expression.

Probably sorry he hadn't caught a shift in eyes, or a slight jump that would reveal guilt, or knowledge of the medicine, Elena thought.

"This particular medicine treats dizziness, lack of coordination."

The mumbles and grumbles that had been increasing in volume stopped.

Stupefied silence reigned.

"Ah." There was a boatful of satisfaction in Harris's remark.

Elena inched closer to the wing. But the policeman standing guard moved to bar her way.

"Miss," he whispered and pointed to center stage.

"Well, Detective," Jake said after the awful pause. "You definitely have our attention."

As if Jake didn't know about the medicine.

"Medicine that can be prescribed in tandem with others to treat other illnesses. Normally Ménière's disease..." He scanned their faces and let drop the other shoe. "Vertigo."

If silence were an abyss, they'd be plummeting down its eternal darkness about now.

Elena had to make a conscious effort to look shocked. After all, she wasn't supposed to know about this. Well, she didn't know about Ménière's disease, just the vertigo part of it. That shocked her.

But, every dancer here, right now, understood those prognoses were career enders. Total ruination.

"You can't be serious," Derek exploded. "Ménière's disease. Vertigo. What rubbish. No one in this company has that. We would have noticed immediately, not to mention the company's doctor."

"Your company doctor can be bypassed easily, Mr. Michaels. Haven't you heard of Telehealth?" Harris again shook the evidence bag.

"But, on the off chance this was not obtained through the Internet, we issued a warrant to all pharmacies, narrowed down in scope, to flag if the meclizine was refilled or recently prescribed. And it was."

No. Please, don't let it be. It can't be...

Jake was beside her in a flash. "What's wrong?" he whispered.

"Oh, Jake."

"Sir?"

As one, they all pivoted to the policeman on stage right. He hovered near Martina's earlier purchases, the ones she'd thrown down next to Elena's and Francesca's things. In one hand he had an open paper bag, in the other, a plastic bottle, similar to the one Elena had found.

"It's meclizine, sir," he said, extending it to Harris after reading the label.

"Whose property is that?" Harris pointed to the floor next to his officer.

Absolute silence.

"Whose stuff is this?" Harsher.

"My stuff," Martina answered.

All turned to her.

"Why you look at me?" she said, near a screech. "That is *not* mine."

The detective's look of disdain was something to watch.

"You deny this is yours?"

"Yes. Went shopping." Martina pointed to what Detective Harris held. "Picked that up for someone else."

But Elena's attention was not on the drama that was unfolding on stage, she was peering at the paper bag the policeman still held. The logo came into full view. Elena's heart somersaulted. The DR told her all she needed to know.

Oh, no, no, no.

"Elena?" Jake sensed her rising despair.

"Oh, Jake. No."

"You deny the evidence?" Detective Harris almost yelled. "Deny it's yours?"

"Actually, Detective, that is mine," interrupted a voice from inside the theater. Elena looked up from where the voice had issued. There, on the descending steps of the third balcony, stood a figure in shadow.

Harris ordered the stage crew to turn the house lights on.

"Anne," Elena whispered.

"What?" Jake said, unbelieving.

"It's Anne, Jake." Elena's voice caught. "She's the one."

"I foolishly asked Martina to pick that up for me today," Anne said, no longer in shadow. She stepped closer to the guardrail at the edge of the balcony. "Shouldn't have done it, I know, but I ran out of the medicine and I've been a bit fuzzy today. Lethargic. I apologize." She looked at Elena. "You guessed a minute ago, didn't you? Saw you staring at the paper bag the policeman held."

"Yes," Elena said, heartbroken.

"You?" Detective Harris couldn't quite fathom the curveball just pitched. "This is yours?"

"Why so surprised, Detective? You see, desperation is the mother of all influence. And once you start lying, and hiding, and getting rid of obstacles...well..." She waved her arms to encompass all the theater. "I need this. Unfortunately, I won't have it for long. I've been diagnosed with MS, you see."

The shock waves going through every member of the company had to be as brutal as Elena's felt.

"MS, as in multiple sclerosis?" Jake asked.

Anne nodded.

"Good God." Jake was beyond shocked.

"Anne, please. Come down," Elena pleaded. "Let's..."

But Derek Michaels stepped in front of Elena.

"You?" he said, his voice a mix between offense, perturbation, and incredulity. "You've been behind all these catastrophes—the fake letters, the cutting of ribbons... everything?"

"Indeed, I have."

"You're sick," Analisse said loud enough to be heard.

"Yes, dear. Deathly sick," Anne answered.

"Why?" Derek asked. The perplexity behind the question was there for all to hear. "Why have you done all this?"

"Ah, the man who uses, abuses, and discards." Anne couldn't get rid of the bitterness in her own voice. "Then again, you've always been an egotistical narcissist, haven't you?" She paused a second, considered her words for a moment. "That's a redundancy, isn't it?"

"But, Anne, I loved you. Always loved you. Why would you do this to me?"

Anne's laugh was bitter. "Love? What do you really know about love, Derek? I was a tool to expend your base passions on. And, shame on me, I went along with my secondary role. Had to make my own opportunities, so I had to be a parasite, as well. But all toe shoes disfigure with use, lose their luster, especially when brighter, newer ones beckon. And your true love is the company: ageless, demanding, voracious. Your own Scylla."

"But I kept you. Gave you roles."

"You mean the pitiful charity roles you offered?" Anne laughed without humor. "Please. And, if I'd come to you with my diagnosis, would you have kept me on your payroll? Paid for my treatment? Kept me in the apartment?"

Silence. Absolute silence from Derek.

"You see, I know you better than most."

"But, Anne," Elena asked. "You found someone good. You told me. I'm sure..."

"Ah, my beau. Well, dear, something happens to people the moment you reveal the happily ever after will be marred with illness. Especially when you have a short history together. He dumped me the day Detective Harris took you to the precinct. I have no one now."

"Were you responsible, Ms. Ruskin, for Mr. Bakare's attack?" Harris asked.

"I was indeed," she admitted.

Harris nodded to Murdock, who nodded to the police officers near him to go fetch Anne.

"You don't really have to give me an escort, Detective," Anne said. "I'll come down shortly."

"Anne," Elena said. "Why Justin? What did he ever do to you?"

"It is unfortunate that the good doctor, my doctor, moves in the same circles as Justin. He let the cat out of the bag, so to speak, at a dinner. You see, the good doctor has a fondness for liquor, and he was sufficiently inebriated that night that doctor-patient confidentiality went out the window, especially when he saw Justin, my colleague, a person he admired. He asked how I was doing, commiserated about how terrible my condition was for an aging dancer." Anne visibly shrugged. "Justin, ever the opportunist, thought it would be good sport to use that knowledge to coerce and blackmail me. He wanted me to influence Derek into making him Martina's partner."

"But he's *old*," Martina said. "He no longer excited people on stage."

"The term you want is 'has been,' dear," Anne said. "And you are correct. He was on his way out, you see. So, he approached me in the rehearsal room. Warned me if I didn't help, he'd go directly to Derek and I'd be thrown out of the company faster than a *fouetté*. So, I pushed him while he was practicing his *cabrioles*. It was an added bonus when his head hit the piano." She chuckled. "He landed so hard the strings of the piano vibrated."

Caroline's choked cry echoed around the stage.

"And in the studio? It was you who turned off the breaker, wasn't it?" Elena said. "You who wanted to come in?"

"I was so angry after I heard about *Black Rhapsody* and Fauchier's marriage to your mother, I really wanted to hurt you," Anne said, in such a matter-of-fact voice that it chilled Elena. "But then, after thinking about it, there was no need to harm you. You were the perfect tool to help me destroy Derek's dream. And, believe it or not, I'm very fond of you."

"And Tess?" Jake asked. "Did you attack Tess?"

"Wanted her out of the way," Anne admitted. "With Tess indisposed, I could ask Derek to replace me as Moyna or Zulma in *Giselle*, since Lauren would be promoted to the Myrtha role. My last hurrah, sort of. Unfortunately, that didn't pan out. I'm still dancing in the corps."

"And the vandalism in my dressing room?" Elena asked.

"Oh, Caroline did that out of spite, my dear," Anne said. "She confessed when I confronted her. She's been under a lot of stress, you see. Without Justin, or marriage to him, she has nothing. She can't even collect from his life insurance." Anne cocked her head. "Ah. I hear my police escorts arriving."

"Oh, Anne," Elena said.

"My dear, don't fret. I'm ecstatic that I was able to steer you away from Terpsichore and this heartless animal," Anne pointed to Derek. "You have a wonderful future ahead of you. Use it well. Choreograph to your heart's content. Love well too. And Jake, please propose soon? You're perfect for each other."

With that said, Anne climbed several steps, turned, and with a beautifully executed *saut de chat*, arms outstretched in final farewell as if to embrace the career and the world she loved, she leapt over the low guardrail of the upper balcony and plummeted to her death.

Chapter Fifteen

"THAT WAS WONDERFUL," ELENA SAID TO THE ENSEMBLE, AS they finished their run-through of *Black Rhapsody* in the rehearsal hall of Ballet Etudes in Monaco. "Thank you, everyone. Great rehearsal. See you tomorrow."

One by one, the members of the company dispersed, clapping as they went.

Fred's wife, who was currently a stand-in for the lead role in *Black Rhapsody*, gave a goodbye kiss to her husband and to Elena. She was beginning to show her pregnancy.

"That was amazing, Elena," Fred said, mopping up his sweat. "And you're going to kill me with that variation."

Elena chuckled. "Nothing you can't handle."

"It's challenging and beautiful. Perfect for men. Can't wait to rehearse it with Francesca." He guzzled down whatever mixture he had in his drinking bottle. Fred was into bizarre smoothies and weird vitamin waters. Today, the mixture looked red. "When is she arriving?"

"Friday."

"Can't wait," he said, and with a brief *ciao,* went off after his wife.

Elena sat, glancing around the hall, now void of sound and movement, and thought it would be good to see Francesca again. It had been three months since Anne's final, tragic curtain call. Three months since performing in a gala marred by misfortune. Three since Fred and she had skipped town to return home to their familiar spaces. And two since hearing Justin had passed away, a life unnecessarily snuffed out like a burned-out wick.

This week also marked the end of all legal tribulations with Terpsichore's director and owner. Derek had finally agreed to her last counteroffer and signed all the documents. From now on, Elena wouldn't hold one single share of Terpsichore. She'd negotiated full price for the portion her mother had inherited up to her death, instead of what Derek had wanted, up to the time of Fauchier's death. She had forgone all proceeds of ticket sales, and profits from the school, in exchange for a ten percent cut of all the staging of Fauchier's works at other companies from the time of his death. She'd get the same percentage for any works staged in the future, as well, unlike the year limit Derek had imposed. In exchange, Elena had agreed to stage *Black Rhapsody* at Terpsichore. A little give and take. That had been Jake's suggestion.

So, it was finally over.

Her sigh was deep and painful.

She would not cry. Not anymore. That had been done privately and on Jake's shoulders. Now was a time to celebrate life and honor the dead.

In memoriam...

Elena swapped the music from *Black Rhapsody* and replaced it with the Prelude No. 4 in E Minor from Frederick Chopin. Perfect music for the piece she was choreographing in remembrance of Anne.

The idea had come to her several weeks ago. It would be Elena's tribute to her friend, filmed and distributed for the world to see through social media, her brother at the piano keys, with Fred and Jean-Pierre, from Ballet Etudes, partnering her.

She didn't care if the company picked it up, or if any other ballet company did so.

It was Elena's cathartic memento to Anne's life. Her *honoris causa* for a friend's last hurrah.

During the next half hour, Elena danced what she had visualized, stopping at intervals to mimic with hands, body, and arm movements the instances where Fred and Jean-Pierre would enter, lead, lift, and move to the melancholia of the piece.

The music stopped. Silence reigned in the rehearsal hall once more.

Elena stared at her reflection, alone in the vast space, her heart heavy, and yet, strangely content.

Anne would have been pleased.

A moment later, she shook away her doldrums and bent to unlace her toe shoes.

"We really must stop meeting this way."

Elena looked through her legs and smiled at the upside-down figure of the man she loved. Her Romeo. Her scherzo man with the killer smile.

And, without bothering to finish unlacing, Elena turned and sashayed her way to an even brighter future.

A Note from the Author
IN MEMORIAM

This novella has been a labor of love. It is also a tribute.

It's a tribute to an incredible prima ballerina and choreographer, who lost everything in order to give her daughters a good life and future. A tribute, long coming, to a talented, gifted, and extremely brave woman, who set aside her standing and fame, both in the ballet world, and in television in Cuba, so her daughters wouldn't suffer under a communist regime.

This novella is my homage to my mom, Elena del Cueto.

Elena del Cueto, fixing her ballet toe shoes before a performance at Sociedad Pro-Arte Musical in Cuba. Photograph by Célida Villalón.

Ballet dancer, choreographer, and instructor, my mom, Elena del Cueto, was born in Havana, Cuba, on February 9, 1927. From an early age, she wanted to dance, dance, dance. She was barely fourteen when she was accepted at the ballet dancing school in Havana's Sociedad Pro-Arte Musical and soon became an accomplished ballerina and principal dancer. She demonstrated her talent, her determination, and her fresh approach to the art in many performances in Havana. In 1946 she was named auxiliary teacher at the Sociedad and that same year she married my father, the school director, choreographer, and dancer, Alberto Alonso, brother-in-law to Alicia Alonso, Cuba's prima ballerina and wife of my uncle, Fernando Alonso.

With the arrival of television in Cuba, my mom was featured on weekly TV broadcasts of various musical productions such as *El Güije, Rapsodia Negra* (Black Rhapsody, ergo, the title of my novel and the ballet I mention in it), its music composed by the famed Ernesto Lecuona, and her performances turned her into a favorite of Cuban audiences. She not only danced in, but choreographed with incredible success, variety programs that were so popular in 1950s Cuba (*Casino de la Alegría, Jueves de Partagás* and others), but, as a leading member of the Ballet Nacional de Cuba, she also starred in numerous ballets on Havana's most distinguished stages. She made history with her own choreography of *Variations on a Theme by Haydn* (Brahms) and *Fantasía Cubana* (P. Csonka) among other superb ballets in the company's repertoire. She was also the first, together with my father, to incorporate elements of Cuban dance into her choreographic works.

In 1962, my mom faked a contract to dance in Mexico and managed to escape Cuba with my sister and me. She never looked back. We danced with her, and her troupe, for many years, until life took us in different directions.

So, I'll recap by saying this is but a small peek into all her accomplishments. It is unfortunate that, even today, the Cuban government and the Ballet Nacional de Cuba continue to ignore and disregard my mother's history and contributions to the art due to her anti-communist ideals.[1]

Thus, now that I have become a writer, I decided to honor her with this novella.

Love you, Mom. Keep dancing in heaven.

----

1. Portions of this mini-biography of Elena del Cueto are by Mark Martin, https://www.imdb.com/name/nm6773092/bio/

About the Author

Maria Elena Alonso-Sierra is an award-winning author with a unique point of view: to give her readers and fans thrills and kills, with a twist. Her characters are placed in danger in ingenuous ways while, at the same time, her novels are set in locales across Europe and the United States, reflecting her international upbringing and extensive time as a Cuban exile and global traveler.

The author's writing career began circa age thirteen with a very juvenile science fiction short story; but the writing bug hit, and she has been writing, in one capacity or another, ever since. She has worked as a professional dancer, singer, journalist, and literature teacher in both the university and middle school levels (and not necessarily in that order) and holds a Masters in English literature.

All her novels have received different accolades, including gold, silver and bronze medals, as well as honorary mentions from respected book award institutions. Ms. Alonso-Sierra is currently writing full-time and loves to hear from her fans and readers. When not writing, she roams around to discover new places to set her novels.

Also by Maria Elena Alonso-Sierra

The Coin

The Book of Hours

The Fish Tank: And Other Short Stories

Hanging Softly in the Night